Firefly Summer

Center Point
Large Print

Also by Nan Rossiter and available from
Center Point Large Print:

Nantucket
Under a Summer Sky
More Than You Know
Words Get in the Way
The Gin & Chowder Club

**This Large Print Book carries the
Seal of Approval of N.A.V.H.**

Firefly Summer

Nan
Rossiter

CENTER POINT LARGE PRINT
THORNDIKE, MAINE

This Center Point Large Print edition is published
in the year 2016 by arrangement with
Kensington Publishing Corp.

The text of this Large Print edition is unabridged.
In other aspects, this book may vary
from the original edition.
Printed in the United States of America
on permanent paper.
Set in 16-point Times New Roman type.

ISBN: 978-1-68324-139-3

Library of Congress Cataloging-in-Publication Data

Names: Rossiter, Nan Parson, author.
Title: Firefly summer / Nan Rossiter.
Description: Center Point Large Print edition. | Thorndike, Maine :
Center Point Large Print, 2016.
Identifiers: LCCN 2016028931 | ISBN 9781683241393
    (hardcover : alk. paper)
Subjects: LCSH: Sisters—Fiction. | Large type books.
Classification: LCC PS3618.O8535 F57 2016 | DDC 813/.54—dc23
LC record available at https://lccn.loc.gov/2016028931

Firefly Summer

Part I

I have loved you with an everlasting love;
I have drawn you with unfailing kindness.

—Jeremiah 31:3

July 3, 1964

"Mom-mom-mom!" Easton shouted, tumbling into the kitchen, his face lit with happy exuberance. "Mom-mom-mom!" he repeated, grinning the grin that stole everyone's heart. He was wearing his favorite Red Sox cap—a permanent fixture on his blond head—and his sky blue eyes were sparkling with life. Even at the tender age of seven—just an evening shy of eight—Easton had an irrepressible way of filling a room with his unbridled enthusiasm, but on this particular evening, Martha Quinn was a little short on patience.

"What is it, Easton?"

"Look!" he exclaimed, turning off the kitchen light and proudly holding up a mason jar blinking with tiny golden-green lights.

Martha looked up from pouring cake batter into two round pans. "I see. Now turn the light back on or I'll have batter all over the table."

The screen door swung open again, and because the spring was broken, banged against the house, allowing two more jostling children trailed by a big yellow Lab to tumble in.

9

"If Willow's feet are muddy, please keep her outside," Martha commanded.

"Mo-om," howled six-year-old Piper. "Sailor took my jar!"

"That's because mine broke and you weren't catching anything anyway," eleven-year-old Sailor said defensively.

"I was so," Piper protested. "Mom, do you have another?"

"I do . . . somewhere. Sailor, how'd you break your jar?"

"It fell."

"You mean you dropped it," Martha corrected and then glanced down at their bare feet. "Did you clean it up?"

"Yes."

"Did you use a dustpan?"

"There weren't any small pieces."

Martha eyed her skeptically.

"Pipe, you should've put your name on your jar, like I did," Easton said, holding his jar so she could see his name scrawled across the lid. He opened the refrigerator. "Here's another jar," he said, taking out a half-eaten jar of bread and butter pickles. "Mom, can I dump these into something else?"

Martha eyed her middle child again. "Sailor, please ask Birdie and Remy to come in."

"Birdie! Remy! Mom wants you!" Sailor hollered through the screen.

"I could've done that," Martha said.

A moment later, the screen door swung open, banging against the house again, and the two oldest Quinn girls clambered in, giggling and elbowing each other, but as soon as they sensed the tension in the kitchen, they stopped, stood straighter, and waited for instructions.

"I need you two to keep everyone outside. I have a million things to do tonight."

"We've been trying, Mom," thirteen-year-old Remy and fifteen-year-old Birdie—whose real name was Martha—protested, "but they—"

"No buts!"

A car door slammed, and Martha sighed. "Thank goodness!"

"Dad!" the girls shouted, clambering around their father as he came through the door. "What kind of ice cream did you get?" they asked.

"Did you get strawberry?"

"Coffee?"

"Vanilla?"

"I hope you were able to get chocolate!"

"Hold on!" Whitney Quinn said, laughing good-naturedly and holding the bag above their heads. "Whose birthday is it?" he asked, eyeing his four daughters.

"Easton's!" they chorused.

"That doesn't matter," Sailor protested. "On

my birthday, we . . ." but Whitney held up his hand and her voice trailed off in defeat.

"It's Easton's birthday, so the flavor of the day will be . . ."

"Did you find black raspberry?" Easton asked hopefully.

Whitney smiled. "You only turn eight once . . ."

"You did! All right!" he exclaimed.

⊰{ Chapter I }⊱

Piper Quinn looked up from pulling on a dandelion —whose roots, she decided, reached all the way to China—pushed a shock of her short dark hair out of her eyes, and waved. Nat McCabe looked in the rearview mirror of his pickup and waved back. She smiled. Nat had stopped home for a late lunch, but before he left, he'd pulled her into his arms, murmured how good she smelled, and teasingly told her he'd been craving rice pudding all morning, and Piper, who'd been satisfying Nat's cravings for nearly forty years, laughed. She'd been planning on working in the garden that afternoon—they'd had a wet spring and the weeds were thriving—but as she watched Nat pull away, she thought about the rice pudding her mom used to make, and an image of her mom's old *Good Housekeeping* cookbook—

faded red and missing its dust jacket—filled her mind. Her mom had used that cookbook as faithfully as she'd used her Bible.

Piper glanced at the weeds poking their seedy heads up above the fence and briefly entertained the idea of looking for a recipe online. There were several sites she liked, all with wonderful recipes and reviews, but she quickly dismissed the idea. There was only one rice pudding recipe she wanted to make, and it was in her mom's favorite old cookbook.

Piper gave the mulish weed one last tug and it defiantly snapped off at the ground. She sighed, tossed it in her basket, and eyed the offending root. "I'll be back," she warned, "*and* I'll have my weeder!" She rinsed her hands under the outdoor faucet, dried them on her shorts, and looked at the big golden retriever sprawled across the sunny grass. "Are you staying out here, ol' pie?" The sweet old dog, hearing one of the many names she associated with herself—ol' pie, ol' girl, sweets, pupster, and of course, her official name, Chloe—opened one eye, yawned, and closed it again. Piper shook her head and smiled. "I'll take that as a yes." She climbed the two wooden steps to the wraparound porch and straightened the wooden sign that was hanging next to the door. The carved and painted green-and-white sign had been welcoming friends to the Quinn summer home in Eastham for as long as she could remember.

Whit's End was the whimsical name her father had given the rambling Nantucket-style house when he learned that their fifth child would also be their fourth daughter! He'd carved the sign that same summer, and although it had been repainted several times, it was due for another fresh coat.

Piper went inside, kicked off her tattered running shoes, and walked over to scan the cookbook shelf. On it was everything from *Mastering the Art of French Cooking* by Julia Child to the infallible Irma Rombauer and her daughter Marion's *Joy of Cooking*, and tucked next to that was a dog-eared copy of *The Joy of Sex—what in the world is that doing down here?* Piper pulled it from the shelf and continued looking for the cookbook, but when she didn't see it, she picked up the groundbreaking sex manual from the early seventies and leafed through it, remembering, with a smile, how she and her sisters had spent hours poring over the iconic illustrations, trying to decide whether some of the positions were even anatomically possible. She started to feel aroused, closed the book, and tucked it under her arm. Nat would get a kick out of it . . . and maybe even a new craving!

Piper climbed the stairs to the second floor and gazed resignedly up the worn, narrow stairs to the third. She hadn't been in the attic in years. She'd even tried to forget its existence, but she knew forgetting wouldn't change anything—the attic would still be full of stuff . . . and *stuff* was the gentle word she and Birdie and Remy used when referring to the attic's contents. Sailor used a more colorful noun. For years, she and her sisters had talked about going through everything, but somehow, they'd never gotten around to it. Life always got in the way.

Piper pushed open the door and pulled the string dangling from the rafters. Nothing happened. She peered around the dimly lit room and made her way toward the window—the only other source of light—but as she walked between all the boxes, her heart sank—she was never going to find the cookbook in this mess.

She bumped into an old seamstress mannequin, and when she reached out to steady it, she inadvertently touched the unfinished neckline of her mom's last project—a sundress for Remy's daughter Payton. Her mom had been working on the dress that fateful rainy, spring day when she'd stopped to make a cup of tea and get the mail. Piper had been away at college at the time, but Birdie had called to tell her what happened. "Thank goodness she put the kettle on *before* going out to get the mail, because it was the whistling kettle that alerted Mr. Moody—who found her lying in the driveway."

Martha Quinn had suffered a stroke, and although Dr. Sanders had assured her four daughters it was a mild one, the stroke had turned out to be the first of many that, over time, irreversibly damaged the tiny blood vessels in Martha's brain and stripped her of all her motor and cognitive skills—from sewing and cooking, to writing and walking, to remembering and recognizing, and finally, to swallowing—but it was that first stroke that made it difficult for Martha to hold and thread a needle; and later on, when Remy asked Payton whether she'd like to have the dress finished by someone else, Payton had said no—the dress would just remind her of the day Gran stopped sewing.

Piper moved the mannequin to one side and saw her mom's hope chest pushed up against the wall. She lifted the heavy lid, and the sweet, woodsy scent of cedar drifted into the room, transporting her back to her parents' bedroom in the big old colonial in New Hampshire—their year-round home.

Nestled in the top of the old chest was a wooden tray filled with jewelry and beads. Piper picked up a string of pearls and slipped it over her head. Her sisters had loved putting their mom's beads around their necks, donning her fancy hats, clunking around in her high heels, and admiring themselves in the full-length mirror behind the door. Piper, however, had only liked to watch; whenever her sisters had tried to put the beads around *her* neck or the bright red lipstick on *her* lips, she'd always shaken her head and turned away—there was no way they were putting that stuff on her! She'd much rather play the games her brother played—games that involved hitting or bouncing balls and running.

Piper laid the beads back in the tray and noticed a stack of envelopes with her father's long, elegant handwriting scrawled across them. They were addressed to Martha Lane—his seventeen-year-old sweetheart. Piper slipped off the faded ribbon and began to read the letters her father had written to her mother when he was a navy pilot flying Hellcats off an aircraft carrier in the Pacific during WWII. She smiled at his sweet words and the way he professed his love and told her of the future he hoped they'd share one day. Piper smiled sadly—back then, her parents had been blissfully unaware of the tragedies that lay ahead in their lives.

An hour later, Piper slipped the last letter back into its fragile sheath, retied the ribbon, and looked out the window. She saw Chloe, far below, moving to her favorite spot under the towering oak trees her father had planted when each of his children was born, and then realized the trees' long shadows were stretching across the grass—the afternoon was slipping by. *Five more minutes,* she thought, turning back to the chest. She lifted out a pile of sweaters and found an old leather photo album. She pulled her father's dusty old mission-style rocking chair up to the window, sat down, and opened the book. The album was full of black-and-white photos that had been carefully mounted on black construction paper. She slowly turned the pages and smiled—her dad looked so handsome in his navy uniform, and her mom looked absolutely stunning in a long fur coat, back when fur was not only acceptable, but fashion-able. Women weren't caught dead wearing fur anymore.

Piper slowly turned the pages, reading the captions her mom had neatly printed in white ink: *Grand Central, 1945, Hanover, N.H., 1947, Fenway Park, 1948* . . . and then there was one with just the year: 1949. The picture was of her parents, and her mom was holding a baby. They looked so happy. Piper studied the photo; they were standing on the porch of Whit's End, and in 1949, the baby had to be Birdie. She shifted the book in her lap and a pile of loose photos fell on the floor. She picked them up and as she slowly looked through them, she realized they'd all been taken in front of Nauset Lighthouse. The first one was of Birdie when she was about two; then Remy stood beside her. Soon, the pictures included Sailor . . . and then Easton . . . and finally, there was one with her.

She turned the page and another photo fell out. She picked it up, and the late afternoon sunlight cast its golden rays across it. It was of all of them—older now—a formidable crew! They had their arms around each other's shoulders and they were laughing. Sailor was making bunny ears behind Remy's head. They looked so happy. Piper's eyes glistened—she'd only been five at the time, but she'd been old enough to know that her world—and the people she loved most in it—would never be the same.

❧ Chapter 2 ❧

"It's just a sprain," Dr. Sanders said, slipping the X-ray back into its folder. "You need to be more careful, though, Birdie. You're not a spring chicken anymore."

"You're not a spring chicken, either, my dear," Birdie Snow snorted. John Sanders had been Birdie's doctor most of her life. He'd been fresh out of residency and new to her parents' doctor's practice when she'd switched over from the family's pediatrician. At the time, Birdie had felt a quiet pride in being the handsome young doctor's first patient, and through the years, she'd wondered if the teasing relationship they'd always shared might've blossomed into something more if David hadn't come into her life.

"Indeed, I'm not," John said with a chuckle. "I'll be seventy this year . . . *and* I'm going to retire."

"You are?!" Birdie sounded horrified.

"Yes, I might even see if I can find a girl to marry. I think it would be nice to have a little companionship in my old age. I've always wanted to travel, and it would be more fun with a companion."

Birdie didn't even hear his last sentence. She was too busy feeling as if the rug were being pulled out from under her . . . *again!* She'd always appreciated that her doctor was growing old alongside her, and she fully expected him to be there till the bitter end. It never occurred to her that he might retire. And as far as finding a girl to marry—that was an entirely different subject . . . and a frivolous one at that. "You can't retire! Who's going to take care of me? My ailments are only going to get worse, and I definitely won't be able to trust some young, new whippersnapper who doesn't know my history."

"Yes, you will," John said, slipping a blood pressure cuff on her arm. "I've got a fine young man lined up, too—Dr. Joshua Hart. He'll be starting next month and we're planning to have an open house so everyone will have the opportunity to meet him. Besides, Birdie, you have my cell phone number, so if something serious comes up, you can always call me." He put his stethoscope under the cuff and squeezed the bulb. "You're the first patient I've told," he said, eyeing her, "and I'd like to be the one to tell my other patients, too."

"Don't worry, John," Birdie said with a sigh.

"I'll take your secret to my grave, which will be a lot sooner now."

"No, it won't be," John countered, looking at her chart. "Let's see, you're going to be sixty-seven next month." He looked up. "And you're *already* retired, I might add."

"Semi-retired," Birdie countered. "I'm still very involved in Cornell's bird count, feeder watch, nest watch, *and* tracking snowy owls on the Cape in the winter, as well as continuing to serve as director emeritus on the ornithology board." She paused. "Not to mention helping David rehabilitate all the orphaned and injured birds that somehow find their way to our house."

John smiled as he wrapped an Ace bandage snugly around her swollen ankle. "You're as busy now as you've ever been, Birdie, which is wonderful, but your blood pressure is still elevated—one sixty over a hundred—and with your family history, you need to do a better job of keeping it under control." He secured the bandage. "Have you been taking your Lisinopril?"

"Yes, yes," she said, waving him off. "Even though I hate taking pills."

John eyed her skeptically. "There *are* other ways to lower your blood pressure. . . ."

"I know, I know—I could lose some weight. You don't need to remind me."

"That's one way," John agreed, "but it would also help if you cut back a little on the red wine."

"Ha!" Birdie snorted. "Did David tell you there was more to my sprained ankle than just tripping on the rug? Because if he did, I—"

"Not at all," John said, holding up his hand in defense of his old golfing partner.

"Good! Because he'd be in a heap of trouble, and besides, I just read an article that sang the praises of red wine. Not only is it good for your heart, but it lowers cholesterol, helps prevent cancer, *and* staves off dementia."

"That *may* be true," John said, although he wasn't entirely convinced by the recent studies trumpeting the health benefits of red wine, "but that's only when it's consumed in moderation."

"I hardly ever have more than one," Birdie said, feigning innocence, even though she knew John knew better—after all, they traveled in the same circles.

John raised an eyebrow. "One glass . . . or one bottle?"

"Ha!" Birdie said, reaching for her crutches. "You know, maybe it *is* a good thing you're retiring. You're getting awfully fresh in your old age."

John put his hand on her shoulder and looked in her eyes. "Birdie, you know I love you, and I know the curves life's thrown your way, but it's not worth risking your health over. You have a lot of life left to live."

Birdie knew John had her best in mind. "We'll

see," she said, looking away. "Now, do I get anything for pain?"

"I thought you didn't like taking pills," he teased.

She eyed him and he chuckled.

"For a sprain you can just take ibuprofen every four to six hours and make sure you keep your foot elevated. Remember R.I.C.E.—rest, ice, compression, elevation?"

"I remember," she said gloomily.

"Good," John said, opening the door. "And you also need to remember that anything stronger than ibuprofen will not mix well with alcohol."

"You take the fun out of everything, you know that?" she said, trying to maneuver the crutches.

"Don't hurt yourself on those," he said, reaching out to make sure she didn't fall.

"Don't worry, I'm fine," she muttered. "For an old hen."

⚜{ Chapter 3 }⚜

Remy Landon stood in the hallway, trying to remember why she'd come upstairs. She walked into her bedroom, hoping it might trigger her memory, and then realized she hadn't made the bed yet . . . and it was almost two o'clock! She started to smooth the sheets, and as she fluffed the starboard pillow, she thought of Jim. She always thought of Jim when she made the bed—it was as if there was a short circuit in her brain and the simple act of fluffing his pillow triggered it. And it was always the same memory, from their wedding night.

"Do you mind if I take the starboard side?" Jim asked uncertainly. "You can have the port. . . ."

She smiled at his use of nautical terminology in reference to their bed, but she wasn't surprised—Jim loved sailing. "Only if I can be captain," she teased, remembering the game Port and Starboard from her childhood.

"You can always be my *captain," he said, pulling her into his arms.*

"Captain's coming," she teased.

"Aye, aye, captain," he said softly, kissing her neck.

"I think you're supposed to salute," she murmured.

"I am saluting.*"*

She felt him press against her and smiled shyly. "I guess you are. . . ."

Jim had been gone twenty years now, but every time Remy made the bed, the same memory filled her mind, and try as she might, she couldn't seem to stop it.

She propped Thread-Bear, the old teddy bear Jim had given her when they were dating, against the pillow and walked around to open the window.

It was a beautiful day—perfect for gardening—but she would definitely need to change first. She pulled open the cardboard box—out of which she'd been living for almost two weeks now—and decided, since it had been reaching eighty degrees every day, it was safe to transfer her turtlenecks and jeans into the box and her T-shirts and shorts into the bureau. Her mother had always warned her not to make the switch too soon because it would jinx the weather. It was the same with flannel sheets—if you put cotton sheets on before mid-May, the temperature would surely drop and there might even be a frost!

Remy rummaged through the box. She'd been wearing the same clothes *forever,* and every season, when she dragged the box out, she promised herself she'd get rid of some of the things she didn't wear anymore—jeans that were way too tight, turtlenecks that were so saggy they should be called hipponecks, sweaters that were pilly—and treat herself to some new things, but then she'd think of all the elderly women who worked at the thrift store. Those hard-working ladies certainly wouldn't appreciate a box of sweaters and jeans dropped off when it was eighty degrees out, or capris and tank tops in October, so she always ended up packing everything back into the box and telling herself she'd try to lose some weight over the summer and fit into those jeans again. Just because it hadn't happened yet didn't mean it couldn't.

Remy pulled out her favorite gardening shirt—a threadbare heather-gray T-shirt she'd bought at the Middlebury College bookstore when she'd gone back for her fifteenth class reunion—and shook it open. It had been the year after Jim died—and although some of her classmates had known, others hadn't. *"Where's ol' Jimbo?"* they'd asked jovially, and then their faces dropped when she'd explained that Jim—her beloved, sweet Jim—had died of a sudden heart attack. "He had a ninety percent blockage in his left artery," she'd explained, just as it had been explained to her. "Yes, a true widow maker," she'd agreed, nodding uncertainly. Even though she'd heard the term *widow maker* before, she'd never associated it with Jim's artery. And then fresh tears had welled up in her eyes and her classmates had hugged her and told her how sorry they were, and how strong she was to come to the reunion so soon after his death.

But Remy hadn't felt strong. She'd felt miserable. And after her classmates walked away, she watched them nodding in her direction and knew they were quietly warning one another over their chardonnays and cabernets not to make the same unfortunate mistake of asking her about Jim. And suddenly, feeling as if she couldn't breathe, she'd mustered a weak smile, excused herself, and fled to her car. Why had she thought she could handle it? She'd driven to her hotel, slipped off the new dress she'd spent hours picking out, left it in a crumpled heap on the bed, and driven all the way back to Wellfleet, where the house had never felt emptier.

Remy unbuttoned her blouse and pulled the T-shirt over her wavy silver hair. Thank goodness that was all behind her. In the years since, she'd raised three children, refurbished their old house, volunteered at the library—a position from which she'd recently retired—and hardly ever dwelled on the life she and Jim might have had. And if she decided to grace her old class-mates with her presence at their next upcoming reunion, she'd be able to show them that life hadn't gotten the best of her. She'd gotten the best of life!

⊰ Chapter 4 ⊱

Sailor Quinn-Ross pushed her drawing table up against the window. *Just like Edward Hopper,* she thought, *or any of the countless other artists and writers who'd come to Cape Cod for inspiration and stayed for a lifetime.* The little Truro cottage had been a rare find *and* a steal! When she'd called Josiah Gray—the real estate agent she'd met at the Buzzard's Bay Dunkin' Donuts back when "pay it forward" was popping up everywhere (he'd paid for her large black coffee and then given her his business card)—and left a message that she was looking for something to get her out of Boston and away from her loser and soon-to-be ex-husband, she'd never expected him to call back and say he had just the place. In fact, he'd added, if he wasn't going through a divorce, too, he'd buy it himself.

Sailor had called Josiah right back and met him that evening. She'd walked around the sandy yard covered with scrub oak, gnarled pitch pine, and rambling beach plums, took note of the once lovely—but now overgrown—gardens, and, enchanted by the sunlight filling every room, signed the papers before an ad could even hit the papers. And even though the cottage would need winterizing, it was solid, *and* it was the best thing that had happened to her in a long time.

Sailor stood in the middle of the bright, airy bedroom she'd envisioned as her studio and looked around. Her old oak drawing table—which she'd had since college—fit perfectly under the window, but it also took up half the room. And this was the bigger room! She'd already ordered a twin bed for the smaller room because there was no way her bed from home would fit, not that she even wanted it after she'd found Frank on top of his secretary in it! In fact, there wasn't much she wanted from the four-thousand-square-foot house in Cambridge. Everything she wanted, she'd already packed up and moved. The house in Cambridge, she'd decided, was much too big anyway, especially since the kids had moved out—*and* it was too full of memories that just didn't matter anymore. The kids mattered, but Frank—well, let's just say she was tired of pretending. "Sell it all," she'd said as she walked out. "I'm done! I am *so* done!"

The simple cottage, on the other hand, was perfect. It was a true beach cottage—a place to crash when you weren't at the beach or out exploring the Cape. It had hardwood floors throughout and a sunny deck with an outdoor shower, and in addition to the two bedrooms, it had a cozy living area that opened into a small kitchen, and although the bathroom was barely big enough to turn around in, she'd manage.

Sailor picked up a cardboard box marked *BOOKS* and put it down in front of a small oak bookcase she'd set up next to her drawing table. She pulled open the flaps, lifted out a pile of children's books, and stood them up on the shelves. *A lifetime of work,* she thought, *and it fits on two shelves!* What would happen to her career now? Frank had always been her editor. He'd been the one who called her that snowy afternoon in early December all those years ago, when she didn't know how she was ever going to pay for Christmas gifts. He'd been the one to tell her he loved *Don't Put the Cart before the Horse—*

a silly children's book she'd written and illustrated her senior year at RISD—and ever since that day, they'd been a team—in more ways than one. Any idea she'd had for a book always breezed right through the publisher's meetings. What about now, though? Would Frank make things difficult for her? Would he try to have her blacklisted? She would definitely need to find a new editor . . . maybe even a new publisher. With her library of work, though, and her connections, she shouldn't have too much trouble . . . or would she? Her connections were getting older—some were even retiring—and she was getting older, too. The publishing world was changing. Nothing was certain anymore.

Sailor sighed, stood up stiffly, and made her way through the boxes to the kitchen. The electricity had been turned on that morning, so she'd picked up some basics for the fridge—cheese, butter, eggs, and then she'd stopped at the package store and picked up a couple of bottles of chardonnay. She looked at her phone. It was 4:45 . . . and five o'clock somewhere just off the coast. She opened a bottle, rummaged around in one of the boxes for a glass, and carried both outside to sit on the steps. *Whatever happens happens,* she thought resignedly. *I can't worry about it. Besides, I'm sitting on the steps of my new beach cottage with a bottle of wine, the smell of the ocean, and a new life—it doesn't get any better than this!*

❈{ Chapter 5 }❈

Piper sat on the mudroom bench, trying to tie her running shoes while Chloe's tail banged against her head. "Hey! You're silly, you know that?" Piper said, pulling her into a hug and making her wiggle even more. "I love you, too," she whispered, holding her head in her hands and looking into her sweet brown eyes. "Are you ready to go for a run?" Chloe danced around and pushed the screen door open with her nose, making it bang against the house . . . and making Piper wince. "Remind me to fix that later."

As soon as Chloe got outside, she picked up a stuffed animal that was lying on the porch, gave it an affectionate shake, and began prancing around with it. "I'm sorry, Chlo, but you have to leave Zoe here," Piper said, eyeing the big floppy toy. Zoe—once a soft, cream-colored stuffed dog with squeakers in her nose and tail— was Chloe's prize possession. When Nat first brought her home, Chloe had immediately fallen in love with her, and ever since then, whenever someone stopped by, Chloe always hurried off to find her beloved stuffed animal and then paraded through the house with her in her mouth, wagging her whole hind end. Unfortunately, Zoe had spent a couple of nights out in the rain and her creamy color had turned a dingy shade of gray. She'd also started to smell a little funky, and in addition to these unpleasantries, her eyes, ears, and squeakers had been surgically removed when no one was looking. Piper didn't have the heart to throw Zoe away, and although Chloe constantly tried to sneak her inside, Zoe was banished to the great outdoors, so whenever Chloe went outside and saw her, she acted as if she'd found a long-lost friend.

"Chlo, leave Zoe here," Piper repeated firmly and Chloe gently set her down. "Good. Let's go." Piper started to trot down the driveway, but when she looked back, Chloe had picked her up again. "Leave Zoe," she commanded, and this time, Chloe set her down for good and trotted after Piper.

Piper glanced back at the house. She'd always loved the lovely Nantucket-style home her parents had left her—as the only unwed daughter, they'd wanted to be sure she always had a place to live—but what Piper loved even more about the house was its location. It was right next to the bike trail and within walking distance of Rock Harbor—one of the best places on the Cape for watching the sun set. In fact, Birdie's husband, David, an ornithology photographer, had often taken a picture of the Quinn sisters every year at Rock Harbor when the sun was setting, and he always teased Birdie, "I'm taking a picture of my big bird today!"

Chloe led the way down the path, and as they neared Bridge Road, sat down and waited for Piper to clip her leash to her collar. The sun was just starting to slip behind the trees, and as they turned toward the harbor, Piper's thoughts drifted to the next day. Nat had called from the marine sanctuary—where they both worked—to tell her there'd been a possible sighting of a loggerhead turtle near First Encounter Beach. He said he'd already been out looking but hadn't seen anything so they'd need to head out first thing in the morning to make sure the turtle—if there was one—wasn't in distress.

Sightings of loggerheads off Cape Cod were rare, but not unheard of—a female, weighing nearly three hundred pounds, had been found on First Encounter Beach two years earlier. Unfortunately, she'd already been in distress for some time—she'd had only one good fin, compromising her ability to swim—and she'd died before they could help her. Twenty years before that, a smaller loggerhead, weighing just a hundred pounds, had washed up onshore in the same area. There were also recordings of leatherbacks—weighing up to seven hundred pounds—in Cape Cod Bay, but the most common turtles in the Bay were Kemp's ridleys, and she and Nat had rescued countless numbers of these smaller sea turtles.

Piper had worked at the Cape Cod Marine

Sanctuary ever since she'd interned as a rising senior at the University of New England in Maine. It was during her internship that she first met Nat, the soft-spoken marine biologist, eight years her senior . . . *and* engaged. It hadn't occurred to Piper that Nat might be involved with someone else, and by the time she figured it out, it was too late—she'd already fallen for him.

Piper would never forget that first day. Nat had been wearing faded red swim trunks and a snow-white T-shirt, and he was already very tan—even though it was only May. She'd been standing on the dock with the other interns, admiring his sun-streaked chestnut brown hair and carefree demeanor when he looked up and asked if she would hold the turtle he was trying to untangle. Piper had knelt next to him, her heart pounding, and held the turtle—whose legs were churning as fast as they would go—and watched as he carefully snipped the fishing line and gently unraveled it from the little turtle's shell and fin. "Thanks," he said, smiling at her with slate blue eyes that seemed to see right through her.

"You're welcome," she said, blushing.

Later that day, when she was heading to her car, he'd called her name. "It *is* Piper, isn't it?"

She'd nodded.

"I don't know if you have time right now, but someone just called in a possible leatherback sighting and I could use a second set of eyes. Want to come along?"

Piper had jumped at the chance, and from that day on, she and Nat had been inseparable. Anytime there was an errand to run, a sighting to check, or a turtle to rescue, Piper had been by Nat's side, learning the hands-on work she'd do—and *love* doing—for the rest of her life, and although she loved every minute she spent with Nat, too, she never told him. Nat, for his part, seemed innocently unaware of her feelings. It wasn't until the end of that summer, when the staff went out for pizza together and Nat drove her back to her car, that she got up the courage to tell him how she felt. They were leaning against the hood of his truck, and she shyly told him she was going to miss him. Nat had put his arm around her, kissed the top of her head, and told her he was going to miss her, too, but then Piper had leaned up and softly kissed him. Nat had pulled away in surprise, but then he'd searched her eyes, and gently kissed her again.

"Are you sure about this?" he murmured when she pulled him against her, and she nodded, and on the last night before she headed back to Maine, the innocent friendship they'd shared all summer spiraled into intimacy.

"Now I'm *really* going to miss you," Piper murmured, feeling his lingering heat between her legs.

He smiled. "I'm going to miss *you,* too, but you need to focus on your schoolwork and *not* think about me. I'll still be here when you graduate."

"That's a long time from now."

"Good things come to those who wait," he teased.

"Maybe you could come to Maine."

"I don't have a reason to come to Maine."

"You could give a talk."

"That's a nice thought, but I think we'd be asking for trouble."

"We're already asking for trouble. . . ."

"That's what worries me, Pipe."

Piper had smiled wistfully, and then he'd pulled her close, kissed the top of her head, and wondered how he'd let it happen.

When Piper reached the harbor at the end of Dyer Prince Road, she unclipped Chloe's leash and the big golden raced ahead, loping through the dune grass like a porpoise. Piper followed her down the sandy path, and when she came to the beach, Chloe was standing on the water's edge, waiting. "Okay," Piper said and Chloe charged into the water.

Piper continued to run along the wet sand, and when she looked back, she saw Chloe, wet and sandy, racing after her. "Oh, no, you don't!" she said, but Chloe raced past, knowing right where, in the tall grass, Piper had hidden a tennis ball.

She got there first, picked it up, and pranced around triumphantly. "You beat me," Piper said, laughing breathlessly, and Chloe dropped the ball at her feet and raced toward the water. Piper picked up the ball and threw it as far as she could, and the golden plowed through the shallows. Time and again, Piper threw the ball, and time and again, Chloe raced after it.

"Okay," she said finally. "Time to head back," and the big golden turned on a dime and raced past her. "You are so full of energy tonight. Maybe you should act your age before you hurt yourself," she said, laughing as the blur of wet fur blasted past her again. Piper trotted along after her wet dog, looked up at the evening sky, blazing with orange and pink streaks, and smiled. "Thank You for *everything*," she whispered.

⍦ Chapter 6 ⍦

Birdie sat on the back deck of their old saltbox-style house in Orleans with her sprained ankle up on a chair, watching the birds fluttering back and forth between the scrub pine and the bird feeders. She noticed a flash of bright blue and sat up—an indigo bunting was on the feeder! Indigos were rare on Cape Cod, as were scarlet tanagers and orioles. Birdie opened her laptop, logged in, and entered the sighting—including the date and time—and leaned back to watch. The elusive indigo fluttered down to the birdbath, took a drink, and flew away.

Birdie sighed. "Maybe he'll come back." She refilled her wine glass and thought about the conversation she'd had with Dr. Sanders that afternoon. She couldn't believe, at this stage of his life, he would start looking for a woman to marry. He was seventy years old, for heaven's sake, and through two-thirds of those years, every single woman in town had tried to get him to go out, but he'd never accepted any of their invitations. She shook her head. He'd also been out of line to imply that she drank too much. She didn't drink nearly as much as some people in their circle, and she could stop anytime she wanted. The only problem she had was that she didn't want to stop. She looked forward to having a glass of wine at the end of the day—it was her way of celebrating, and there was always something to celebrate—a gorgeous sunset, a good book, a thunderstorm, a rare bird sighting, the first snow, finishing her Christmas shopping. The reasons were endless—that's how life was. And having a *bad* day was also a good reason—a glass of wine helped her get over whatever was bothering her.

She took another sip. Even though John denied it, she'd bet anything David had said something to him when they were playing golf that morning. She could just hear her husband: *I'm worried about Birdie. She didn't* just *trip on that rug . . . she had a few too many drinks and took a looper!* David never said anything to *her,* though. He didn't have to—she knew what he was thinking. She could feel his eyes watching her whenever she poured a glass of wine, and she knew he kept track of the bottles in the recycling bin. She shook her head. Those two should just worry about themselves. After all, they were the ones who went to the clubhouse for a martini lunch every time they played golf—and that was in the middle of the day! And what about the time David backed into the lamppost? Too many gin and tonics at the Mitchells' clambake, that's what happened! At least she stuck to wine; none of that hard stuff for her—*"headache in a bottle"* she called it—and she'd never backed into anything. She knew when she'd had enough, and she knew when she shouldn't drive. She took another sip and watched a female cardinal flutter from the feeder to a branch where a juvenile was waiting. The female landed right next to him and promptly dropped a seed into his open beak. Birdie smiled sadly. "I would've been a good mother, too," she murmured, looking heavenward. "If You'd only given me the chance."

David opened the screen door and an old black Lab with a snow-white face moseyed out and rested her head on Birdie's lap. "Hello, Bailey," Birdie said, stroking the dog's velvety ears and looking into her cloudy chocolate-brown eyes. "How was *your* day?" Bailey—who was named after the famous ornithologist Florence Merriam Bailey—wiggled her arthritic hind end and Birdie smiled. "No matter how much it hurts, you'll never stop wagging that old tail of yours, will you?" The old Lab licked her hand and then wandered over to a sunny spot, dropped into it like a sack of bones, and proceeded to watch the birds—her name suited her!

David noticed a prescription bottle on the table next to the wine bottle and picked it up. "I thought you weren't supposed to mix alcohol and Vicodin."

"It's no big deal," Birdie said, waving him off. "I'm sure the combination will only dull the pain *more*—which is just what I need."

He looked at the date on the bottle and frowned. "This is from 2010. Did John say you should take this?"

"Motrin wasn't helping and this was in the cabinet."

David shook his head and sighed. "Shall I heat up dinner then?"

"Yes, there's leftover chicken in the fridge . . . and rice pilaf."

"The lemon chicken we had last night?"

"Yes. And asparagus, too."

"Do you want a salad?"

"If you feel like making one."

David slid the screen door closed and Birdie listened as he puttered around in the kitchen, warming up their supper. It was nice to be able to relax and let him make dinner for a change. She was lucky to have a good husband—a husband who didn't cheat, like Frank; or die, like Jim; Nat was a different story—she couldn't figure out why he and Piper had never married. Nonetheless, even though her sisters had all been blessed with children—even unmarried Piper had sweet Elias—she'd been blessed with a good and faithful man, and Lord knew, a man like that was hard to find. She took another sip of her wine. Yes, having David—even with all his faults— was definitely a reason to celebrate!

⊰ Chapter 7 ⊱

Remy looked out the kitchen window and whispered, "Red sky at night, sailor's delight. Red sky in the morning, sailors take warning."

"What does that mean?" she'd asked Jim one time when they'd been coming back from a sunset sail.

"It's old weather lore," he'd explained. *"When there's a red sky in the evening, it's because the sun's rays are streaming through a high concentration of dust particles—which is indicative of a high pressure front and stable conditions . . .*

aka good weather; but when there's a red sky in the morning, it means either the good weather has passed and a low is moving in or that the sunlight is streaming through a high concentration of water vapor. Either way, it means a storm is possible."

Remy smiled. Jim, the science professor, had always been good at explaining things. Since that night Remy had discovered, to her surprise, the same weather lore was in the Bible. She'd stumbled across it in the book of Matthew: *Jesus replied, "When evening comes, you say, 'It will be fair weather, for the sky is red,' and in the morning, 'Today it will be stormy, for the sky is red and overcast . . .' "* She couldn't believe the lore went back that far, but then again, most of the disciples had been fishermen, so they must've kept an eye on the weather.

She filled a glass with cold water, squeezed a slice of lemon into it, reached for her book, and stepped out onto the screened-in porch to settle into her favorite chair. A moment later, Edison— the handsome gray tomcat with snow-white boots that had appeared on her doorstep one snowy November evening ten years earlier—hopped up on her lap, pressed his nose against hers, and promptly curled up. Remy stroked his soft fur. She'd come to believe that Edison watched and waited for her to sit down, because every time she did, he appeared. "Where've you been hiding?" she asked, but he just purred. His exploits were a well-kept secret.

Remy opened her book and started to read, but almost immediately, her thoughts began to stray. Why was she having so much trouble concentrating lately? She used to devour books—three in a week, at least! Recently, though, she'd had trouble getting through one page without dozing off, and if she did make it through a page, she often had no idea what she'd read. And if she had a glass of wine—which she rarely did anymore—there was no point in reading at all, because she'd be asleep before she even opened the book. She didn't know how Birdie and Sailor did it. They could drink a whole bottle of wine and stay up late reading—or in Sailor's case, working.

She looked down at the page. She'd always loved Anne Morrow Lindbergh's timeless meditation on the stages of a woman's life, but this time, she couldn't seem to concentrate on the lovely words. She ran her hand lightly over the page—maybe it was because she'd read the book so many times, or maybe it was because her tired old brain didn't work as well as it once had. Maybe she was actually developing early-onset Alzheimer's—it couldn't be regular Alzheimer's because she was only sixty-five—but she'd certainly become more forgetful lately. She had to write everything down. In fact, she had lists all over the house, and if she went to the store and forgot her list, she might as well turn around and go home. And then there was the clutter that was accumulating in the spare bedroom—she didn't know how it had happened. She'd always prided herself on keeping a tidy house, but that room was an embarrassment—so much so she had to keep the door closed. Heaven forbid her kids ever saw it. They would think she was losing it!

Remy looked at the darkening sky and sighed. She'd read somewhere—she couldn't remember where—that clutter was another symptom of dementia or Alzheimer's. Heaven help her if she had Alzheimer's! What would happen to her? Would any of her children—Payton or Eliza or Sam—take her in? They were so busy with their own families and she definitely didn't want to burden them . . . but she didn't want to be in a nursing home, either. She hated nursing homes; when Birdie had insisted on putting their mom in one, Remy had been against it. As far as she was concerned, nursing homes were a miserable, lonely, end-of-life existence.

"Oh, dear God, don't let me have Alzheimer's," she whispered, "*or* be a burden to my children. Just let me die in my sleep . . . on the port side of my own bed!"

Her cell phone started to play "In the Mood" and she picked it up and looked at the screen. It only showed a number. "Hello?" she said quizzically. "I'm sorry. Who did you say?" she asked, frowning, and then her face lit up. "Oh, Sam! I was just thinking about you. . . . Yes, I know, I need to put your name in my phone. . . . I just can't seem to figure out how. . . . Yes, I know you showed me. . . . Maybe you could show me again the next time you're here. . . . Yes, everything's fine. It's *so* good to hear your voice!"

❧ Chapter 8 ❧

Sailor poured the last of the bottle into her glass and looked up at the wispy streaks of purple drifting across the coral sky. "You sure know how to paint a sunset, Lord," she murmured. "We muggle artists can't even begin to compete!" She took a sip of her wine, realized "Smoke Gets in Your Eyes" was drifting from inside the house, and followed the sound to her studio. She picked up her phone, looked at the screen, and promptly turned it off. She had nothing to say to Frank, and she certainly didn't want to hear what *he* had to say.

As she walked back through the cottage, she plugged in the lamps she'd brought from home—two floor lamps in the living room and a small lamp on the bedroom floor next to one of the kids' old sleeping bags, her accommodations until her bed arrived. She'd always hated gloomy, dark rooms; although she'd never been officially diagnosed, she was convinced she suffered from seasonal affective disorder, and she was equally certain that being an artist didn't help either. Everyone knew artists tended to be more sensitive. Look at all the artists, writers, and performers who'd fallen into the grips of substance abuse—it was because they all felt life too keenly.

Now that she was up and moving, Sailor could feel the effects of gravity on her bladder. She hurried to the bathroom—the old storage tank definitely wasn't the iron vault it had once been! Back in college, she could drink her friends under the table and still not need to *go,* but now, if she laughed or coughed without crossing her legs, she sprang a leak. It was a good thing she worked from home because there was no way she was going to wear panty liners or, heaven help her, diapers!

Sailor would never forget the time she'd had to help her mom after they'd first moved her into the nursing home; it was before the damn dementia—as she called it—had completely robbed her of every bodily sensation, so she still knew, and was able to signal when she needed to *go.* Sailor had called the nurse, but she'd been slow in coming, and finally, sensing it was urgent, she'd wheeled her mom into the bathroom, helped her stand up, pulled her pajama bottoms down, and realized she was wearing a diaper—no wonder the nurse hadn't been in a hurry! "Oh, Mom," she'd murmured in dismay. "Is this what it all comes to?" She pulled the bulky diaper down, felt its heavy weight, and realized it was already too late.

Martha had stood, hunched over and staring straight ahead while Sailor pulled off the wet diaper and slipped on a fresh one from a package in the corner. "I'm sorry, Mom," she whispered, tears filling her eyes. "I'm so sorry all this is happening to you." If her mom couldn't feel humiliation, she could certainly feel it for her.

"Damn it, God!" she'd railed as she drove home. "Why did You have to make getting old suck so much? Why can't people get old with their dignity still intact? Is it too much to ask? It's pretty poor planning on Your part! I don't think You thought the 'getting old' stage through very well!" And when she finally got home, she called her youngest daughter and told her what had happened. "If I ever get like that, Merry, just shoot me!"

Meredith had laughed. "Oh, Mom, that's not gonna happen to you."

Now Sailor sighed—it already *was* happening.

She reached for the toilet paper, realized there wasn't any, and shared her favorite expletive with the silence. "I guess it's drip-dry today," she mumbled, pulling up her underwear and shorts in one swift motion. A moment later, she opened the box on the counter labeled *TOILETRIES* and realized she'd stuck a half a roll in the box—just in case. She shook her head, slipped it onto the holder, and made a mental note to buy more.

She finished unpacking the box—her soap, shampoo, facial cream, toothpaste, and toothbrush —and stood in front of the mirror, studying her reflection, trying to decide if it was the mirror or the lighting that was more forgiving than the one at home. She touched her short salt-and-pepper hair and then lightly traced the wrinkles around her eyes. "I shouldn't have smiled so much in life," she said to her reflection. "All those fake, forced smiles at parties and reunions . . . and now, I'm paying the price." She turned her head. "I'm just one big wrinkle! Maybe that's why our vision gets worse with age," she mused, "so we can't see our wrinkles!" She shook her head. "So You *do* have a plan," she said in a voice edged with sarcasm, "a flawed plan, but a plan nonetheless."

She turned off the light and went into her studio. "Ah, where to begin?" She reached for the glass she'd left on the drawing table, took a sip, put it on the bookcase, and set to work securing her lamp to her drawing table. The black "combo" lamp, as it was called, had an incandescent and a fluorescent bulb that, when on at the same time, illuminated her work surface with light that was similar to pure northern light, but after she tightened the clamp, slid the arm into its sleeve, crawled under the table, plugged it in, crawled back out, and pressed both switches, only the incandescent came on. She shook her head in dismay. "Geez Louise! If it's not one damn thing, it's another!"

"Moving on!" she declared. She took another sip of her wine, opened the flaps of an old box she'd plopped onto her chair, paused, realizing the contents, and began to slowly unwrap a collection of framed photos. Sailor had always loved the black-and-white photographs David had taken of the "Quinn Sisters," as he called them. It had been a summer tradition to walk out on the dunes of one of the beaches or out to Rock Harbor at sunset and have their picture taken. It was also a Christmas tradition for David to give them each a framed copy of that year's photo. Birdie and Remy and Piper usually hung the photos up here and there in their homes, but Sailor had always thought they should be hung together. Unfortunately, she'd never wanted to hang them up in the house in Cambridge. For some reason, the sprawling house she and Frank shared never "fit" the way she felt about her family—so she'd always kept them tucked in a box. Now, as she looked around the room, her eyes settled on the wall next to her drawing table—it was the perfect spot.

She looked down at the photos again. When viewed together, they were an extraordinary collection—it was stunning to see how she and her sisters had changed over the years. She picked up the very first one and realized she must've been around eighteen at the time—which would've made Birdie twenty-two, Remy twenty, and Piper only thirteen. Look at them! They were all so slender . . . and gorgeous . . . and independent. Although the family resemblance was strong, the similarities ended there—they were all so different. The only lasting similarity was the solemnness in their eyes, a solemnness that revealed a shared sorrow—one of which they never spoke. Sailor never understood why her parents never talked about that night . . . why they never even said Easton's name, and through the years, whenever she or her sisters said it, they were given looks that said *"don't go there."* Eventually, they learned not to mention him, and looking back now, it was an absolute wonder they weren't all more messed up. She'd tried to work her issues out on her own. She'd even gone to therapy for a while, hoping that a therapist would be able to help her relax and not be so afraid to express her feelings, but it hadn't helped. She couldn't even tell *him* about Easton. Her parents' silence, she'd decided, was so ingrained in her psyche that she felt like she was betraying her family if she said anything. Maybe she was more screwed up than she thought!

She looked back at the picture and searched her sisters' eyes. They were definitely all products of the same upbringing and shared family history, and as a result, they loved each other fiercely.

Maybe that was the one good thing that had come from the tragedy of losing their brother.

She put the photo back with the others and looked at them again. Even their clothing was an unintended study in the fashion of the times—from college T-shirts and L.L.Bean polo shirts to linen blouses and flowing sundresses—their clothing revealed roots firmly planted in the soil and sands of New England, and as they'd aged, they looked more and more like the strong New England women they'd become.

Sailor picked up one of the more recent photos and smiled—it was, by far, her favorite. At the time, however, she hadn't even wanted to be in it. She gazed at it now. She was very thin, hollow-cheeked, and gaunt, and her sisters all had their arms around her. Without looking, she knew the photo had been taken in 2006 because that was the year she'd had a double mastectomy and then endured twenty-eight rounds of chemo. She hadn't wanted to be in the picture because she'd lost all her hair and she'd thought she looked terrible, but her sisters had insisted, saying it was more important than ever. Birdie had found a soft hat for her to wear, and as they'd all stood on the beach, her sisters had wrapped their arms around her and held her tight . . . and her eyes had filled with tears—she'd never felt so much love.

❧ Chapter 9 ❧

Piper tossed the forward line into the launch, pushed off, and hopped in.

"Not bad for an ol' girl," Nat teased, swinging the boat around and heading out into the bay.

Piper rolled her eyes. "You're one to talk."

"How old are you going to be this summer?" he teased. "Sixty?"

Piper gave him a wilting look. "The best way for you to remember *my* age is to take *your* age—which is sixty-six—and subtract eight."

"Ouch!" Nat said, shaking his head.

Piper laughed as she pulled her Windbreaker over her head. The early morning air was cool and misty—not great for boating, but they'd definitely been out in worse. She reached for her binoculars and scanned the slate gray water. First Encounter Beach was in Eastham—the next town over—so they'd be there in no time, but the turtle could be anywhere by now, and with the Memorial Day weekend looming, the Bay would soon be full of boats and much more dangerous for a big sea turtle.

As they neared the beach, Nat slowed down and reached for his binoculars, too. They drifted along, scouring the coastline, but the only sign of life was a woman throwing a tennis ball for her dog. "I wish I had his energy!" Nat said, watching the dog plowing into the surf.

"That's what happens when you get old," Piper teased.

"I'm still young enough to keep up with you!"

"You think so?" Piper teased as Nat pulled her into his arms. "Hey," she said. "We're supposed to be looking for a turtle, you know, one of those reptiles with a hard shell."

"Actually, loggerheads have soft shells," Nat said, sliding his hands down her back. "Kind of like you . . ."

"Very funny," Piper murmured. "There are people around, you know. . . ."

"There's no one around," Nat countered softly.

Piper looked back at the beach and realized the woman and the dog had disappeared and fog was starting to roll in. "Sheesh, what happened? It's getting to be like pea soup out here."

"Mmm," Nat agreed. "I don't think we're going to find our turtle today."

"I guess not," she said resignedly. "The tide's starting to turn, too, so we better head back."

"What's your hurry?" Nat asked.

Piper smiled, remembering the time they hadn't paid attention to the tide because, like now, Nat had been distracting her and before they knew it, the boat had stopped rocking.

"Nice!" Nat teased, shaking his head. "Now, look what you've done!"

"Me?" she countered. "You started it!"

"You're the one who wore that tight, white tank top. . . ."

"You're the one who didn't wear a top," she countered, eyeing his tan torso. She sighed. "What should we do?"

They debated walking to shore, but then realized they'd have no way of getting back to the boat when the tide came in, so, with nothing to do, they followed the receding water, stood on its edge, shed their clothes, swam in the shallows, and as the sun set, made love on the cool, wet sand. An hour later, flushed with lovemaking, they walked back to the boat and watched the stars grow brighter as the coastline—from Boston to Provincetown—blinked to life. They pulled on sweatshirts, leaned against the boat's windshield, and gazed at the canopy of lights twinkling all around them. Six hours later, they woke up to gentle rocking . . . and one month after that, Piper realized she was pregnant.

"I don't want to be stranded for twelve hours," she said. "I have stuff to do—I want to see Sailor's new place and Elias is coming home tonight so I need to go food shopping."

"I thought he wasn't coming home till tomorrow."

"Change of plans," she said with a shrug. "He misses his mom."

"He misses *Chloe*," Nat teased with a grin.

Piper laughed. "Yeah, you're probably right," she said, knowing how much their son missed Chloe when he was away at college.

Nat pressed against her and she felt how aroused he was. "Are you sure you want to head back right now?" he asked softly.

"I guess I could stay a little longer," she murmured with a smile. "As long as you're quicker than the tide."

❧ Chapter 10 ❧

Birdie could tell, when she woke up in the middle of the night, that trouble was brewing. She rolled to her side and felt her ankle throb, but it wasn't nearly as bad as the pain looming behind her eyes. She made a fist under her pillow and pressed her temple into it. "Please, no," she murmured. "Please don't let me get a headache." She hadn't had a migraine in years—not since she'd been perimenopausal—but she remembered the symptoms all too well, and she knew she needed to get up and take something—early intervention was key—but getting up seemed so . . . impossible . . . and what should she take? What *could* she take? The only thing that had ever worked for her head was Imitrex, and it had been so long since she'd needed some, she didn't even know if she still had any. She sat up and groaned as the change in blood flow increased the pounding in her temple. "Not good," she murmured, easing to the side of the bed and reaching for her crutches. One thing was certain—the pain in her head was making the pain in her ankle seem like a walk in the park.

David felt her moving. "What's the matter?" he murmured.

"Migraine," she said.

"Want me to get something?"

"No, no . . . go back to sleep."

He rolled over, and before Birdie had even made it across the room, he was snoring again.

"Must be nice," she muttered, maneuvering around Bailey, who was sprawled out across the hall. She made her way gingerly down the stairs in the darkness, but when she turned on the kitchen light, she blinked at the brightness and promptly turned it off again. She felt her way to the stove, closed her eyes, switched on the hood light, squinted at the clock, and groaned again. It was 3:20—much too early to be awake. She wouldn't be able to function in the morning . . . when the *real* morning arrived.

She pulled open the medicine drawer full of pills and rifled through it, praying she'd find an old blister sheet of her migraine medicine. They had everything from prednisone to Prozac and Valium to Xanax—"We could open a damn pharmacy!" she muttered. Like a possessed woman, she pulled out the remaining contents of the drawer—three pill splitters, one pill crusher, two heartworm pills, and an old inhaler. She peered into the empty drawer, and to her surprise, spied a small rectangular foil packet in the back. She pulled it out and squinted at it but she was unable to tell without her glasses whether it was Imitrex; she could, however, make out the date: "Discard after 06/00"—*Really?* Could it *really* be sixteen years old? Was it safe? Was it safe to take *with* Vicodin? Had it lost its potency? Her aching head spun with questions.

Maybe the Vicodin had caused her headache . . . or maybe it was the combination of Vicodin and alcohol. For the first time in her life, Birdie regretted ignoring John's warning. Why hadn't she listened? She could feel the pressure building behind her eyes. Maybe she didn't have a migraine at all. Maybe it was a brain aneurysm! One of her colleagues had died from a brain aneurysm, and at her funeral, her husband said the only symptom she'd had was a severe headache. Birdie found her glasses and studied the foil packet. Maybe she should wait and call John in the morning. Then again, if she had an aneurysm, maybe she should go to the emergency room. She looked at the clock, wondering if John would mind a call at this hour. Surely, if he knew she had a brain aneurysm, he wouldn't mind. Another wave of nausea swept over her, and she felt as if someone were tightening a vise grip on her head. She leaned against the counter and folded back the corner of the packet, trying to separate the hard plastic from the paper, but the ancient seal had melded together. She looked in the junk drawer for scissors—they were never where they were supposed to be!

In desperation, she pulled a sharp knife out of the dish drain, and almost immediately, the old familiar voice in her head started to sound the alarm. She knew that voice too well—she'd been listening to it, and ignoring it, for sixty-seven years. *Be careful!* it warned. *Don't do anything stupid!* "Of course, I'll be careful," she muttered. "Do I ever do anything stupid?" She paused. "Don't answer that." She pointed the tip of the knife into the edge of the plastic bubble, but just as she started to apply pressure, the knife slipped and sliced into her finger. Birdie cried out in surprise and pain, dropped the knife in the sink, turned on the cold water, held her finger under it, and watched the white porcelain turn bright red. *For heaven's sake, how can there be so much blood? I wonder if I need stitches?* With her free hand, she reached for a paper towel and wrapped it around her finger. *If I go to the ER for stitches, maybe they'll do a CAT scan and find my aneurysm, too.* She squeezed her finger, trying to decide which part of her body hurt most: her finger, her ankle, or her head. With her throbbing finger wrapped in a bloody paper towel, she ditched her crutches and limped to the bathroom, where, in the process of looking for a Band-Aid, she found the scissors. She rinsed her finger again, dried it, quickly applied the Band-Aid before more blood spurted out, and limped back to the kitchen with the scissors. She looked at the clock, and thinking more clearly now, made the executive decision to *not* call John at this ungodly hour. She carefully cut open the package with the scissors, swallowed the pill with a gulp of water, dumped the rest of the water in the sink, retrieved her crutches, and headed for the living room. Collapsing on the couch, she propped her foot on a pillow and leaned back.

"Please make it go away," she prayed, pressing her knuckle into her temple. The pressure behind her eye was explosive—even the tears sliding down her cheeks didn't relieve it. She listened to the ticking of David's clocks. They seemed so loud. The old grandfather clock in the hall chimed its familiar Winchester chime, followed by four loud bongs; her bird clock from Orvis—the one David had given her for her birthday years ago—chirped with the song of her least favorite bird, the house wren, whose favorite pastime was filling bluebird houses with sticks. She didn't know how that fool wren had any time to make a nest and raise a brood of its own when it was so busy ruining other birds' nests. Finally, a couple minutes later, the cuckoo—perpetually late-to-the-party, no matter how carefully David adjusted the pendulum—opened its door and cuckooed four times. Birdie silently counted each chime, song, and cuckoo. There was so much she wanted to do today. She'd wanted to stop and see Sailor's new cottage *yesterday* and bring her a celebratory bottle of chardonnay (Sailor always switched to white in the summer), but those plans had gone right out the window when she'd tripped on the rug and spent all of the next morning at the doctor's office. And now, if her headache didn't go away, she wouldn't get to see her today, either. She also had a backlog of work to finish for the ornithology board, but if she had a headache, she definitely wouldn't be able to look at a computer screen.

She stared into the darkness, wondering how human beings had survived before painkillers, antibiotics, and antianxiety pills. She could still remember peeking anxiously into her grand-mother's darkened bedroom when she'd been rendered helpless by debilitating and days-long headaches. Back then, there'd been no relief for her poor grandmother—she'd just had to wait it out. Oh, the misery she'd endured!

The clocks chimed again, and Birdie felt a cool breeze drift through the window. The sky was growing brighter and the ever-punctual songbirds —whose internal summer clocks were set for

4:30—started to sing. She closed her eyes and listened. Mr. Cardinal was first—she could picture him tapping his baton and giving the others his first cheerful note; soon, the grosbeaks, chickadees, and titmice all joined in, and then, not to be left out, the house finches, wrens, nuthatches, and bluebirds added their songs, too, until the woods were alive with a symphony . . . and then there was another haunting sound. Birdie caught her breath and listened, remembering a long-ago night when she and her siblings had been camping in the backyard—all five of them in one tent! Easton had been lying next to her and she'd just fallen asleep when he nudged her with his elbow.

"Birdie?" he whispered urgently. "What's that sound?"

"What sound?" she murmured sleepily.

"Listen."

She listened but all she could hear were crickets. "I don't hear anything."

"Shhh!"

And then, there it was—a long mournful wail. "Oh my," she whispered.

"What is it?"

"It's a loon," she said, her voice filled with awe.

"A loon?"

"Yes. Dad said they're on the Cape, but I've never heard one before."

"It's so cool," Easton said. "It sounds like a whale."

"It *does* sound like a whale," she agreed, smiling. They'd lain still, listening to the lonely loon until it was silent and all she heard was her brother's peaceful breathing.

Birdie listened to the loon now. It had been years since she'd heard the long, sad call. She breathed in deeply through her nose and exhaled slowly through her mouth, trying to take her mind off the pain. Finally, she felt the sensation she'd been waiting for—her throat tightening as the blood vessels constricted; it was an odd sensation —the first time she'd felt it, she'd panicked, but now she welcomed it, knowing it meant her headache was going away. She closed her eyes and felt Bailey nuzzle her hand. "Hey, there, sweetie pie," she murmured, stroking her soft ears. Five minutes later, she drifted off, and when she woke up, Bailey was lying beside her and David was making coffee.

"How's your head?"

"Better," she said in a relieved voice. "Thank goodness I had something to take."

"Well, it looks like you had trouble finding whatever it was," David said, nodding to the pill bottles all over the counter. "Did you cut yourself, too?"

Birdie looked at her finger and realized the blood had almost soaked through the Band-Aid. Her memory of that frantic hour in the kitchen, however, was just a blur. "Yes, I guess I did."

"There was blood all over the sink."

"There was? I thought I rinsed it out."

"Well, you missed some," David said as he poured coffee into two mugs. "It looked like someone was murdered."

"It *did* bleed quite a bit," she said, suddenly realizing she really needed to go to the bathroom. She'd forgotten the effect headache medicine had on her bladder. She reached for her crutches and winced—her head might be feeling better, but her ankle and finger were still throbbing.

She returned from the bathroom and sat down and David put a cup of coffee in front of her. "How about an English muffin with some marmalade?" he asked.

"Sounds good," Birdie said, smiling, and then she remembered hearing the loon . . . and her little brother lying beside her. The memory made her heart ache.

⊰ Chapter 11 ⊱

Remy opened her mom's *Good Housekeeping* cookbook, turned to the earmarked "Pie and Pastry" section, and began to jot down the ingredients for rhubarb pie. She had plenty of rhubarb—the big, leafy plants had loved all the rain they'd had that spring—but she still needed to pick up an orange; she always forgot the recipe called for orange zest. She set her pen down and opened the cabinet to see if she had any quick-cook tapioca but when she heard a plaintive meow she stopped her search to open the back door and Edison sauntered in, expecting breakfast.

"I'm going out," she said as she scooped kibble into his dish. He settled in front of it. "I won't be long," she added, opening the back door again and stepping out, but a moment later, she was back. "I forgot my list," she said as she pulled her shopping list off the top of her notepad. "See you in a bit." She closed the door again and made it all the way out to Ol' Bess—her ancient Subaru Outback—before remembering she forgot her phone. She stood in the driveway, debating. Did she need it? No one ever called. Then again, if something happened and she needed help, she wouldn't have it. She went back inside and unplugged it. "I'm *really* leaving this time," she assured the cat as she opened the door again. This time, Edison—who'd grown accustomed to her habit of repeatedly leaving—took advantage of the opportunity to scoot back outside. "Stay away from the road," she called as he sauntered away. "I'm sure *he* didn't forget anything," she murmured. "It's all the trappings we humans can't live without."

Ten minutes later, she found a parking spot right in front of the Wellfleet Marketplace. She gathered her things, made sure she had every-thing—list, glasses, and wallet—and then surprised herself by remembering her canvas bags, too. "I remembered and I haven't even had my tea yet!" she murmured proudly, fully believing that tea made her mind sharper. She went into the store, grabbed a basket, and made her way through the produce section, carefully consulting her list. Since she hadn't taken the time to make breakfast—*or* have her tea—she stopped at the bakery and bought a blueberry muffin, which came with a free tea. From there she headed to the deli and ordered a small container of the market's famous Cape Cobb salad. Then, as she stood in the checkout line, she compared her list with the contents of her basket and realized she'd forgotten the orange. With a sigh, she left her place in line and went back to the produce.

Twenty minutes later, she pulled into the sandy driveway of the house she and Jim had had built on Great Island when they were first married. The house was a rambling bow-roof Cape with cedar shake siding on the ends and back, and weathered cedar shingles on the roof. In keeping with Cape Cod tradition, the front of the house was painted. When they'd first built it, Jim had painted it a dark rustic red, but after he died, she'd asked Sam to paint it tan; and most recently, despite the protest of her sisters, she'd had it painted white. Sailor had been especially critical. "White is so boring," she'd moaned. "It's so . . . vanilla!"

"That's me," Remy had countered with a resigned smile. "Boring vanilla," and that was really how she thought of herself. She wore the same clothes, year in and year out, took the same walk around the island, day in and day out, ate the same breakfast every morning—Bob's Red Mill steel-cut oatmeal, and went to bed at the same time every night. If that wasn't *vanilla* she didn't know what was. Even her favorite flavor of ice cream was vanilla.

Remy carried the groceries into the house, set her tea and muffin on the counter, and as she began putting everything away, noticed that the cabinet door was open. She frowned, trying to remember why she'd been in there. She glanced at the cookbook and then it hit her—she'd been looking for tapioca! Her heart sank as she scanned the shelves—she had everything from cornstarch to corn syrup and baking soda to baking powder, but she couldn't find the little red and white box of tapioca beads. "Sugar!" she exclaimed. "Now I have to go back out!"

With a growl of frustration, she warmed up her muffin in the microwave, spread a little butter on it, and ate it while sipping her lukewarm tea. Then she washed the dishes, set them in the dish drainer, wiped the crumbs off the counter, and headed back to her car, returning only once this time, for her keys.

She pulled up in front of the store and looked

around. The prime parking spot she'd had before was long gone, and because there wasn't a parking spot anywhere, she was sure the checkout lines would be long, too. "So much for an early start!" she muttered.

When she finally got back to her car, she tossed the plastic bag with the one box in it onto the passenger seat—she'd forgotten to bring a canvas bag, and although she'd told the bagger she didn't need a bag, he'd still given her one.

She started the car, put on her seat belt, and pulled out into a long line of traffic. "It's not even Memorial Day!" she moaned. She dreaded the long lines summertime brought and tried to avoid venturing out at all on the weekends. She pushed back her damp hair, and because her air conditioner didn't work, rolled down her window.

Saturday was travel day on the Cape. It was when all the rentals changed hands and all the vacationers flooded the supermarkets, stocking up for the week. One time, Remy had forgotten it was Saturday and made the mistake of going to Stop&Shop to pick up some deli meat. The line at the deli counter had been at least forty deep!

She pulled back up the driveway, brought the tapioca inside, stuffed the plastic bag in the recycling, put on her apron, and reached for a sharp knife. The sun felt hot on her shoulders as she broke off several long stalks of rhubarb and sliced off their gigantic leaves with a quick swipe of her knife. She left the leaves wilting in the sun and carried the stalks inside. She rinsed them under cold water, dried them quickly with a paper towel, and chopped them into inch-long pieces, quickly filling her biggest measuring cup. Then she looked at all the rhubarb she still had left—|not to mention the abundance still in the garden—and decided to make two pies. She'd find someone to give the second one to, and if not, she'd eat it herself—she loved rhubarb pie!

She masterfully rolled out the dough, laid and pressed two perfect circles of dough into pie plates, and then rolled out two more, which she'd cut into strips and weave across the filling into fancy lattice tops. Finally, setting her rolling pin aside, she grated enough orange zest for two pies and reached for her ceramic sugar canister, but when she picked it up, it felt light. Her heart sank again. She didn't even need to look, but did anyway—there was barely half a cup. "Sugar!" she exclaimed.

❧ Chapter 12 ❧

Sailor lay in bed, watching the sunlight and shadows dance on the walls and listening to a pair of cardinals calling back and forth. She smiled— even though she'd just spent the night on a hard-wood floor, she'd slept better than she had in months. She sat up and looked around the room, reveling in the lovely realization that this bright, airy space situated on a patch of sand on a curving peninsula of land on the edge of a great thundering ocean in a great big crazy world was *her* refuge, and no one could take it from her.

When she was young, she and her sisters had all dreamed of living on the Cape, full-time, and even though their friends were skeptical—"I bet it gets pretty desolate in the winter," they'd said, or "I've heard all the restaurants and shops close and it becomes a ghost town"—their words of warning only made the sisters feel more drawn to the idea. Solitude was good for the soul, they believed, and they knew they'd never be alone; they would *always* have each other. Besides, there was something sacred about Cape Cod.

Piper had been first to move. It had been easy for her because all she'd had to do was move back home when she finished college. Remy was next—in 1989 she and Jim moved from Vermont to the bow-roof Cape they'd had built in Wellfleet. Birdie, on the other hand, took a while. She wasn't able to convince David until 2004. She'd been asking for years, but it wasn't until they turned fifty-five and she warned him that if they didn't move soon they might never get the chance. He finally relented and they sold their home in Ithaca, bid their colleagues good-bye, and moved to a rambling old saltbox in Orleans.

Finally, it was Sailor's turn. She hadn't wanted to leave Boston. That is, until she very much *did* want to leave Boston!

She climbed out of her sleeping bag, stopped at the bathroom without bothering to close the door, and then shuffled to the kitchen to make coffee. She filled her red teakettle with water and put it on the back burner, and while it heated, rifled through a box labeled *KITCHEN* and found her can of Cafe Du Monde coffee. She measured a scoop into her coffee press, poured steaming water on top of it, and let it sit—she liked her coffee strong.

Five minutes later, carrying her favorite Black Dog Tavern coffee mug, she headed back to the bathroom, and leaving the door open again, turned on the shower. She'd just climbed in and started to suds up her hair when she heard a familiar voice calling, "Hellooo!"

She peeked around the shower curtain. "I knew I should've locked the door!"

"That wouldn't have kept me out," Piper said with a grin.

"I'll just be a minute," she said, ducking back behind the curtain.

"Okay, I'll help myself to some coffee," Piper replied, reaching for another mug. "Do you have any cream?" she called, opening the refrigerator.

"No, sorry, no pollutants here."

Piper walked through the rooms, sipping her

coffee and smiling at her sister's simple furnishings —an Adirondack chair and two floor lamps in the living room, a crumpled sleeping bag and a pile of clothes in the bedroom, and a bookcase and drawing table in the studio. She stepped closer to look at the photographs that were spread out across the table—she'd never seen them side by side before. She looked at each one, and then her eyes were drawn to one in the middle. Without looking, she knew the photo had been taken in 1992. She knew because that was the summer she'd been pregnant with Elias, and in the photo, taken on July fourth, she was *very* pregnant— Elias had made his grand entrance on August first. Piper picked up the photo and smiled. She was wearing one of Nat's old oxford shirts over a very tight tank top and her sisters each had a hand on her belly. She'd always loved that photo—it was probably her favorite.

Sailor came into the room, drying her hair with a towel, and looked over her shoulder. "I remember that day," she said with a smile. "You were having Braxton Hicks and you insisted your baby was coming."

Piper laughed. "That was before I found out what a real contraction feels like."

"You mean like having your insides ripped out?"

"Or being stabbed with a white-hot poker."

They laughed and gave each other a long hug.

"So, how're *you* doing?" Piper asked, searching her sister's eyes.

"Okay," Sailor replied. "Pretty good, actually. I'm totally in love with this place."

"I know," Piper agreed, looking around. "It's perfect. I love your furnishings," she teased.

Sailor laughed, knowing her sister meant her *sparse* furnishings. "I'm trying to simplify," she said defensively. "Life with Frank was way too complicated—we had too many *things*. Now I'm feeling much freer *and* happier."

Piper smiled. "You *look* happier."

"Thanks," she said with a nod. "Now, what are you doing here so early? I thought you were coming tonight."

"I am but I had to be at the sanctuary this morning to help Nat look for a turtle, and then it got foggy . . . but now it's beautiful."

Sailor laughed. "Yeah, I know what happens when you and Nat go looking for turtles," she teased.

Piper laughed. Her sisters had always inferred that "Looking for turtles with Nat" was code for something much more intimate, and over the years, whenever she said it, they raised their eyebrows and nodded knowingly.

Piper rolled her eyes. "So, anyway, I knew you'd have fresh coffee, and since I didn't get a chance to have any this morning, I thought I'd stop by and check out your new digs." She looked around at all the boxes. "Do you need help unpacking?"

"No, thanks," Sailor said, following her gaze. "It looks worse than it is."

"That reminds me," Piper began. "I was in the attic yesterday . . ."

"How is it up there?" Sailor said with a grin.

"A disaster!" Piper said. "We really need to get through that stuff."

"Well, maybe now that I'm living out here, too, we can light a fire under Birdie and Remy and spend some time up there."

"That would be great."

"Why were you up there anyway?"

"I was looking for Mom's old cookbook."

"Did you find it?"

Piper shook her head. "Do you have any idea where it might be?"

Sailor frowned. "I don't know. I haven't seen it in years. Why are you looking for it?"

"Nat had a craving for rice pudding."

"Ahh," Sailor teased. "One of Nat's famous cravings . . ."

Piper laughed—her sisters knew all about Nat's cravings, too . . . well, maybe not *all*.

"Why don't you just look online for a recipe?"

"Because I want Mom's recipe."

"Well, if anyone has the cookbook, it's probably Remy."

Piper sipped her coffee and nodded. "Remind me to ask her."

Sailor went back to the bathroom to hang up her towel and retrieve her coffee. "C'mon," she said. "You have to see the gardens." Piper followed her outside and they walked out through the over-grown yard, trying to determine what flowers were coming up. "I think those are peonies," Piper said, pointing, "and look at all the hydrangeas! You need to get in there and prune out the dead stalks."

Sailor nodded. "Sometimes the stalks still have life in them. I know they look dead but they might still shoot out some leaves. I think I'll wait."

They heard a car pull into the driveway. "Who's that?" Piper asked, frowning.

"I don't know," Sailor said, eyeing the black SUV.

The door opened and a man wearing sunglasses stepped out. He was wearing a light blue oxford shirt and stone colored khakis. He was tan and his dark hair was streaked with silver. He smiled and Sailor suddenly recognized him. "Oh! It's Josiah Gray—my real estate agent."

"Really!?" Piper whispered conspiratorially and then felt a sharp elbow in her ribs. "Ouch!"

"Hey, Josiah, what brings you out here?" Sailor said pleasantly, walking toward him.

"Hey," he said, glancing at his watch. "I hope I'm not too early. I was in the area and I thought I'd stop by to see how you're doing and if you're getting settled and"—he reached into his car and produced a bouquet of sunflowers and a box of

Dunkin' Donuts Munchkins—"to thank you for your business."

"I *love* sunflowers!" Sailor said. "Thank you!"

Josiah smiled. "I thought you looked like a sunflower girl."

"I am. I'm a Munchkin girl, too," she said, taking the box of bite-size doughnut holes.

Piper watched their exchange with surprised amusement. *A Munchkin girl?!*

Sailor suddenly remembered her manners. "Josiah, this is my sister Piper," she said, motioning to Piper.

Josiah nodded. "It's nice to meet you."

"It's nice to meet you, too," Piper said, stepping forward and shaking his hand.

Josiah looked back at Sailor. "So, how *is* it going? Are you unpacked?"

Sailor laughed. "Well, not quite, but I'm getting there." She paused. "Would you like a cup of coffee?"

"Oh, no," Josiah said, putting up his hand. "I have to get to work. I just wanted to stop by and, like I said, thank you for your business."

"Okay, well, you're welcome . . . and thank *you* for the flowers and treat."

"You're welcome." He opened his car door and started to get in. "I may take you up on that coffee another time, though. . . ."

Sailor looked surprised. "Okay. Anytime."

Josiah nodded, and as he drove away, waved.

75

"Wow, Sail, he's cute!"

"He *is* cute," Sailor said, handing her the flowers. She opened the box of Munchkins and held them out.

Piper picked out a chocolate glazed doughnut hole, took a bite, and with sugary lips, teased, "I never knew you were a Munchkin girl!"

⚜ Chapter 13 ⚜

After stopping at the farmers' market for heirloom tomatoes, Piper turned onto Main Street and drove past the road that led back to the sleepy cemetery in which her parents were buried. Feeling oddly drawn to stop, she turned in and parked under the majestic pine trees. She hadn't visited her parents' graveside in years. Like the attic, it was a place she avoided, but now, it was as if the letters and pictures she'd come across had stirred something deep inside her, and as she walked on the pine needle–covered path, she recalled that long-ago time.

Whitney Quinn had retired from being a Pan Am pilot right after Piper had started her freshman year at the University of New England. Soon after, he and Martha had sold the family home in New Hampshire and moved to Whit's End full-time. Six months later, though, as so often happens when someone retires, Whitney was shoveling the heavy, wet snow of a late March storm when he suffered a massive heart attack. Martha was standing at the kitchen sink, washing the dishes, and she looked up and saw him leaning heavily on his shovel. A moment later, he crumpled onto the wet snow.

"Whitney!" she cried, running out and trying to lift him up.

"I'm sorry . . ." he murmured.

"Sorry for what?" she cried, cradling his head in her lap.

"I'm sorry about Easton," he whispered, his voice racked with pain, his eyes full of sorrow.

"Oh, Whitney, it wasn't your fault," Martha cried, rocking him back and forth. "I asked you to take those kids. If it was anyone's fault, it was mine." She looked down, realized his eyes had closed, and shook him. "Don't you leave me, Whitney Quinn!" she cried, tears streaming down her cheeks. "Don't you dare leave me!"

Birdie, Remy, and Sailor—who were all married by then—had been devastated when Martha called them with the news, but Piper had still been in college—and three years away from meeting Nat—so her father was still the center of her world, and Martha couldn't bring herself to call her youngest daughter and tell her on the phone.

It was snowing when Piper returned to her dorm that evening and found Birdie and David waiting for her. "What's wrong?" she asked, seeing the strained looks on their faces. Her heart pounded. "Why are you here?"

Birdie explained as gently as she could what had happened, but Piper had shaken her head in disbelief. "No, you're wrong," she said angrily. "I just talked to Dad. He said he was picking me up on Friday for spring break."

Tears filled Birdie's eyes as she listened to her sister try to make sense of it all. Then she wrapped her arms around her and held her as she sobbed inconsolably.

Whitney's funeral was held at the Federated Church in Orleans on a foggy, slate-gray Monday, and in spite of the dreary weather and the fact that it was a weekday, the historic old church was filled to capacity with family, friends, fellow pilots, and veterans. Years earlier, Whitney had offhandedly told Martha he didn't want a wake, so when the family walked into the sanctuary that morning, it was the first time Piper saw the dark mahogany casket—visible proof that her father wasn't coming back. She'd cried out in shock—his body was in that box! It was more than she could bear and her knees had started to buckle, but Jim, who was right behind her, had caught her and gently guided her into the pew next to her sisters.

Whitney Easton Quinn was buried with full military honors, and as the haunting sound of "Taps" was played, Piper had gazed at her brother's tombstone beside her father's open grave.

EASTON LAURIE QUINN
JULY 4, 1956–JULY 3, 1964
BELOVED SON AND BROTHER

Piper couldn't believe it had been fifteen years and she remembered thinking that her tortured father was finally reunited with his only son. After the guests left that day, it became evident to everyone in the family that Piper would need more time to grieve, and at Birdie's suggestion, Martha arranged for her youngest daughter to take time off from school and stay home with her through the summer, their shared grief drawing them even closer.

Piper stood solemnly in front of the three sun-bleached tombstones now, her brother cradled between their parents, and listened to the wind whispering through the pines. Her parents hadn't been able to protect him in life, but they were forever by his side in death.

⊰ Chapter 14 ⊱

"Did you fall in?" Birdie called up the stairs.

"Very funny," David called back from behind the closed bathroom door.

"I'm leaving."

"Do you want me to drive you?"

"No, no," she said. "I'll be fine."

"Well, let me know if you want me to pick you up."

"Why would I want *that?*" she asked, sounding annoyed.

There was a pause while they read each other's minds. "Okay," he said resignedly. "Have fun. Give your sisters a hug."

"I will," Birdie said more cheerily, feeling briefly emancipated from his judgment.

"Call if you change your mind."

There it was again. "Okay," she said to appease him, but as she limped to the kitchen, she muttered, "I *won't* change my mind, *and* if you remember correctly, I'm *not* the one who backed into the lamppost."

She checked her bag to make sure she had everything, eyed her crutches, decided she didn't need them, slipped the bottle of pinot grigio that Alec, the new owner of the package store, had described as "crisp and elegant with hints of apple and citrus," and the bottle of "PM" he'd said was "all the rage" into her bag. "It's from the Patagonia region," he'd said. "You'll *love* it!" and although Birdie was old enough to be Alec's grandmother, he was just so darn cute, with his short blond hair, blue eyes, and those stylish rectangular glasses—*and* so passionate about his recommendations—that she believed he could talk her into buying Boone's Farm!

Birdie limped toward the door, trying to balance everything, and realized Bailey was waiting expectantly. "Oh, hon," she said, kissing her sweet forehead. "You have to stay home with Dad tonight." The old Lab gazed at her solemnly. "I know you want to come," she explained, "but I'm not going to Piper's. I'm going to Sailor's . . . and Chloe's not going, either, so don't look so sad."

Bailey folded her old limbs, clunked heavily to the floor, and put her head between her paws. "I'm sure Dad will take you for a walk, though," Birdie consoled. Then she called through the ceiling, "Please take Bailey for a walk!" She listened to her husband's muffled reply, assumed it was *yes,* and said, "See, I told you . . ."

She opened the door. "I'll be home soon," she said as the Lab's forlorn eyes followed her out the door. "Next time, Bay, I promise." Bailey sighed heavily and Birdie shook her head as she limped toward her ice blue MINI Cooper Clubman with the license plate that read: SNWOWL. "Even the dog knows how to make me feel guilty!" she muttered, looking heavenward. "My life is just one big guilt trip, Lord. I should've been born a Catholic."

On a normal day, Truro was a twenty-minute ride, give or take, from Orleans, but as Birdie pulled onto the rotary and turned onto Route 6, she groaned—traffic was bumper to bumper. "Who *are* all these people?" she mumbled, and

81

then she remembered it was the Friday before the Memorial Day weekend. She heard her phone *beep* and looked down. Piper had texted: Want me to pick you up? She merged into the right lane, stopped in the barely moving traffic, slid her finger across the screen, and started typing: Already left. Traffic is . . . She heard a loud honk behind her and looked up. The car in front of her had moved all of ten feet and she hadn't kept up. As she rolled forward, she looked in her rearview mirror, gave the man behind her a wilting look, and resumed typing: terrible. See you th . . . There was another long, impatient honk, and when she looked up, she saw they'd moved another ten feet. She looked back down, finished typing her message, hit Send, and then looked in her rearview and held up her middle finger. As they continued to creep along at a snail's pace, she looked back to see how the disgruntled driver behind her was doing, decided he was on the verge of blowing a gasket, and took her almighty sweet time the next time, too. She was sixty-seven, after all, and she deserved a little respect . . . *and* she was a full-time resident! "Someone needs to take a chill pill," she muttered, shaking her head.

Moments later, the left lane started moving and the man pulled into it, and as he blew by, he returned her gesture and raised her one rude expletive.

"Back at ya," Birdie said with a smirk as she clicked on her radio.

People began to gradually turn off Route 6 toward their destinations and the traffic began to move. Birdie glanced over at Arnold's as she drove by. She couldn't believe there was already a line curling around the building. "It's definitely summer," she said with a sigh.

A few minutes later, she turned onto Old County Road and into a sandy driveway straddled by a white picket fence. "Can you believe I finally got my picket fence?" Sailor had said when she'd been giving Birdie the directions.

"This is nice," Birdie murmured as she parked behind Remy. She could see her sisters look up from where they were standing in the garden. She reached for the plate of Caprese salad— fresh tomatoes, mozzarella, and basil, drizzled with balsamic vinegar—and handed it to Sailor through the window.

"Mmm, this looks good," she said, smiling.

"The basil's from my garden," Birdie said as she picked up her cumbersome bag, clanking with bottles, and gingerly stepped out.

"Where are your crutches?" Remy asked, frowning as she gave her a hug.

"Oh, I don't need those old things," Birdie said. She turned to Sailor, hugged her, too, and pulled out the bottle of pinot grigio with the festive ribbon tied around its neck. "I'm told the palate is full and ripe," she said with a smile.

Sailor chuckled. "Is that what your favorite gay package store owner told you?"

"It *is*," Birdie admitted with a grin. Then she frowned. "Do you really think he's gay?"

Sailor nodded. "I love the label," she said, admiring the da Vinci drawing. "And I do because he's way too cute to be straight."

Birdie laughed. "You're probably right."

"And what did you get for yourself?" Sailor asked, eyeing the second bottle.

"Malbec," Birdie said, holding out the bottle of Phebus.

"Did he talk you into it?"

She chuckled at how true her sister's observation was. "He said it's all the rage!"

"So you're betraying your beloved merlot?" Sailor teased, feigning shock.

"Just expanding my horizons," Birdie said. "Do you have a corkscrew? Because I brought one just in case." She started to reach back into her bag.

"I have one," Sailor assured. "Come on in and we'll crack these bad girls open!"

Remy offered Birdie her arm and she gladly took it, and as they followed Sailor into the little cottage, Sailor turned. "Do you want the grand tour now or in a little bit?"

"In a little bit," Birdie said, sinking wearily into the only chair in the kitchen—a folding beach chair. "My ankle's a little achy."

"That's why you should be using your crutches," Remy scolded. "It's only been a couple of days. . . ."

Birdie waved her off. "I'm fine. It's just because I had to push the damn clutch in so many times on my way here—traffic was terrible! In fact, it'll probably be a half hour before Piper gets he—"

"Hello!" a voice called cheerily.

Sailor looked out the window. "Here she is now!"

"Hey!" Piper said, sweeping in and giving her sisters hugs. She set down a platter of bruschetta and a bottle of the Black Dog Tavern's new wine, Great White Chardonnay—it had a picture of the iconic black dog with a shark fin on his back.

"Where'd you get that?" Sailor asked, admiring the label.

"Package store."

"Birdie's package store?"

Piper laughed. "Yes, that cute new French owner tried to talk me into something else, but when I saw this label, I knew I had to get it. I don't know how it tastes, but I'm easily swayed by labels." She eyed Birdie's ankle. "How're *you* doing?"

"I'm doing . . . but I'll be *doing* a lot better after your sister gets that bottle open."

Piper looked over and realized Sailor had broken the cork. "What the heck *are* you doing, girl?" she teased.

"I'm a beginner . . . *obviously!*" Sailor said, laughing.

Piper reached for the corkscrew and Sailor stepped back. "Oh my, look at that bruschetta! Where'd you get the recipe?"

Piper glanced over her shoulder. "Allrecipes .com."

"I love that site," Sailor said. She offered the plate to Birdie and Remy. "Did you see Remy's pie?!" she asked, nodding over her shoulder.

Birdie sat up to see. "Is that rhubarb?" she asked in happy surprise.

"It is," Remy confirmed.

"Look at that fancy latticework," Piper said, handing a glass of the red wine to Birdie and admiring the pie. "We should take a picture and send it in to a magazine!"

Remy smiled. Her sisters' enthusiastic compliments made all the trouble—even going out the third time to get sugar—worth it!

"I can't remember the last time I had rhubarb pie," Birdie mused, taking a sip of her wine and immediately feeling the strain of the day exit her body like an evil spirit. "Mmm, this *is* good," she said. "You should try it."

Piper took a small sip and nodded. Then she looked at the bottle. "I've never had malbec."

"You can have a glass," Birdie offered, but Piper knew Birdie was a tad possessive of her wine and declined.

"No, thanks, I think I'll just stick to white tonight—it *is* summer, after all."

"It is indeed!" Birdie said, smiling.

Sailor handed glasses to Remy and Piper, and Birdie held up her glass in toast. "To Sailor's new home!"

"To Sailor's *lovely* new home," Remy corrected.

They clinked their glasses and Piper added, "And to finally getting her to move out here!"

"Hear, hear!" Sailor said, laughing and taking a sip.

She put her glass down, uncovered the dip she'd made, and pulled open a bag of tortilla chips. "Want to sit on the deck?"

With everyone carrying a dish, they went outside. "Where'd all this outdoor furniture come from?" Piper asked, setting the plates on the table.

"The previous owner left it, even the grill. I think he must've rented the house out to people. There were some plates and pots and pans in the kitchen, too."

"How come he sold it?" Remy asked.

"He died."

"Oh," Remy said softly.

"Happens to the best of us," Birdie said, her voice edged with sarcasm. She paused. "So, ladies, I have a tidbit for you, but you have to promise not to tell anyone."

Sailor looked up from scooping dip. "Oo-oo! *Promise not to tells* are the best kind of secrets."

"Well, it's not that big a deal. It's just that I was sworn to secrecy."

"Do tell," Piper pressed.

"Dr. Sanders is *retiring!*"

"Oh, no!" Remy groaned. "Who are we going to go to?"

"He's hiring some young new whippersnapper to take his place."

Sailor shook her head. "I hate changing doctors. So much so, I've even driven out here from Boston just to get my thyroid prescription refilled. It's bad enough we have to go to a doctor at all, but to have to start all over with someone new." She shook her head. "Did he say when?"

"October. But you can't tell anyone . . . *and* you have to act surprised—or dismayed—when he tells you."

They all nodded.

Piper sipped her drink and looked over at Sailor. "Have you heard from Frank?"

Sailor started to scoop some dip but broke her chip. "He called but I didn't pick up," she said, fishing it out.

"Are you going to sell the house?" Birdie asked.

"We are, unless he wants to buy me out. I'm only communicating with him through my lawyer."

"How are the kids taking it?" Remy asked.

"Merry said she doesn't know what took so long and Thatcher is so busy I don't think he's had time to think about it, but it's not like they're kids anymore. They both have spouses and Merry has the girls *and* they've both been in previous relationships that didn't last, so they know how it is."

"This is a little different," Remy said, seeming to mourn her sister's failed marriage more than she did.

"Rem, I can't spend any more time agonizing about it. Frank is not like Jim—he cheated on me more times than I can count—he even cheated on me when I was having chemo. Life is too short. I've known it was coming, and now I'm relieved it's over. Plus, God obviously has a plan; just look at this place—it's the perfect retreat."

Piper scooped some dip. "I think God has a bigger plan for you than just a beach cottage. You guys should've seen the handsome Realtor who stopped by to give her a box of Munchkins *and* these lovely flowers," she said, motioning to the sunflowers on the table. "Not only that, but Sailor told him she was a *Munchkin girl!*"

Birdie raised her eyebrows. "A Munchkin girl? Really?"

Sailor laughed. "I guess I did. We met at a Dunkin' Donuts—that's probably why he brought them."

"What's his name?" Birdie asked.

"Josiah Gray."

"Any relation to Christian Grey?" Remy asked.

Sailor laughed at the reference. "OMG, Remy, did you read *Fifty Shades of Grey*?!"

"I did," Remy said sheepishly. "I wanted to see what all the hubbub was about."

"What did you think?"

Remy shrugged. "It wasn't anything to write home about."

"That's for sure," Sailor said.

"Did you read it, too?" Remy asked in surprise.

"In a moment of weakness," Sailor admitted. She looked at Birdie. "And you?"

"Pshaw! I don't have time for such nonsense," Birdie said indignantly.

They all turned and looked at Piper, who just smiled. "I have my own Christian Grey."

Sailor chuckled. "I don't think Nat's cravings are *quite* like Christian Grey's . . . but if they are, I'd rather not know."

Piper's phone made the sound of a cricket chirping and she picked it up and looked at the screen.

Birdie raised her eyebrows and Piper laughed. "Elias's home—he says since I'm out with the girls, he and Nat are going out for boys' night."

"Tell them to come here!" Sailor said.

Piper continued to read. "They're going to Yarmouth Pizza—he has a craving."

Sailor grinned. "He takes after his father!"

Piper laughed. "I hope not. Some of Nat's cravings are pretty X-rated."

"Yes, we know," Birdie said, chuckling as she refilled her glass.

The sisters whiled away the evening, catching up on each other's news and relishing each other's company. It had been several weeks since they'd all been together on a Friday night, but now that summer was here—and Sailor had moved to the Cape—they hoped it would become a weekly occurrence.

"Who's ready for pie?" Sailor asked as the evening wound down.

"Let me help you," Remy said, getting up.

She followed Sailor inside and took the ice cream she'd brought out of the freezer. "Anyone want ice cream?" she called.

"What flavor?" Birdie asked.

"What flavor do you think?" Remy asked, peering out the window.

"Vanilla!" they chorused.

❧ Chapter 15 ❧

When Piper pulled into the driveway, Nat and Elias were sitting on the porch with Chloe stretched out between them. She parked behind Elias's old pickup—a hand-me-down from Nat—and saw Nat say something to him, and then they both looked up and grinned.

"You two look like cats that ate canaries," she said as she stepped onto the porch. Chloe thumped her tail in greeting but didn't move from her spot near Elias's feet. "Don't get up," Piper teased, looking down. "I'll come to you." She knelt down and scratched Chloe's ears, making her flag of a tail thump even harder. She stood up and looked at her son. "*You,* on the other hand, *do* have to get up to give your mother a hug."

Still wearing a grin, Elias stood, his lanky body —just like his dad's—towering over her petite five-foot-two frame. He wrapped her in a hug. "Hi, Mom," he said.

"Hi, hon," she murmured. "Missed you."

"Missed you, too."

She stepped back and held him at arm's length. "You look like you grew another four inches . . . and you're so skinny! Have you been eating? We spend a lot of money on that meal plan, so you better be making the most of it!"

"I've been eating," he assured her.

She smiled. "How was traffic?"

"Not bad. Pennsylvania, New York, and Connecticut were fine. It didn't get bad till I got to the bridge."

"Tappan Zee?"

"No," he said with a laugh. "Sagamore."

"That's because it's Memorial Day," she said matter-of-factly, just in case he hadn't looked at a calendar lately.

"I know," he said, rolling his eyes. "It'll be a lot easier when I'm able to fly home."

"There's no eye-rolling," Piper teased. "And I

doubt you'll be able to fly home because you don't have a plane."

"I don't yet," he said with a grin.

Now it was her turn to roll her eyes.

"Hey, there's no eye-rolling," he teased.

She laughed. "Touché! So, what did Chloe do when you pulled in?"

"She launched herself into his cab and sat down on his lap," Nat said, chuckling.

Piper laughed. "That's the best welcome there is." She knelt down again. "You missed him, didn't you, old pie?" and Chloe thumped her tail some more.

She looked back at Elias. "She's been sleeping on your bed, you know . . . so I don't know where you're going to sleep."

"She's just going to have to move over," he said, loving the easy feeling of being home with the people who loved him most.

"Want a beer?" Nat asked, motioning to their bottles as she pulled a chair up next to them.

"No . . . no, thanks. I had a glass of wine at Sailor's and I can hardly stay awake. I'm sure if I have anything else, I'll just fall asleep sitting here."

"That's all right," Nat said. "We'll just throw a blanket over you, won't we, E?"

"Maybe," Elias teased.

Piper leaned back and listened contentedly to her husband and son talk about school, running, flying lessons, and the funny noise his truck was making. She didn't feel the need to say anything. It was more than enough to just sit and listen to the lovely voices of her two favorite men. Suddenly, she felt her face flush as a wave of heat washed over her. "Are you guys hot?" she asked, sitting up.

They both looked up and shrugged. "Not really," Nat said. "There's a nice breeze out here."

"Well, I am," she said, getting up to get a glass of cold water.

She came back and sat down and watched Chloe rest her chin on Elias's shoe. It reminded her of how, when she was a puppy and Elias was at school, she used to curl up on his shoes in the mudroom—the smellier they were, the better! She'd never forget the day Nat brought Chloe home. It had been in the fall—she remembered because she always thought the best time to get a puppy was late spring or summer so you didn't freeze when they had to go out in the middle of the night, but Nat had showed up with the soft, golden ball of fur in his arms in early November. Chloe had been just eight weeks old, and although she'd been the only female in a litter of ten, her mom's owner said she was just as rough and tumbley as her brothers. The first night, however, you'd never have guessed it because she cried and cried for her brothers, and although Piper tried to comfort her with an old, soft blanket, it wasn't until Elias snuck her up to his bed that she finally fell asleep. After that, Chloe happily adopted Elias as her *new* brother, and they became inseparable.

Inseparable, that is, until Elias went off to college; then Chloe was lost. Every day, when she heard the school bus rumbling down their street, and even though Elias hadn't taken the bus in years—he'd driven to school his junior and senior years—her ears would perk up and she'd hurry over to rest her chin on the window stool, watching and waiting and wagging her tail. It was heartbreaking to watch—Chloe's heart was so full of hope, but then the bus would pass by without stopping and she'd turn and walk sadly back to her bed, lie down, and rest her head between her paws.

One more year, Piper thought. *One more year and Elias will move back home.* Piper knew that most parents hoped their children would become independent after college, but Piper hoped Elias would find a job nearby and move back home. She'd dreaded him going away to college and now she dreaded him moving out for good. There was something so final about it, and besides that, it made her feel old.

"I bought Chloe a present," Elias announced, suddenly remembering the gift he'd left in his truck.

"You did?" Piper said as Chloe lifted her head.

He nodded and stood up. "Want to come see?"

he asked softly, looking down at her. Chloe clambered to her feet and trotted after him. A moment later, Piper and Nat heard squeaking, and the moment after that, Chloe emerged from the shadows, proudly carrying a floppy, cream-colored stuffed animal.

"A new Zoe!" Piper exclaimed as Chloe wiggled happily up the steps.

❧ Chapter 16 ❧

In the fall of '78—after Piper had gone back to UNE for her senior year—Nat gently broke off his engagement to Katie Markham, the girl he'd been dating since college, and drove to Maine to give a talk to the marine biology students at New England University about the plight of the sea turtles in New England waters.

Piper had known he was coming, but she hadn't had a chance to see him before he spoke, so when she saw him walking into the lecture room, her heart skipped a beat; and as she watched him stand in front of her classmates and describe what it was like to untangle a turtle from floating debris or try to put a dropper full of medicine into a sharp beak, her heart pounded. His hair was longer, she noted, and it was so odd to see him wearing real clothes—faded jeans, hiking boots, and a cobalt blue Cape Cod Marine

Wildlife Sanctuary fleece —instead of swim trunks and a T-shirt . . . or *no* shirt. She was mesmerized by his easygoing mannerisms and his soft voice as he clicked through a slideshow of the turtles he'd rescued, including an old leatherback whose neck and beak were so entangled it couldn't close its mouth; and when there was a collective chorus of surprise at the sight of the jagged stalactite spines in the leatherback's throat, his smile stole her heart all over again. "Can you imagine putting antibiotics in there?" he asked and everyone laughed, including Piper, whose heart was now flopping like a flounder out of water.

After the lecture, Piper hung back while Nat fielded questions and spent time with students who were interested in becoming marine biologists, but after everyone left, he pulled her outside, searched her eyes, and with snowflakes swirling around them, kissed her for a very long time.

The following spring, Piper accepted a full-time position at Cape Cod Marine Wildlife Sanctuary and announced that she was moving back to Whit's End. Her mom—widowed three years by then—was delighted, and her sisters—who were still living off the Cape—were relieved. Not only did their mom's health seem to be in a steady decline, she was also very lonely.

Life at home, though, was hectic. Piper worked long hours at the sanctuary and often went out with Nat after work, but she constantly worried about her mom. Martha, for her part, loved having one of her daughters back home—it gave her life purpose again—and as she packed Piper's lunch, washed and folded her laundry, and kept a plate of supper ready for her to heat up when she got home, she thanked God for her blessings.

As the months slipped by, Piper's concerns grew. She constantly pictured her mom puttering around the house alone all day—she didn't sew anymore, and although she'd once been an avid reader, she barely read her *Guideposts* magazine when it came, never mind a book. Piper also began to feel selfish for spending most of her free time with Nat—time that she could be spending with her mom. She knew how much her mom would enjoy her company, too. To alleviate some of the guilt, she tried to convince her to join the senior center or go out to lunch with her friends, but Martha wasn't interested. She said she'd much rather spend time with her daughter, and although she meant well, it only made Piper feel worse . . . *and* a little resentful. She loved her mom with all her heart, but where were her sisters in all of this? Their lives weren't the least bit affected, and they certainly weren't dragging around guilt like an old, barnacle-covered anchor over their mom's loneliness.

Sometime during her second summer home, Piper noticed Martha was becoming much more forgetful. She constantly forgot to take her pills. She also forgot essential ingredients in recipes that she'd been making for years and should know by heart; and she was always misplacing things—on more than one occasion, Piper had found her pocketbook in the kitchen cabinet and her glasses under the bathroom sink.

Finally, not knowing what else to do, Piper decided to cut back her hours so she could spend more time at home. She bought a pill tray and began keeping track of her mom's meds. She did all the food shopping, baking, and cooking; she kept the house tidy and the laundry under control, and she mowed the lawn. *And* she had had little time for anything else, especially Nat. Sometimes, during the day, she'd find her mom sitting, slightly slumped in a chair. "Mom, what's wrong?" she'd ask in a worried voice.

"I don't know," Martha would mumble. "Just tired, I guess . . ."

And then she'd rebound and be herself again and Piper would be relieved, but the irreversible damage of every unrecognized mini-stroke was taking its toll; and years later, when Piper looked back, she wished she'd had a better understanding of what was happening. She wished someone had sat her down and explained how much damage mild—and barely recognizable—strokes would do.

Finally, Birdie came out to the Cape for a visit

and immediately realized how much strain their mother's care was putting on Piper. By then, Martha was spending most of her time just gazing out the window. Her gait was unsteady and her once-beautiful handwriting was barely legible. Piper had cut back her hours to part-time, and sometimes, she didn't go in at all.

"Why didn't you tell us?" Birdie asked in dismay after she'd helped Piper get Martha ready for bed.

Piper shrugged. "I don't know—you're busy . . . *and* far away."

"Honestly, Pipe, I don't think Mom should be left alone at all. It's not safe," Birdie said, pouring a glass of wine.

"I know, but I *have* to work," she said, dunking her tea bag. "Do you think we could get someone to stay with her while I'm working?"

Birdie took a sip of her wine. "I don't know," she said softly. "She's only going to get worse. I think we should think about looking into a nursing home."

"We can't do that," Piper countered. "She always said she never wanted to be in a nursing home."

"I know, Pipe, but her care is getting to be too much."

Piper bit her lip. "Why can't we at least *try* having someone come in?"

"It's expensive."

"So is a nursing home."

Birdie shook her head. "I don't know what the answer is."

"There is something *so* wrong with the cost of elder care!" Piper said in frustration.

"I agree," Birdie said, nodding.

"I think we should try having someone come in. . . ."

Birdie sighed. "Piper, the day is coming when she won't even recognize us. . . ."

"Well, until that happens, I want to have someone come in. I will pay for it myself."

Birdie smiled sadly. "Okay, we'll try having someone come in, but you're not paying for it all. I'm sure Sailor and Remy will help." She paused and eyed her sister. "But when it gets to be too much or safety becomes an issue, then we have to move her into a nursing home."

"Okay," Piper agreed, relieved that her sister was willing to give it a try . . . and relieved that she would finally have a little time to herself.

Six months later, after several falls and several episodes of wandering off—"going home," Martha said—they moved her into a nursing home with a memory care unit, and six months after that, she stopped swallowing, and because her living will ruled out feeding tubes or any other form of intervention, they brought her home. She lasted five days, passing peacefully on the day before her eightieth birthday.

The four heartbroken sisters felt as if they'd

endured more than their share of loss, and on the summer evening after they'd laid their beloved mom to rest beside her husband and son, they gathered at Whit's End. Remy and Jim with their three little ones, Payton, Eliza and Sam; Sailor and Frank, with their two, Merry and Thatcher; and Birdie and David, who had just endured the most recent of three heartbreaking miscarriages—which Birdie believed was God's way of telling her she wasn't fit to be a mother. Nat was there, too, of course.

Nat was always *there* for Piper; he'd helped her when she was overwhelmed with her mom's care. He'd held her tight when she cried after helping move Martha into a nursing home. He'd made her eat something when she wasn't hungry, and he'd made love to her when she felt unlovable. Nathaniel McCabe, Piper believed, was an angel sent from heaven, and her sisters all thought so, too. They also wanted to know when the wedding would be.

Piper loved Nat with all her heart, but when he asked her—and he'd asked several times—something deep inside wouldn't let her say yes. It wasn't until she felt Elias growing inside her—pushing her heart open wide with all the mystery and wonder a child brings—that she felt she *could* say yes. Sadly, by then, Nat had given up.

❦ Chapter 17 ❧

Birdie pulled back the shower curtain and reached for her towel. She started to dry off, but then slid the towel away and looked at her reflection. She sighed. It was no wonder David wasn't aroused by her body anymore—she was an old, sagging, wrinkled woman, and although he insisted it wasn't her, she fully believed that if he had a gorgeous twenty-something lying beside him, it would trigger some signs of life.

She continued to dry off, taking comfort in the fact that she wasn't the only one in the "no-sugar-in-my-coffee" club. Both Remy and Sailor were members, too, although Sailor now had potential sugar in Josiah Gray. Piper, on the other hand, with her "own personal Christian Grey," would probably have sex on her deathbed. "What an awful thought," she chided herself. "What *is* wrong with me? Not only am I old and wrinkled, I'm bitter, too."

She smoothed Oil of Olay under her eyes and onto her tan, ruddy cheeks, and then smoothed more onto her neck, which, she'd decided long ago, was a lost cause. "I'm still putting in the effort, though," she murmured. "I'm still believing there's hope for my wrinkled, old chicken neck."

She pulled on her shorts, buttoned her blouse,

hung up her towel, threw her laundry in the hamper, and went into the bedroom to make the bed. As she smoothed the sheets, she gazed at the center of the bed—once the scene of so much lovemaking. *Never again,* she thought gloomily. David didn't want to take the "little blue pill" or any other color pill for that matter. He was worried about the side effects, and since she didn't want to pressure him into taking something he thought might be harmful, they didn't talk about it. So that, she guessed, was the proverbial *that.* At first, she'd been relieved—she could just go to bed and go to sleep, but now the idea of never making love again left her feeling lonely and grieving for a part of life they'd never share again.

As she pulled the quilt up, she recalled the first time she'd laid eyes on David Camden Snow. Oh. My. Goodness. Was he handsome! They'd both been freshmen at Cornell and they'd seren-dipitously showed up for the same intro-ductory meeting of the ornithology department. It was 1967, but she remembered it as if it were yesterday. She'd been sitting in a row by her-self reading William Styron's new novel, *The Confessions of Nat Turner,* and waiting for the meeting to start when she felt someone standing beside her. She'd looked up and there he was—a handsome, tweed coat–wearing boy with a square jaw and aristocratic nose.

"Excuse me," he said, and when she finally

came to her senses, she realized he wanted to sit down. She stood up so he could get by and then watched as he sat two seats away. He seemed distracted and slightly disorganized, but when he looked over and saw what she was reading, he chuckled, and held up a copy of the same book.

"What do you think?" he asked.

"I'm not very far," she said, "but I think it's amazing. He reminds me of Faulkner."

The boy nodded. "I think it's extraordinary, and to think Styron's a Southerner! It makes it all the more powerful."

Birdie nodded, barely hearing his words because his eyes were so . . . so strikingly blue. "I'm David," he said, extending his hand. "David Snow."

Birdie swallowed. "I'm Bir . . . I mean Martha. Martha Quinn . . . but my family calls me Birdie."

David smiled. "Is that because you love birds?"

"Actually, it is," she said with a smile. "My mom said I loved watching the birds when I was little, and since she and I share the same name, my family just started calling me Birdie. I've loved birds my whole life . . . especially the snowy owl."

"I like owls, too. The barred is my favorite."

"Who cooks for you?" she said with a grin. "Who cooks for you aaaalll?"

David laughed at her mimicking the owl's call. "Hey, that's pretty good!"

She smiled and nodded shyly.

When the meeting ended, David walked out with her and then, with an unassuming confidence, asked her if she'd like to go see a movie that weekend—he'd heard *The Graduate* was pretty good. Birdie had agreed.

A week after that, they went to see *Guess Who's Coming to Dinner* . . . and on their third date, he took *her* to dinner. Afterward, he snuck up to her room because her roommate was away, and they talked all night. One thing had led to another, and before she knew it, they were standing by the back door in the half-light of dawn, kissing good-bye.

Birdie sighed—those were the lovely old days, the days before life had become heavy and full of heartbreak. She straightened out the covers and then sank to her knees, her eyes filling with tears. She lightly traced the pattern on their Amish quilt, closed her eyes, and rested her head on her hands. "I know it's been a long time since You've heard from me, Lord," she whispered. "I'm sorry I've turned out to be such a miserable wretch. I have so many things for which to be thankful . . . but I just wish things had turned out differently. I wish *everything* had turned out differently. I wish You'd blessed us with children . . . and I know, if You'd only let Easton live, all of our lives would be so much better right now."

David—who'd come up the stairs with a cup of coffee for her—stood outside the door, listening to her pray, and tears filled his eyes.

❈ Chapter 18 ❖

Remy smoothed sunscreen onto her speckled arms. It was too late, she knew, to save her tired, old skin from sun damage. She was freckled *everywhere*—some spots were the size of nickels! Not to mention the wrinkles! The last time she saw Dr. Sanders, though, he told her to use sunscreen every time she went outside. Even though her skin was damaged from years of lying in the sun *and* burning, he'd said, it still needed protection. He even gave her the name of a dermatologist and said the dermatologist would be able to spot little things he might not see. Remy had tucked the card away, and now she doubted she could even find it, but she was using her sunscreen, *and* even though he'd said SPF 30 was enough, she'd bought 75!

Remy looked at her reflection and sighed. She'd read a book, or maybe it was a movie she'd seen—she couldn't remember which—about a woman who'd written a letter to her younger self, warning her of all the pitfalls that lay ahead in her life and how to avoid them. Remy had found the idea intriguing, and afterward, she'd thought about the warnings she'd give *her* younger self if she had the opportunity. She remembered thinking she'd warn herself to make sure Jim took better care of his heart. She'd also tell her not to worry so much about the kids, because, after all, Sam *was* found when he got lost at Boy Scout camp, Eliza was able to walk again after she broke her leg skiing, and Payton did get into the college of her choice—Amherst, not Middlebury—despite having low SAT scores. And now they were all happily married with families of their own. Yes, she had definitely spent too much time worrying!

Now, though, she'd also warn her younger self not to spend so much time in the sun; to use copious amounts of sunscreen, wear a hat, rent a beach umbrella, and do everything possible to protect her skin. She'd tell herself to not worry about having a golden summer tan—it wasn't worth it, because if she did, someday, she'd just be an old, brown speckled hen!

She pulled an old T-shirt with cranberries on it over her head—she remembered buying it at the original Cuffy's—before the store closed for a year—*or was it two?* She couldn't remember. She reached for her hat, tied her sneakers, and opened the door. Immediately, she heard little paws padding across the floor as Edison scooted between her legs and out the door. "Good morning to you, too, sir," she said with a chuckle.

She closed the door and headed down the driveway for her daily constitutional around Great Island. She walked the trail every day—no matter what the weather—and she never grew tired of it. There was always something new to see; just the other day, she'd seen a common yellowthroat sitting right in the middle of the path, and when she knelt down to see if it was injured, it fluttered up and latched onto her finger. She decided it must have been a baby, just learning to fly and not knowing enough to be frightened.

Birdie was always interested in hearing about the birds she saw, although she didn't always believe her. "There aren't any of those around here," she'd scoffed when she'd told her she thought she saw a brown pelican. "It was probably a gannet."

As Remy stepped onto the trail that meandered along the coastline of the island, she remembered how her sisters had raved about her pie the night before and even asked her to make another one for the next time. "There's no better compliment!" she'd said, smiling, "but I think I might make blueberry next time." "That would be good too," they'd all said, nodding as they walked to their cars, and then Birdie had tripped and almost fallen. Piper had asked her if she wanted a ride, but she'd said no, she was fine. Thinking back now, Remy wished Birdie had let Piper give her a ride. They shouldn't have let her drive—she'd drunk the whole bottle of wine she'd brought and then she'd started in on the bottle of white she'd brought for Sailor. The problem was, if they'd tried to stop her from driving, she would've been furious.

Remy stepped out into a clearing along the tip of the island—from which there was a gorgeous view of the bay—and stopped to watch a small brown-striped bird walking along the shore, its hind end bobbing up and down as it moved. "What a funny bird," she murmured, wondering what it was. Out of the corner of her eye, she saw something else move and looked up to see a red-tailed hawk watching the little unsuspecting bird, too! "Nooo!" she shouted in horror, clapping her hands and startling both the hawk and the bird. She could almost hear Birdie's scolding voice, *The hawk has to eat, too.*

"I don't care," she mumbled. "He can eat some-where else."

As she passed the rock outcropping she knew to be about halfway, she felt the sudden urge to use a bathroom. She hadn't even had her tea yet! She'd only had a small glass of water, which she now regretted—water always went right through her. *How do you stay hydrated when water doesn't spend any time in your body?* she wondered. *When it just takes a direct route from your throat to your bladder?* She looked around—she knew other people liked to walk the trail in the morning, and now that it was Memorial Day other hikers might come around the bend any moment. She trudged on, looking for a secluded spot into which she could duck and relieve herself. She hated when this happened, because now, instead of enjoying her walk, all she would think about was where she could *go* . . . and she worried what would happen if no opportunity presented itself. Would she make it home? She shook her head in frustration and remembered the time when she was a girl of about twelve. She'd been riding her bike when she suddenly realized she had to *go* right then! There was no way she'd make it home. She tried straddling the crossbar of her bike, but that didn't help, and then, all of a sudden, she panicked and just couldn't possibly hold it anymore. She'd never forget the warm sensation trickling down her legs, soaking her pants. She'd been utterly humiliated . . . and then the situation had gotten worse! A family she knew stopped next to her in their car to see whether she needed a ride home. "No, thank you," she'd said nonchalantly, praying they wouldn't notice her wet pants.

Why did she always remember the awful moments? She looked around desperately, and finally hurried into the scrubby pine underbrush, dropped her shorts, her eyes filling with tears of relief. *What a sight I must be—a sixty-five-year-old woman crouching in the woods with my big butt waving in the wind . . . and if anyone comes along, there's no way I can put the brakes on!* Just then, she heard voices and her heart started to pound. "Oh, Lord, please don't let them see me . . . and please don't let me have a heart attack in this position!"

❧ Chapter 19 ❧

Sailor rinsed out the wine bottles and began washing the dessert plates and glasses. She didn't usually leave dishes in the sink overnight, but after her sisters had left, she'd been too tired to deal with them. She looked out the kitchen window—it was another beautiful spring day and she was anxious to get out in the gardens and figure out what plants were there. But she still had so much to do inside, not to mention she needed to go food shopping.

She dried her hands, popped a stale chocolate Munchkin in her mouth, and washed it down with the last of the cold coffee. Then she looked around for a pencil and a scrap piece of paper. She didn't find either but when she opened the fridge, she realized she didn't need a list because she needed *everything*. She looked at her phone—it was 9:15 . . . *and* it was Saturday, so she'd better just skip her shower and go right to the store or she'd be there at the same time as the thundering herd.

Twenty minutes later, she turned into the Birdwatcher's General Store parking lot. On her way down Route 6, she'd remembered she wanted to get a bird feeder and some seed for her new yard and she'd decided she should do it before she went food shopping. She climbed out of her car and stepped onto the porch of the long gray building.

"Hey, Mike," she said when she saw the owner standing behind the counter.

"Hi!" Mike said jovially, giving her a little wave.

Sailor knew he didn't know who she was, but that was okay—he was really a friend of Birdie's. For many years, Birdie had led guided bird tours on the beaches and marshes of Cape Cod for the Massachusetts Audubon, and she'd even stayed at the famous Outermost House before it washed away in the winter hurricane of 1978 that buried all of New England in snow, so Birdie's and Mike's paths had crossed many times over the years, and Birdie always sent bird lovers to his store.

Sailor had been in the store countless times, by herself *and* with Birdie (in fact, it was the perfect place to find gifts for her bird-loving sister)—which reminded her—she needed to get a gift for Birdie's birthday too! She headed across the worn wooden floor in the direction of the bird feeders. There were so many from which to choose—tube feeders, house feeders, shelf feeders, suet feeders, window feeders, and feeders specifically designed to stymie the efforts of squirrels and raccoons—feeders with perches that dropped when some-thing heavy was on them; feeders in cages; and posts with baffles.

There was even a video playing on a loop in the back of the store of a squirrel hanging on for dear life with his hind feet while his little arms were stretched out like Superman's as the motorized base of the tube feeder spun wildly. *It's truly amazing how much time and energy we humans spend trying to outsmart the pesky little varmints!*

She selected a small, simple tube feeder, a bag of sunflower hearts, and then stood in front of the birdbath display. Finally, she decided she would come back at a later time to get a birdbath, after she straightened out the gardens—it would be her incentive!

While she waited in line, she noticed the cover of a thin volume she'd read years earlier. She'd always been drawn to the simple illustration of a quail on the cover and she picked it up again and glanced through it. *That Quail, Robert* was the true story of a little quail that had been hatched from an egg and raised by a woman on the Cape in the early sixties. Robert—who turned out to be female—had all kinds of funny habits and Margaret Stanger's story was a poignant tribute to the little quail's life and to the love she shared with her humans. Sailor stood there, wondering if Birdie had ever read it, and finally, she added it to her pile, along with a Susan Boynton coffee mug that had her famous characters on it singing "Happy Birdie to You," and stepped forward to pay.

"Did you find everything?" Mike asked.

Sailor nodded and then noticed the silver pencils in a can on the counter. "How much are the pencils?"

"They're free," Mike said, smiling and pointing to a sign above him, "*if* you can tell a good joke."

Sailor frowned, trying to think of a joke. "Hmm," she said thoughtfully, looking around. She spied a hummingbird feeder hanging in the window. "I have one!"

"Go," Mike said and waited with raised eyebrows while everyone around them stopped to listen.

"Why did the hummingbird hum?"

Mike looked puzzled. "Hmm . . . why did the hummingbird hum?" he mused thoughtfully. "I don't know. Why *did* the hummingbird hum?"

Sailor grinned. "Because he didn't know the words."

"Bada-bing!" Mike said, smiling and ringing the bell above the counter—a signal that someone had just told a good joke. Then he handed Sailor a pencil.

She smiled as she walked out, and as she put everything in the backseat, she heard her phone *beep*. She looked at the screen. It was a text from Josiah. **Coffee?**

She got in the car, rolled down her windows, and wrote back. **I'm in Orleans . . .**

Me too! ☺

She stared at the screen, thinking about all she still needed to do—she hadn't even gone to the store yet . . . and soon, it would be mobbed.

She shook her head slowly. **Hot Chocolate Sparrow's?**

Be there in ten!

Okay. See you then.

She sighed. She knew she was going to regret not going to the store, and then, just as she pulled into the coffee shop parking lot, she remembered she hadn't even taken a shower yet! She looked in the rearview mirror and groaned—*what* had she been thinking?!

❧ Chapter 20 ❧

"What happened to your car?" David asked when he came in with the paper.

"Why? What's wrong with it?"

"There's a dent in the bumper."

"There is?!" Birdie got up, frowning, and limped outside. She looked down at her car and then touched the yellow indentation in the bumper.

"It looks like you hit one of those yellow poles on the bike trail," David said, following her outside.

Birdie swallowed, trying to remember the drive home from Sailor's the night before. She *had* gotten a little mixed up in her neighborhood when she left, but the bike trail was nowhere near there. After that, she vaguely remembered pulling into the driveway when she got home because David had left the outside lights on, and she remembered Bailey struggling to her feet to say hello. She also remembered drinking a large glass of water, but the actual drive from Wellfleet was a bit of a blur and she certainly didn't remember hitting anything.

"I don't know," she said, sounding perplexed. She looked at David, but he just pressed his lips together.

"I did *not* have too much to drink," she said defensively.

"I didn't say anything."

"You didn't have to," she said angrily. "I know what you're thinking."

"You don't know what I'm thinking."

"Yes, I do—you think I drink too much. I can see it in your eyes—it's like living with a judge. But I *don't* drink too much. You drink as much as I do, and every time you play golf, you have a drink at the clubhouse . . . and that's in the middle of the day. At least I wait till five o'clock."

David stood silently, listening.

"You should've seen how much my father drank. When he was home, he sat in the dark living room with his damn Scotch and no one was allowed to bother him or turn on the TV. We had to tiptoe around him after dinner. You have no idea how hard it was. Thank goodness he was flying most of the time, and thank goodness my mom eventually arranged for us to go to prep school, because at least there, we were free from seeing the torment in his eyes." She paused. "No one in my family was the same after Easton died."

David slowly shook his head. "For the millionth time, Birdie, Easton's death was *not* your fault," he said softly. "It wasn't anyone's fault."

"Yes, it was," Birdie said, tears springing to her eyes. "You weren't there. You wouldn't know."

"It was an accident. Accidents happen. They're a part of life."

Birdie clenched her fists in anguish. "Don't you understand? Because of me, our family was shattered. Because of me, there was no joy in our house. Any happiness we felt was always shadowed by loss and unimaginable grief. Easton was the only boy. He was my father's *only* son."

David took a step toward her, but she put up her hands. "I don't want your comfort. I just want to be left alone." He pressed his lips together and turned to walk back to the house. Birdie stared blindly at his back and then sank to the bottom step, covering her face with her hands. A moment later, she felt a warm body leaning against her. "Oh, Bay," she said sadly. "How did you end up with such an awful mother?" Bailey wagged the tip of her tail and licked Birdie's salty cheeks, and Birdie wrapped her arms around her neck. "What would I do without you?" she whispered.

Oh, what a gift God made when He created dogs. She had loved—and laid to rest—so many sweet dogs in her lifetime—each with its own personality; each with its own way of bringing comfort; each with solemn, loving eyes that were filled with all the wisdom in the world; and each leaving a gaping hole in her heart when they died and making her vow to never get another, never set herself up for so much sadness again. But she always did.

Bailey stuffed her wet nose in Birdie's ear and Birdie laughed and thought of Willow, the big yellow Lab her family had had when she was growing up. Willow had loved to stuff her nose into their ears, too. She was supposed to be the whole family's dog, but they'd all known she loved Easton best, and when he didn't come home that night, she looked all over for him. She cried and cried and wouldn't settle down, but in the days that followed, it was Willow who nuzzled their ears and gave them solace.

Part II

You will surely forget your trouble,
recalling it only as waters gone by.
Life will be brighter than noonday,
and darkness will become like morning.

—Job 11:16–17

July 3, 1964

"Black raspberry's good," Piper said with an approving nod.

"It's not as good as chocolate," Sailor said dejectedly.

Whitney put the ice cream in the freezer and noticed the frazzled look on his wife's face. "Uh-oh! How come you guys are all inside? Are you driving Mom crazy?"

"Nooo," the younger three chorused innocently. Whitney looked at his wife for confirmation, but she just raised her eyebrows.

"We were just looking for more jars," Piper explained.

"Actually, we were just going back outside," Birdie corrected, motioning for her younger siblings to follow her.

"But I still need a jar!" Piper cried.

"I have one right here," Easton reminded, taking the top off the jar in his arms. "Anyone want a pickle?" he asked, fishing out a sweet pickle and popping it in his mouth.

"I'll have one," Piper and Sailor both said.

"Use a fork," Martha scolded, picturing all the invisible micro-organisms that had just jumped off her son's hand and were now swimming in the pickle juice.

Hugging the jar to his chest, Easton pulled open the silverware drawer, but at the same moment, Piper and Sailor both reached for it, and without the support of his other hand, it slipped and fell to the floor, spilling sticky pickle juice everywhere.

"That's it!" Martha exclaimed. "Out!"

"Out, guys," Whitney repeated, ushering his children around the puddle and in the general direction of the door. Easton was the last in line, but as he reached the door, he picked up his mason jar and turned around. "I'm sorry, Mom," he said, his eyes glistening. "I didn't mean to . . ."

"I know you didn't," Martha said, trying to regain her composure. "It's just that I have a lot to do. . . ."

"You don't have to give me any presents."

Martha's frown softened. "Well, that wouldn't be much of a birthday, would it?"

He shrugged. "C'mon, Willow," and the yellow Lab took a few more quick swipes of the sweet puddle with her tongue, gulped down some pickles, and trotted after him, leaving a trail of muddy—and now sticky—paw prints.

"I'll get this," Martha said with a sigh, setting the empty batter bowl in the sink and reaching for an old towel. "You can get the broken glass."

"I'll get this," Whitney countered, taking the towel from her, "and the broken glass."

"What I'd really like you to do is take them for a hike—they've been underfoot all afternoon and I still have the cake to frost and presents to wrap."

Whitney nodded. "I'll get this, the broken glass, *and* I'll take them for a hike."

"It'll be dark soon. . . ."

"We have flashlights, and it won't be the first time we've gone for a hike at night."

Martha sighed. "Okay, you can get this and the glass, but I'm doing the dishes."

"Okay," Whitney said with a smile. "I'll let you do the dishes."

Ten minutes later, the kitchen floor was cleaner than it had been all week, the broken glass was swept up, Willow's paws were rinsed and dried, and the children were loaded in the station wagon—Easton in front, Sailor and Remy in back, and Piper and Birdie in the "way back," looking out the back window.

" 'Bye, Mom!" they chorused as their father pulled away.

Piper looked up and saw Willow peering through the screen door. "We forgot Willow!"

"She's not coming," Birdie said.

"Why not?" Piper asked, dismayed by the injustice.

"Because Dad just cleaned her up," Birdie explained.

"But she loves the beach."

"Next time," her sister assured.

Whitney turned on the radio, and when the girls heard the song that was playing, they begged their father to turn it up and crooned along with Gerry and the Pacemakers as they sang their melancholy hit song "Don't Let the Sun Catch You Crying."

When the song ended, Whitney turned it down and looked over at Easton. "I didn't know you could sing," he teased.

Easton blushed and looked out the window. The cool breeze felt good on his hot cheeks. "How come there're so many fireflies this year, Dad?"

"Because we had such a wet spring," Whitney surmised. "Insects love wet, mild weather."

"It's neat to see so many—the woods are full of 'em!"

"Lightning bugs are neat," Whitney agreed, "but mosquitoes won't be."

"Ugh! I hadn't thought of that," Easton said. "That definitely won't be fun."

Whitney pulled into the Nauset Light parking lot, and they all piled out and stood around the back of the car, dividing up the pails and flashlights. "I want to take a picture of you guys in front of the lighthouse," Whitney said.

"Aww, do we have to?" Sailor moaned.

"Yes, we *have* to," Whitney said.

As Easton waited for his sisters to sort through the pails, he watched the lighthouse scanning the darkening sky. Red . . . white . . . red . . . white. Rhythmically. Faithfully. Endlessly. *It never stops,* he thought. *It just keeps turning . . . on and on . . . forever!*

"Ready, East?" Whitney said, interrupting his son's thoughts.

"Huh?" Easton turned, saw his dad holding out his pail, and realized his sisters were already walking across the parking lot. He nodded, took the pail, and trotted after them.

They stood together, in age order, jostling for position.

"Ready?" Whitney said, focusing the lens in the fading light.

"Wait!" Easton said, dropping his pail and throwing his arms around his sisters' shoulders. His sisters did the same, and as they laughingly pulled each other closer, Whitney snapped the shutter, capturing a sweet, carefree moment.

"Okay, no funny stuff this time," he said, eyeing Sailor—who'd made bunny ears behind Remy's head.

Sailor squinched her nose and stuck her tongue out at him.

"You won't like it when your face freezes that way, missy!" he teased.

"You won't like it when your face freezes that way, missy," she mimicked, grinning at him.

"Okay, are you ready this time?"

They all nodded.

"Nice smiles . . . on three. One . . . two . . ."

They gave their dad their best smiles, and Whitney snapped the shutter again.

"Thank you for your cooperation!"

"You're welcome," they shouted, happy to be free and laughing as they raced toward the stairs.

⊰ Chapter 21 ⊱

"Oh, my! She's beautiful!" Piper said as they pulled alongside the huge loggerhead turtle swimming in the sparkling blue water of Cape Cod Bay.

"She sure is," Nat said, smiling as they slowed down to get a closer look. "I bet she weighs three hundred pounds."

"How do you know it's a she?" Elias asked.

"Her tail," Piper said, pointing to the turtle's tail trailing along in the water. "The male's is longer and more prominent."

Elias frowned. "It looks like she's only using two of her flippers." He leaned over the side, trying to see what was impeding her ability to swim. "I think she's caught on something."

Nat leaned over the side, too, and saw a buoy bobbing under her belly, the line of which was wrapped around two of her flippers. "It looks like she may've been hit by a boat, too," he said, pointing to a gash on her shell. He frowned. "I think we better bring her in."

Piper frowned. "Do you think you can lift her?"

"If Elias takes one side," he said, pulling a pair of gloves out from under the seat.

He found a second pair, handed them to him, and they both leaned over the side and grabbed onto her shell. It was slippery and covered with barnacles, and the old turtle, unhappy about being pulled into a boat, began working her flippers extra hard, trying to get free. Then, out of the blue, she stopped struggling, and they were able to pull her up into the boat—dragging the entangled buoy and line with her.

Nat surveyed the mess and shook his head. "Poor girl," he murmured.

"How old do you think she is?" Elias asked.

"I bet she's at least thirty, maybe older," Nat said, "and she's been hit more than once," he added, lightly tracing the scars on her shell. He finished examining her and cut off as much of the line as he could, and then Piper soaked a beach towel in the water and laid the dripping towel over her shell and head. Elias poured a bucket of cool seawater over her, too, and Nat turned the launch around and headed back to the sanctuary while Piper radioed ahead to let them know they were bringing her in.

Twenty minutes later, the sanctuary was in full emergency mode as they loaded the big logger-head onto a special cart and wheeled her into their small hospital. They immediately set to work freeing her from the rest of the line that was cutting into her skin and began administering fluids and nourishment. At the same time, Piper smoothed a gentle, healing balm onto her wounds. The old turtle didn't struggle but her solemn eyes watched their every move—it was as if she knew they were trying to help her.

Later that afternoon, Piper suddenly remembered it was Friday, which meant they were supposed to be at Remy's that evening to celebrate Birdie's birthday. She looked around for Nat and saw him on the phone, and when she walked over, heard him making arrangements to bring the turtle to the Boston Aquarium for rehab—their facility was better equipped for big sea turtles in this much distress.

He hung up the phone and looked up. "What's up?" he asked quizzically.

"You're taking her tonight, aren't you?"

He nodded. "I don't think we should wait. Why? Do we have something going on?"

"It's fine," Piper said, looking down at the turtle.

"I think you should take her . . . but I can't go."

"That's okay. I'll take Elias. Why can't you go?"

"We're supposed to go to Remy's for Birdie's birthday."

"Oh, that's right! I forgot!" he said apologetically.

Piper sighed. "It's okay. I'm sure she'll understand," though she knew her sister would be disappointed.

"Do you want me to get someone else to take her?"

Piper shook her head. "No, you take her."

"Dad," Elias said, coming into the room. "I filled up the truck. Are you ready?"

"Yeah, just a sec." He looked back at Piper. "I'm sorry to mess things up."

"Don't be sorry," Piper said with a half smile. "This old lady needs you more than Birdie does. Take good care of her." She knelt down next to the holding tank, looked into the turtle's solemn eyes, and stroked her smooth head. "We'll see you back here in a couple of weeks!"

◄{ Chapter 22 }►

Sailor ran her hand lightly over the cover of her *Upper Room*, admiring the illustration. She pictured her mom reading the little devotional every morning, a habit she'd passed on to her daughters simply by her example . . . *and* because she'd given them each a gift subscription every Christmas. She tucked the little magazine into her Bible and set it on the table next to her chair. She'd fallen a week behind because she'd inadvertently packed her Bible and the little magazine in the bottom of the box of linens and just found them this morning. She always felt as if she raced through the readings, instead of savoring them, when she was trying to catch up. She sipped her coffee, looked up at the puffy, white clouds floating in the summer blue sky, and smiled. "I know I'm usually full of complaints, Lord," she said, "but I can't thank You enough for bringing me to this place."

She looked around at the gardens. She'd spent all of yesterday weeding, pruning, adding topsoil —a luxury for plants on sandy Cape Cod—and mulching. While she'd been up close and personal with all the greenery, she'd discovered a wide variety of old-fashioned perennials: echinacea, bee balm, black-eyed Susans, peonies, irises, lilacs, several varieties of lilies, and of course, an abundance of hydrangeas! Near the back steps she'd also discovered a small garden with a cluster of chives coming up, and around it, small wooden signs telling her that there would be thyme, oregano, cilantro, tarragon, rosemary, and lemon balm, too. But she knew if she wanted basil and cilantro, too—both annuals—she'd have to buy new plants.

She leaned back in her chair and watched the birds flutter back and forth to the new feeder. It hadn't taken them long to find it and they seemed to love their new little sanctuary. She watched a pair of grosbeaks land and sit there peacefully, having breakfast and enjoying each other's company . . . and suddenly, she felt a twinge of envy. *How crazy,* she thought, *jealous of a pair of birds!* But she realized that although she loved her newly found solitude, she missed the easy companionship of someone she loved. It had been so long since she'd had that kind of relationship with Frank—their lives were so hectic and conflicted that she hadn't even noticed what was missing. But now, out here, away from all the madness, and with room to breathe, she decided it would be really nice to wake up next to someone and laze around together, sipping an early morning cup of coffee and reading the paper.

She took a sip of her coffee now and wondered if Josiah might be that person. After she'd met him for coffee the other day—he hadn't been the least put off by her disheveled appearance—he'd invited her to dinner, and the following Wednesday, they'd gone to the Ocean House in Dennis Port. They'd sat at the beach bar, eaten lobster rolls, and drunk Whale's Tail . . . and it was just so amazing and . . . easy. And since he'd been on his way back from Boston, she'd met him there, but afterward, he'd walked her to her car, and like a true gentleman, kissed her . . . on her hand! Couldn't he tell that she was ready for a long, full kiss on the lips? Or was he respecting the fact that they were both still married? She wouldn't be certain that Josiah had true potential until she kissed him on the lips. So far, he had everything else going for him—he was handsome, well dressed, and almost divorced, but his kiss would definitely be a determining factor. Oh well, he'd get another chance this weekend because they were going to Provincetown.

She finished her coffee, carried her Bible inside, and set it on the table. She refilled her mug, grabbed her laptop, and went back outside. The phone company had finally hooked up her Internet and she had a lot of catching up to do. She'd been "off the grid" for over a week, and if she hadn't been so busy working in the gardens and getting settled, she would've probably gone through withdrawal! She sat down, opened her laptop, and checked her mail—she had three hundred thirty-two new messages! Yikes! She quickly scanned the list—nothing urgent; checked the news—always a mistake; and then clicked on her Facebook page and realized she had two friends whose birthdays were that day—one was an old classmate from RISD . . . and the other was Birdie (Quinn) Snow! Oh my goodness, she'd almost forgotten Birdie's birthday! Good thing they were both on FB or there would've been hell to pay! She sent her friend and Birdie quick birthday wishes and told Birdie she'd see her at Remy's later. Then she closed her laptop and hurried inside to take a shower.

❦ Chapter 23 ❧

Remy sifted through a cardboard box full of recipes, looking for her mom's recipe for chocolate glaze. Martha had always kept her recipes in an old L.L.Bean shoe box. She'd also kept recipes that had been cut from magazines, as well as recipes that had been given to her over the phone and jotted on scraps of paper—like the one Remy was looking for now. In her mind's eye, she could see it written on a scrap of blue-lined notebook paper—but Remy had already been through the box once, and now, she was nearing the bottom again. She knew it couldn't be that far down because she'd just made the glaze when she'd made cream puffs for Easter.

She started at the top again and slowly looked through each piece of paper. "Someday," she murmured, "I'm going to get rid of all these recipes that I've never made and put the rest on cards in a recipe box!" It was a project she'd been planning to do for years. Every time she had trouble finding a recipe, she'd renew her resolution but she still hadn't found the time.

She sighed, and then along the front edge of the box she suddenly spied the familiar blue-lined paper. "Here it is!" she said, relieved. She pulled it out, closed the box, and promptly forgot her resolution. She glanced at the recipe, then measured the cocoa, water, oil, and corn syrup into a small saucepan, turned the flame low, and stirred all the ingredients until it was a smooth mixture.

Years ago, when their mom had stopped baking, Remy had taken it upon herself to carry on their birthday traditions. Birdie's cake was Boston cream pie—hence the need for chocolate glaze; Sailor's was devil's food with a home-made orange frosting—the recipe for which was even older and written in her grandmother's handwriting; Piper's was German chocolate, the frosting for which—a homemade buttery coconut and pecan—was *to die for!* Remy would've gladly made her own cake too—angel food with fresh strawberries and whipped cream—but her sisters insisted on taking turns making it.

Remy added a teaspoon of vanilla and a dash of salt to the cocoa, and as she stirred, she thought about Easton's cake—the yummiest cake of all. His had been a four-layer chocolate cake with a creamy chocolate mousse filling in between each layer and a luscious whipped cream frosting on top. Her mom had been making the cake the night they'd gone for a hike on the beach, but they'd never eaten it, and the carton of black raspberry ice cream had just sat in the freezer for months until, one day, she saw it in the garbage. Remy never knew what happened to the cake she'd been making that night and they'd never had it again—it was as if the recipe had been purposely for-gotten. It had always been that way in her family —anything that reminded them of Easton was shut down or silenced. Remy had grown up feeling as if they weren't even allowed to say his name. Often, she'd wondered if this was why she had such a hard time letting go of Jim's memory. She'd loved Jim and her brother so much and she could never understand why God took them away.

Remy added a cup of sifted confectioner's sugar and continued stirring. The recipe called for her to remove the pan from the heat, but over the years, she'd discovered that leaving it on low heat until the glaze was smooth and warm made it easier to pour.

She picked up the pan, turned to the waiting

cake, already cut into layers that had been spread with creamy vanilla pudding, and poured the warm chocolate over the top, letting it drip down the sides. Then she licked the spatula and stood back admiringly. "It looks like a picture, Mom! You'd be proud!"

She heard the stove *click,* realized she'd left the burner on, and turned it off. It wasn't the first time she'd forgotten to turn one of the burners off, and she often worried she'd leave one on *and* leave the house. She also worried that the pilot light would go out and she'd have a slow and potentially explosive leak. Maybe it really was time, like David suggested, that she thought about getting an electric stove.

She set the pan in the sink, filled it with hot sudsy water, and rummaged through her junk drawer, looking for candles. She took out three candles—one for the past, one for the present, and one for the future—and fit them into three little plastic holders. She and her sisters had decided long ago that they were getting too old to light a candle for each year.

She pushed the candles into the cake and set it back on the counter. Just then, Edison wandered in and Remy eyed him. "You stay off the counter, mister," she said warningly as he swished through her legs.

Remy shook her head and pulled open the napkin drawer, looking for birthday napkins. She had napkins for nearly every occasion—from New Year's Eve to Christmas, and from someone turning twenty-one to someone turning sixty, but she didn't seem to have any plain birthday napkins—how could that be? She dug a little deeper and found a small stack of *Over the Hill* napkins, pulled them out, and wondered if Birdie would be offended—it didn't take much! She sighed. The old girl really needed to get a sense of humor . . . *and* she needed to stop living in the past. Remy set the napkins next to the cake and looked at her to-do list to see what was left. She pulled out her old perk pot from under the counter—just in case someone wanted coffee—and untied her apron. All she had left was wrapping Birdie's gift—a lovely book about an owl named Wesley that she'd found at the Birdwatcher's General Store.

Chapter 24

"Are you ready?" Birdie called up the stairs.

"Almost," David called back from behind the closed bathroom door.

Birdie sighed and walked back into the kitchen to refill her wine glass. Then she tucked the bottle behind the coffeemaker so David wouldn't notice. Someday—if she outlived him—she'd be able to drink to her heart's content and no one would be keeping track . . . unless she ended up in a nursing home. She took a sip and looked down at Bailey. "Need to go out, ol' girl?" she asked and Bailey struggled to her feet. Birdie walked over to open the door, and as she followed her outside, she realized how much better her ankle felt. *Thank goodness!*

"Are we bringing Bailey?" David asked, coming out on the porch behind her and startling her.

"Do you want to?" she asked without turning around.

"Sure. We can take my car since it's full of dog hair anyway."

"Okay," Birdie said, trying not to let him see her glass. "Will you please run back upstairs and grab my sweater?" she asked.

"It's eighty degrees out. Do you really think you need a sweater?"

"It cools off when the sun goes down, and if we sit outside, I might need it."

David sighed. "Which one?"

She started to say, "How about the one you just gave . . ." but then she remembered that her new sweater was still in its gift box on the kitchen table and she needed him to go *upstairs*. "On second thought, how about my pink sweater from Bean—it's in my cedar chest."

She listened to him clomp up the stairs and quickly gulped down the last of her wine. Then she went inside, rinsed her glass, and put it in the dish drainer. She picked up the bottle she'd bought to bring with them and the salad she'd made, and headed out to the car. "C'mon, Bay," she called and the old Lab hurried over to David's old Volvo wagon—which he affectionately called Tank—and waited, tail wagging. "Hold on," she said, setting the bowl and the bottle in the trunk. She opened the back door and Bailey eyed the seat as if it were Mount Everest. "Go ahead. You can do it," she said, but Bailey just gave her a forlorn look. "Okay, get your front up," Birdie coaxed and Bailey pranced around and then gingerly set her front paws on the seat and looked back at her, waiting. Birdie lifted up her back legs—which immediately folded under her—and set her gently on the seat, but as soon as she got her footing, the old dog turned around and gave Birdie's cheek a lick.

David chuckled as he came up behind her with the sweater under his arm. "Thanks, Mom," he said in the voice he always used when he spoke on Bailey's behalf.

"You're welcome, sweetie," Birdie replied, making sure Bailey's tail was tucked in before she closed the door. Then, as she made her way around the car, she realized, in surprise, that the quick downing of her wine had given her a buzz. She got in, focused on buckling her seat belt, and opened her window.

David looked over. "All set?"

"Yes," she answered, knowing full well not to talk too much.

David started the car and backed up. "Is everyone coming tonight?"

"I think so."

"Elias?"

"I hope so," she answered, glancing into the backseat and noticing Bailey had her nose pressed against the window. "Can you put the back window down?"

David pushed the rear window button and the old Lab stuck her head out, and with her jowls flapping, breathed in all the lovely scents of Cape Cod. "Oh, to be a dog," Birdie mused. "Life would be so simple."

"Maybe in your next life," David said with a smile.

"Maybe."

They passed the sign for the National Seashore and Birdie smiled. "Do you remember when you came to visit me at the Outermost House?"

David smiled. "It's one of my favorite memories. I loved waking up next to you in that little house with the ocean breeze whispering through the windows and the summer sunlight streaming in. It was magical."

"It *was* magical," Birdie said softly, picturing David—her young, handsome David—lying naked next to her, lightly tracing his fingers across the curves of her body, and smiling his sweet, mischievous smile.

"What's wrong?" he teased. "Should I stop?"

"No," she murmured. "Don't stop."

He leaned forward and brushed a kiss across her lips, still running his fingers along her hips and thighs, circling ever closer. "Shall I stop now*?" he asked softly.*

"No," she murmured.

And then he eased on top of her and hovered above her, fully aroused. "How about now?"

She looked down and grinned. "If you can," she teased.

"I can."

"No, you can't."

He raised his eyebrows and eased to her side with the same mischievous smile.

"No, no!" she said, laughing. "I didn't mean it. . . ."

He frowned. "I thought you wanted me to stop."

"I changed my mind," she said, laughing.

"Are you sure?"

"Yes, yes," she said, pulling him back.

"If you insist. . . ."

David looked over. "A penny for your thoughts."

"Ha! They're worth more than a penny!" she said with a wistful smile.

❧ Chapter 25 ❧

"They're here!" Remy called, holding the door open for her sister and brother-in-law and Bailey, who was taking her sweet time sniffing every plant along the way, but upon seeing Remy, wiggled happily up the rest of the walk to greet her. "Hello there, ol' pie," Remy said, kneeling down. Bailey promptly licked her face and Remy kissed her on her sweet brow.

"Happy birthday, my dear," she said, standing to give Birdie a hug.

"Thank you, Rem," Birdie said, stepping through the door.

Sailor and Piper were inside, waiting, and when Chloe heard new voices, she trotted to the kitchen, carrying her new Zoe, but when she saw Bailey, she dropped her and went right over to greet her *real* friend.

Birdie's three younger sisters all knew Birdie expected a fuss to be made on her birthday, so they each gave her a long hug and wished her a happy birthday.

"Did you see my Facebook post?" Sailor asked.

"No, I haven't been on today," Birdie said.

When Birdie used her computer, it was to correspond with colleagues, catch up on news, or log unusual bird sightings. She rarely visited her Facebook page—which she'd only set up at Sailor's prodding, and had then been surprised by the number of people who wanted to be her "friend." Birdie fully believed that as she'd journeyed through her life, she'd left a trail of people whom she'd summarily dismissed because they'd become too clingy, complained too much, were overly dramatic, manipulative, or with whom she didn't agree; and ever since she and David had moved to the Cape, the circle of people with whom she spent time had narrowed dramatically, making her even more of a recluse. Sometimes, however, when she was bored, she scrolled, or as Sailor called it, trolled—the term used for viewing posts without commenting or liking—through her newsfeed and found out quite a bit about people—some of which she felt should really be kept private. She was haunted by the commandment, *Thou shalt not judge.* She knew she was judgmental. It was probably her biggest fault and she fully believed there was going to be a price to pay when she got to heaven. She could just see Saint Peter, waiting at the gate, checking his iPad, and looking up at her with raised eyebrows. She couldn't seem to help it, though—the older she got, the less tolerant she became. Life was hard enough without having to deal with people who didn't seem to have a clue. She didn't know if it was because of all the things that had happened to her in life, but she just didn't play well with others anymore, and she prayed she didn't grow tired of David, too.

"I think you received quite a few birthday greetings," Sailor continued. "You should look when you get home."

"I will," she said.

"I left one, too," Piper said cheerily.

"You *know* I didn't," Remy said, laughing as she took the salad bowl from her sister's arms. She was a Facebook holdout.

"You're the only smart one," Birdie said.

"So, what's the birthday girl drinking tonight?" Sailor asked. "We're having frozen margaritas," she said, pointing to a blender on the counter.

Birdie eyed the lime green mixture warily. "I think I'd better stick to my usual."

Sailor nodded and turned to David.

"I'll have a margarita," he said with a smile.

"Salt or no salt?" Piper asked, gesturing to a plate of flavored sea salt on the counter.

"Salt," he confirmed.

Piper ran a lime around the rim of a margarita glass, swirled it in the salt, poured the frosty mixture into the glass, and handed it to him.

Meanwhile, Sailor opened the bottle of wine Birdie had brought in, poured a generous amount into a big goblet, and handed it to her.

"Cheers!" Birdie said, holding up the glass.

"Never mind 'cheers'," David said, holding up

146

his, too. "It's happiest of birthdays to our dear Birdie!"

"And many happy returns!" Remy said with a smile.

"Hear, hear!" Sailor and Piper said in unison.

Birdie sighed peacefully—she was never more content than when she had brimming stemware in her hand. It was the ultimate comfort food . . . or drink, as the case might be. She held the stem between her fingers, recalling an article she'd recently read explaining that the only time you should hold the bowl of a glass was when the wine had been served too cold, because the warmth of your hand would take away the chill.

"Look at that cake!" Birdie exclaimed, eyeing the Boston cream pie on the counter. "Remy, you've outdone yourself!"

Remy nodded and watched as her sister also eyed the "Over the Hill" napkins.

"Cute," she said wryly. "Very cute."

Remy chuckled. "It's all I had . . . unless you want 'Fifty' or 'Sixty' . . ."

"Either of those would have been better," Birdie said with a laugh. She still couldn't believe she was closing in on "Seventy"!

"Shall we go out on the deck?" Remy asked and then eyed David. "I hope you'll do the honors," she added, holding up the grilling spatula.

"I'd be happy to," David said.

They went outside and sat down around a glass

table covered with snacks—chunks of sweet pineapple, cheese and crackers, shrimp cocktail, and Sailor's famous layered dip. Piper leaned forward and scooped into the dip. "I love this dip, Sailor! Every time you make it, I mean to ask you for the recipe," she said, popping the chip in her mouth.

"It's easy," Sailor said, nodding as she reached for a shrimp. "The bottom layer is half cream cheese, half sour cream. Then"—she paused to eat the shrimp and then kept talking—"you sprinkle it with taco seasoning, then chopped lettuce, chopped tomato, a small can of chopped black olives, a jar of salsa, and a bag of shredded Mexican cheese."

"How much of the tomatoes and lettuce?" Remy asked, jotting it all down on a scrap of notebook paper.

"Just to cover."

"It's so good," Piper said, taking another scoop.

Sailor nodded. "It doesn't travel well, though. I've found it's better to wait until I get where I'm going before adding the salsa and cheese, otherwise the salsa leaks everywhere."

Remy nodded as she wrote down this tip, and Birdie, who was watching her sister, teased, "Are you going to a party, Remy?"

Remy looked up and blushed. "Well, no . . ." She knew her sisters knew that *they* were the extent of her social life. "But you never know, I *might* get invited to a party," she added, sounding a little wounded.

"I was just teasing," Birdie said.

"I know," Remy said, although her sister's words stung. "I *am* thinking of going to my class reunion, though, at the end of the month."

"You are?!" Sailor and Piper looked up in surprise. Remy was the biggest homebody they knew, so if she was planning to venture off-Cape it was big news.

"In Vermont?" Birdie asked.

Remy nodded. "I haven't decided yet," she added, just in case she changed her mind.

"You *should* go!" Sailor said.

"Yeah, it would be fun," Piper added.

"Maybe," Remy said. "I saw Dr. Sanders last week . . . because after you said he was retiring, I decided I better make an appointment, and Mary, his receptionist, said he'd just had a cancellation so I took it."

"Did he tell you he was retiring?"

"He did," Remy confirmed.

"Did you act surprised?" Birdie asked.

Remy nodded and David looked at Birdie with raised eyebrows.

"I didn't tell anyone . . . *else,*" she said defensively.

Sailor reassured him, "Don't worry, David. We're taking *all* of our secrets to our graves. In fact, you're lucky we let you come tonight."

David chuckled, knowing all too well the impenetrable bond the four women—in whose presence he was blessed to be—shared.

"Anyway, we got to chatting, and I told him I was thinking of going to my reunion, and he said I should definitely go. He said he loves Vermont and looks for any excuse to go there . . . and so then . . . I jokingly told him he should be my escort."

"You did not!" they all said in surprise.

"Well, I was only kidding, but he asked me when it was and then he checked his calendar and said if I decided to go, he'd love to take a drive up with me. Did you know he went to Dartmouth?"

"I did," Birdie said, finding this turn of events—in light of John's comments at *her* appointment—*very* interesting.

"Yes, I've seen his degree in the office," Sailor added.

"Well, now you should definitely go," Piper said. "You'd have a great time! It would be so much more fun to go with someone."

"That reminds me," Birdie said, looking at Piper. "How come you're flying solo tonight? I thought Nat and Elias were coming."

"They were," Piper said, "and they said to tell you they are very sorry. But we rescued a beautiful old loggerhead this morning—she was all tangled up in buoy line and netting, and after we got her stabilized, Nat thought she should go to the aquarium, so he and Elias took her to Boston late this afternoon. They said they will make it up to you."

Birdie nodded. "Do you often see loggerheads in the Bay?"

Piper shook her head. "No, it's pretty rare, but this one was so weighed down, the ocean swells probably pushed her off course. Two of her flippers were so badly injured she could hardly swim, and there were several scars from boat strikes on her shell—she looked like she'd been through the war."

"Poor thing," Remy said sadly.

Piper nodded. "If she survives and heals enough to be released, you should come watch. It's amazing to see."

"I'd like that," Birdie said, taking a sip of her wine. "Well, please tell Nat and Elias they are forgiven. They're good men doing a good deed, helping an old sea turtle."

Piper nodded. "She really *is* a grand old lady."

Remy stood up. "So, what do you think? Should we start the grill?"

"Yes," they all said in unison.

David finished his margarita and stood to help.

"Want a refill?" Piper asked him as she reached across the table for Sailor's glass.

David considered and then shook his head. "It was good but I'm all set."

"Party pooper," Birdie murmured.

"I'm not a party pooper. I'm your designated driver and I probably shouldn't even have had one. The designated driver isn't supposed to have *anything* to drink."

"Oh, please," she muttered.

David ignored her comment and turned his attention to the grill while Sailor followed Piper inside to help Remy. "So, I have some news," she said.

"Ooo! Do tell!" Piper said, her ears perking up.

"Well," Sailor said, refilling all of their glasses, "Josiah texted me last week and we met for coffee. On Wednesday we went to the Ocean House for drinks and lobster rolls . . . and tomorrow we're going to P-town."

"Wow!" Piper exclaimed. "That's moving fast."

"When are we going to get to meet him?" Remy asked.

"*I* already met him," Piper quipped.

Remy frowned. "You did?!"

"Yes, remember . . . I was there when he brought the Munchkins?"

"Oh, yeah," Remy said, sounding deflated, and then her face lit up. "You should've brought him tonight!"

Sailor laughed. "He's definitely not ready to meet all of you. You'll scare him off!"

"No, we won't," Piper said. "He'd be lucky to be included."

Sailor handed them each a refilled glass. "Well, one of these days . . . *if* it continues. In the meantime," she said, holding up her glass, "here's to a fun summer."

They each took a sip and then Piper headed out to the porch with the wine bottle. "Need a refill?"

"Please," Birdie said, holding out her glass.

❧ Chapter 26 ❧

When the phone rang, Remy was stirring her steel-cut oatmeal and sipping a mug of warm water—into which she'd stirred one tablespoon of honey and one tablespoon of the elixir she'd just ordered from the Vermont Country Store, *Strength of the Hills*. She'd seen an ad for the liquid supplement in *Yankee Magazine* . . . or maybe it was *Vermont Life*—she couldn't remember which—and it had touted the elixir's wonderful health benefits. She turned the burner down, left the oats simmering, and answered it.

"Hello? Oh, hi, Dr. Sanders," she said, her face brightening. "How are you . . . Yes, everything's fine. . . . Oh, you're so welcome. . . . Rhubarb's my favorite, too. I'm glad you liked it . . . I had so much rhubarb this year, I didn't know what to do with it all. . . . No, I haven't decided yet, but I'll definitely let you know." She paused, frowning, and listened as he spoke.

"Okay . . . Do you want me to go today?" She nodded. "That's fine . . . an ultrasound . . . one o'clock . . . drink lots of water and fast for four hours." She looked at the clock. "I can do that." She nodded. "Okay, I won't worry. Thank you."

She hung up the phone and stared out the window. Not worry?! How could she *not* worry when there was blood in her urine? She remembered giving a sample when she'd had her physical—it had been no big deal and she certainly hadn't noticed any blood. She glanced at the clock—it was already eight thirty and she hadn't showered or even had breakfa—*her oatmeal!* She hurried back to the stove and picked up the spoon she'd left in the pan, but the spoon was hot and she dropped it, spattering oatmeal on the floor.

"Sugar!" she exclaimed, removing the pot from the burner and reaching for another spoon. She stirred the oatmeal—which was sticking to the bottom, so she scraped vigorously, salvaging what she could, and plopped the thick clump into a bowl. Then she turned to clean up the mess on the floor but Edison was already licking it up. "It's hot," she warned, but the little cat was undeterred.

She looked at the clock again and quickly did the math—she had a half hour before she had to start fasting and then she had to make sure her bladder was full—which was never a problem. She sprinkled flaxseed meal and chopped walnuts onto her oatmeal and poured a little extra almond milk on top so it wasn't quite so clumpy. Then she took her supplements—fish oil and a probiotic—and wondered if it was something in her diet that was causing the problem. Maybe it was the *Strength of the Hills*—that was the newest thing she'd added. She opened the refrigerator and studied the ingredients: Vermont apple cider vinegar (made from organic apples), grape juice, apple juice, American ginseng, black cohosh—whatever that was—black walnut, chickweed, cinnamon, clove, echinacea, fenugreek—another question mark—ginger, star anise, and turmeric—which she'd read somewhere was supposed to be good for arthritis, but none of the ingredients sounded harmful.

She opened her laptop, propped it up in front of her, and as she ate her lumpy oatmeal, Googled *"black cohosh."* It was an herb—the root of which had been used by Native Americans for medicinal purposes, namely women's health issues, so that could only be helpful. Next, she Googled *"fenugreek"* and learned it was another plant used for all kinds of ailments—from digestive issues to hardening of the arteries to kidney ailments—another positive as far as she was concerned. She looked up *"star anise"*—which, it turned out, was a star-shaped fruit from an Oriental tree, used in all kinds of medicinal teas, and extolled for a whole host of healing properties—another winner! Finally she looked up *"causes for blood in urine"* and the first possible cause that came up was urinary tract infection. *Of course!* she thought with a sigh of relief—*that's what it must be!* She probably even had some antibiotics left from her last UTI. She got up to look in the cabinet and found a bottle from three summers ago—*had it really been that long?* She opened the bottle—there were six pills left. She read the directions and popped one in her mouth—she'd fix the problem all on her own.

Already feeling better, she sat back down to finish her oatmeal. Then she started scrolling through some of the other potential causes. Dr. Sanders had assured her that it was probably nothing, but according to the Internet, there were all kinds of possibilities, and the one that stood out like a sore thumb—and made her heart pound —was bladder cancer. Maybe she shouldn't have taken that antibiotic. Maybe she should've waited, because now, she suddenly didn't feel so well.

She typed in *"side effects of ciprofloxacin"* . . . and discovered there were many—the most common of which was diarrhea, followed by a very long list of rare but other possible inconveniences—everything from change in urination to nausea, dizziness, dark stools . . . you name it! Why was she so stupid? Within ten minutes of receiving Dr. Sanders's call, she'd already taken matters into her own hands and quite possibly upset the entire apple cart. She looked down at her oatmeal. The thought of finishing it made her feel sick. She looked at the bottle again. It plainly said, "Do not take with dairy." Almond milk wasn't a dairy . . . or was it? Maybe she hadn't finished the pills three years ago because it had bothered her stomach then, too.

She stared blindly at the screen. Someone had told her never to look up symptoms or ailments on the Internet. Whoever it was, was right!

She called the doctor's office back and asked Mary whether Dr. Sanders thought it might just be a UTI. Mary asked her to hold on and went to ask, but when she came back, she said he didn't think so because there would be other indications. Remy nodded, thanked her, and hung up. Well, that confirmed one thing—she shouldn't have taken the antibiotic. She wondered how hard it was to make yourself throw up.

She scraped the rest of her oatmeal into the garbage, poured her glass of water down the drain, scrubbed the oatmeal stuck to the bottom of the pot, and washed the rest of the dishes. As she dried her hands, she saw something moving in the corner of the window, and when she looked more closely, realized a spider was wrapping a bug with its silk—a practice Remy considered to be utterly macabre! She put her reading glasses on and tried to discern the species of bug—if it was only one of those pesky greenheads, she would look the other way . . . but if it was something else . . .

"Oh no, you don't!" she said, sweeping her hand into the web, startling the spider. She put the mummified ladybug on the counter and gently worked it free from the spider's sticky thread. Moments later, she had most of the silk off its back, but its legs were still stuck to its belly—that was the tricky part—pulling the sticky thread off without pulling off any legs. At last, she was able to get it all off, losing only one leg in the process. She gently flipped the ladybug over, and it immediately hobbled back across the counter in the direction of the window. Horrified, she scooped it up again. "Didn't you learn anything the first time?" she scolded. She carried the ladybug outside and blew on it. Off it flew into the sky—freedom! Then she went back inside, caught the spider, and put it outside, too. "You can catch all the bugs you want *outside!*" She came back in, remembered her appointment, looked at the clock, and hurried upstairs to shower.

The next three hours ticked by slowly. Foremost on Remy's mind, besides the worrisome presence of blood in her urine, was *when* she should start drinking. She didn't want to have to stop on the way to the clinic to find a bathroom—which was usually what happened. She knew the location of every public bathroom on Route 6. Her favorite restroom—although not the most convenient—was the one in the back of the Birdwatcher's General Store—it was wallpapered with funny bird cartoons; one time she'd stayed in there so long, reading them, Birdie had called through the door to see if she'd fallen in! Finally, just before leaving the house, she went to the bathroom one last time, drank a very large glass of water—at least sixteen ounces—and then filled her water bottle to drink on the way.

An hour later, she checked in to Imagery and Radiology, and after finding a seat in the waiting area, continued to sip her water. "Mrs. Landon?" a voice called and Remy looked up and gave a little wave to the stout woman holding a clipboard. "Come with me," she said in a foreign accent that Remy couldn't quite place, but as she stood up, her nerves kicked into gear. She hated anything that was outside her usual routine, and this entire trip was light-years out of her routine. "Is your bladder full?" the technician asked.

"Yes," Remy said.

They walked into a small, dark room and the woman directed her to lie down and unzip her pants. Remy obliged and the woman squirted warm gel on her belly. Remy took a deep breath as she felt her run a quick scan over her abdomen. "Your bladder is completely empty," she said abruptly.

"It can't be," Remy said in a flustered voice. "It's *always* full *and* I drank a big glass of water before I left."

The technician shrugged as if she'd been expecting it. "I will do your kidneys. Roll to your side."

Remy rolled and waited. There was no way her bladder was empty—that was impossible!

The technician finished taking pictures of what looked to Remy like a dark, ominous cave filled with diseased tumors and instructed her to go to the cafeteria and drink more water.

"This isn't enough?" Remy asked, holding up her water bottle.

The technician looked at the half-full bottle and shook her head dismissively.

Remy zipped her pants, walked to the cafeteria, and bought a bottle of cold water for a dollar fifty—"What a rip-off!" she muttered—and drank it as fast as she could. She went back to the waiting room, and by the time the technician came to get her a second time, she was shivering.

After more dark pictures—which also looked cancer-ridden—the technician told her to empty her bladder and come back in. Remy obeyed and two pictures later, she was set free.

On the way home—because she deserved it—Remy stopped at Sundae School in Dennis Port and treated herself. She almost ordered her usual, vanilla, but at the last second, she threw caution to the wind and ordered a large amaretto nut waffle cone.

❧ Chapter 27 ❧

Birdie listened as David picked up the phone early Thursday morning. "Are you sure it can't fly? And there are no other fledglings around . . . or parents?" He nodded, listening. "Do you think it's injured?" More nodding. "Where did you say you found it? Mm-hmm . . . Okay, well, if you'd like to bring it over, we'll be here." Birdie raised her eyebrows and continued to listen as he gave directions to their house. For months they'd been trying to cut back on the number of orphaned and injured birds they took in, and the last two weeks had been the first time *ever* that they hadn't had a little flock of birds in their small aviary barn and fenced-in sanctuary.

David hung up the phone and saw her eyeing him. He smiled. "How could I say no? She was very upset."

"The only way we're going to be able to stop people from calling is if we put a note on the website that says we're not taking in any birds at this time."

"Do you really want to stop helping?" David asked.

"Well, no, but you have to admit, the last couple of weeks without any responsibilities have been kind of nice."

"I don't know. I've kind of missed having some little creatures to look after," David said, smiling.

"What kind of bird is it?"

"She wasn't sure—she thought it might be a ruffed grouse or a quail."

Birdie sighed. "Is it injured?"

"She said it was flopping around next to the road so it might've been hit, but it wasn't bleeding."

The phone rang again, halting their conversation, and David answered it. "Yes, this is he." He nodded. "Are you sure its parents aren't around? No other fledglings? That's odd . . . they don't usually abandon their young. . . . Of course . . . where are you? Let's see . . . Mashpee . . ." He started to give directions again, and as Birdie poured a cup of coffee, she shook her head. She sat down, waiting for him to finish, and when he finally hung up, he was smiling like a boy on Christmas morning. "He thinks it's a baby barred!"

"Wonderful!" Birdie said, shaking her head. She knew how thrilled David would be if it really was an orphaned barred owl, she also knew how much two baby birds would tie them down.

"It's not like we have anything pressing going on," David said, pouring a cup of coffee and sitting across from her. He looked at the pile of birthday presents still sitting on the table. "How come you're not using your new mug?" he asked, holding up the Susan Boynton mug.

"I will," Birdie said, smiling.

"Haven't you already read this?" he asked, leafing through *That Quail, Robert.*

"Years ago. Have you?"

"I don't remember."

"You'd remember."

"Maybe I'll read it next."

"You should, because we might have our own Robert heading our way right now."

"We might. That would be fun."

Birdie smiled. *It would be.*

Twenty minutes later, a young woman slowed down in front of the house, obviously trying to decide whether she was in the right place, and then pulled into the driveway. Bailey scrambled to her feet, sounding the alarm, and as the woman got out, carrying a cardboard box, David and Birdie both went out to greet her. David carried the box onto the porch and carefully opened it. A small bird blinked at him from where it sat huddled in the corner of a bird poop–covered towel. "What do you think it is?" she asked.

David smiled. "It's a ruffed grouse chick," he said, picking it up and gently examining it. "And its wing *is* injured." He saw the concern on the woman's face. "But not beyond repair," he assured. "I'm sure we can help her."

The woman sighed and smiled. "Good. I didn't know what to do. I was on my way to work and I saw it by the side of the road and I couldn't just *leave* it."

Birdie nodded. "Would you like to leave your number and we'll keep you posted?"

"Yes, I'd love to," the woman replied.

Birdie went inside to get a piece of paper and a pen, and the woman wrote down her name and number. After she left, Birdie looked at the paper and smiled—she didn't think anyone was named Martha anymore.

David was in the barn with the little injured grouse when a man pulled into the yard and got out of his SUV with another cardboard box. David opened it, peered inside, and a juvenile barred owl blinked at him and flapped its wings in alarm. David smiled. "It's okay, missy. We're not going to hurt you." He closed the box and had the man write his name and number on top of the box. "When she's a little further along, she should be released where you found her."

The man nodded.

"Are you sure her parents weren't around?"

"I'm pretty sure, but I can't be positive," he answered, sounding a little less certain than he had on the phone. "I didn't want anything to happen to her. . . ."

David nodded. "Well, I bet she'll be ready to be on her own in a week or so. I'll give you a call and you can meet me."

"That sounds good. Thank you," the man said, extending his hand.

David shook it and the man turned and hurried back to his car. As David watched him go, he shook his head. He was willing to bet that at least half the birds they took in weren't truly orphaned. He was certain that most had parents nearby watching anxiously as well-meaning humans scooped their babies into cardboard boxes and whisked them away to parts unknown. He often wondered how helpless and worried the parents must feel. Caring for young birds was the closest experience he'd ever had to parenting, so he could only imagine how difficult it was for a human to raise and release their offspring.

"Is it a barred?" Birdie asked, coming up behind him.

"It is," he said, half-smiling, "but I bet she wasn't really an orphan."

Birdie nodded and peered into the box. "Don't worry, little girl. We'll get you home."

❧ Chapter 28 ❧

Sailor woke up to the sound of plaintive meowing outside her window. She lazily pushed her covers down and lay still, listening. Maybe it's a cat*bird,* she mused. Catbirds—she'd learned from Birdie —sounded just like cats, hence their very original name. She sat up, swung her legs over the side of her new bed, and as her warm feet brushed the cool floor, looked around—as she'd done every morning since moving—unable to believe her good fortune. She shuffled to the kitchen and peered out the window. Sure enough, there was a cat sitting on one of the Adirondack chairs, sunning himself. *But what was that on the ground?* She stared at a lifeless brown lump, trying to decide if it had feathers or fur. "You better *not* have killed one of my birds!" she warned, praying it wasn't the female grosbeak she'd seen a few evenings earlier, but when she opened the door, she realized it was a mole. The skinny orange tiger cat looked at her with sage green eyes and swished its tail.

"What are you doing here, mister?" she asked, but he just blinked at her. She stepped closer, not wanting to startle him, but he didn't move, and when she reached out her hand, he gave it a sniff, and then a thoughtful lick. She ran her fingers over his ears and realized one was half missing. "What happened here?" she asked softly, gently stroking his head, which made him purr so loudly it sounded like a truck had turned onto the road. "You certainly are a friendly fellow," she said softly, feeling for a collar but not finding one. "Are you hungry?" she asked, trying to think of what she had. "How 'bout some milk?" The cat stood up, stretched his long, lanky body, hopped down, and padded after her as if he'd lived there all his life.

Sailor held open the door and he followed her inside, and as she poured some milk into a dish, he sat on his haunches and waited patiently. She set the dish in front of him and he leaned forward and politely lapped it up. When he finished, he licked his paws and wiped them over his ears. Sailor chuckled and shook her head. "You're quite the gentleman . . . and as much as I'd like to keep you, I bet someone is missing you very much."

She went to find her phone, tapped the camera icon, made a sound so he would look up, and took his picture. She looked at it. "Maybe we'll make some lost cat flyers," she said. Then she frowned. "I mean, *found* cat flyers"—she tapped through the prompts to e-mail it to herself—"and put them around the neighborhood."

The cat padded softly into the living room, hopped up on the new soft chair she'd bought, circled around to curl up, and closed his eyes. "And while I do that," Sailor said, "you go ahead and make yourself at home." She sighed, filled the kettle with water, reached into the cabinet for the coffee can, measured some grounds into her coffee press, sprinkled a little cinnamon on top, and while she waited for the water to heat, found a scrap of paper. She located her new silver Birdwatcher's General Store pencil in the drawer and started to jot down a list; at the very top, she wrote *cat food*. Then she looked out the window at her feeder and wondered how much of a threat the cat would be to her new little flock. "I'll just have to make sure you have plenty to eat."

She poured steaming water over her coffee, waited a few minutes for it to steep, pushed the press all the way down, and poured a mug. She reached for her Bible, picked it up, and went out on the deck to read that day's passage—which happened to be from the book of Job. She read it once and then ran her fingers lightly over the page and read it again. . . . *"But ask the animals, and they will teach you, or the birds in the sky, and they will tell you; or speak to the earth, and it will teach you, or let the fish in the sea inform you. Which of all these does not know that the hand of the LORD has done this? In his hand is the life of every creature and the breath of all mankind."* She looked up, wondering what message it held for her. Was it possible God wanted her to take in the cat?!

She sighed, and as she continued to watch the birds fluttering back and forth to the feeder, her thoughts drifted to the date she'd had with Josiah the night before. They'd gone to Provincetown for drinks, walked around downtown—which was always an adventure—and then stopped at Arnold's for ice cream. Josiah had been a perfect gentleman—holding the door open for her at every turn and insisting on paying for everything;

she couldn't imagine why his wife was divorcing him. In the three dates they'd had, he hadn't talked about his marriage—but she'd shared everything there was to know about Frank. She needed to learn to talk less. She'd always been one to speak her mind—it was one of her biggest faults—and she often left a trail of wreckage behind her. Why was it that she always seemed to say the first thing that popped into her mind without considering how much pain it might cause? How many times, over the years, had she told Birdie to let go of the past—as if it were a balloon she could just release and watch float away? And how many times had she told Remy to stop worrying, even though she herself was probably a bigger worrywart? And how many times over the years had she asked Piper why in the world she wouldn't marry Nat? Her sisters knew her too well, and loved her anyway, but would someone like Josiah be willing to put up with her constant sarcastic, off-the-cuff remarks? Oh well, she was sixty-three *and* stuck in her ways. If the wisdom of saying less—or nothing at all—was ever going to sink in, it would've by now . . . and if Josiah was meant to be, he'd have to get used to it, too.

She sipped her coffee, making a mental list of the things she wanted to get done that day—finish working on the final sketches for her new children's book, get going on setting up book signings for the one that was coming out in a couple of weeks, catch up on her correspondence, and most importantly, figure out how she was going to proceed in her working relationship with her publisher without having to deal with her soon-to-be ex-husband. Her newest book was well under way *and* she had a contract. If she could work exclusively with Leslie, the art director, she wouldn't have to deal with Frank at all.

She heard a *meow* and got up to open the door. The orange cat sauntered outside, and without looking back, trotted toward the woods. "Will I see you later?" she called, but he didn't seem to hear her. She shook her head, gathered up her things, and went inside to shower.

She refilled her mug and carried it to the bathroom, but when she set it on the counter and looked in the mirror, she frowned. What was that bright pink stripe on her cheek? She touched it and realized it was bumpy. "Oh no," she murmured. "Please don't tell me . . ." She turned her face and lifted the silver strands of hair that covered her forehead and saw another stripe near her eye. "I don't believe it!" she said, shaking her head. She turned on the shower, got undressed, and carefully surveyed her brown limbs and her snow-white torso—everything looked okay—but ten minutes later, when she turned off the water and looked at her reflection again, she gasped—there were angry red welts everywhere—it was as if the warm water had activated them. In her mind, she could hear her father's warning voice: *Leaves of three, leave them be!* His words had been especially directed at her because she'd proven to be the child most prone to poison ivy. "That's what I get for working in the garden," she muttered remorsefully. "No good deed goes unpunished!"

⊰ Chapter 29 ⊱

Piper kicked off the sheet with her foot and sat up. Her favorite old T-shirt—the one with *CELEBRATE FREEDOM* across the top, *READ A BANNED BOOK* across the bottom, and listed in between, all of the offending books—everything from *TO KILL A MOCKING-BIRD* to *THE GREAT GATSBY*—was soaking wet. "What the heck?" she muttered, pushing her damp hair off her forehead.

"What's the matter?" Nat asked sleepily.

"I don't know. I'm just so damn *hot*."

Nat rolled onto his side, opened his eyes, and looked at her. "Do you have a fever?"

"It sure feels like it. I just want to rip my clothes off!"

"Well, feel free," he said. "I won't mind."

"Very funny," she said in a voice that wasn't amused. She went to the bathroom and then padded quietly downstairs with Chloe trailing hopefully behind her. "It's too early for breakfast, if that's what you're thinking," she said matter-of-factly, pushing the door open to let her out, but when the big golden came back in, wagging her tail expectantly, Piper looked at the clock, realized it was almost five, and relented. "Okay," she said, "but you're going to be hungry later."

As she measured kibble into the dog bowl, she heard a distant rumble of thunder. She set down the food and went back outside to stand on the porch. A breeze was picking up and the dawning sky was an ominous gray.

The cool air felt good on her flushed skin so she sat down. A moment later, she heard a soft cry and stood up to let Chloe out. "Stay here," she said and the big golden flopped down next to her. Piper was glad Chloe wasn't afraid of storms. Willow—the old Lab they'd had growing up—had been terrified of thunder and had always tried to hide under the bed. Unfortunately, only her head and shoulders fit, leaving her whole hind end sticking out . . . but she thought she was safely hidden!

Piper leaned back and watched a circle of leaves swirling in the dark sky as the thunder rumbled closer and lightning flashed every few seconds. She heard Nat close the upstairs windows, and moments later, saw him peering through the screen. "Still hot?"

"I'm better out here," she said.

"Want some coffee?"

"Sure," she said. "Is Elias awake?"

He shook his head. "Sound asleep."

Piper nodded. Elias had always been a sound sleeper, even when he was a baby—fireworks, thunderstorms, loud music—if he fell asleep, that was it. He was out!

A few minutes later, Nat appeared carrying two mugs and sat down next to her. "Maybe you're hot because it's your time. . . ." he said.

"My *time?*" she said, looking up—just the way he said it raised her hackles.

"Yeah, you know." He paused. "Change of life."

"You mean *menopause?*" she asked, the prickliness in her voice growing sharper. Why do men have such a hard time saying words like *menstruation* or *menopause? Men* is actually in these words!

"Yes, that," Nat said nonchalantly, sipping his coffee. "You haven't gone through it yet, have you? You must be due. . . ."

Piper frowned. Yes, it was true that she hadn't "gone through" menopause . . . and yes, it was indeed possible that was the reason she was so damn hot—in fact, right this very minute, she could feel her temperature rising like a thermometer left out in the sun, but who was he to suggest it? What did he know about it . . . really?

Nat felt her eyes on him and looked up. "What?" he asked innocently.

"Nothing," she said.

"Well, even your mood has been a little bit . . ."

She waited but he seemed to have trouble finding the right word. "A little . . . ?"

He swallowed. "Not your usual cheerful self, I guess."

"Really?"

"Don't take it the wrong way," he said defensively. "I'm just throwing it out there because you seemed upset that you were . . . well, hot . . ."

She nodded, affirming she understood, but she still had trouble wrapping her mind around his observation that she was moody. Had he actually begun to use the word *bitchy* or was that just her imagination?

"You are in your late fifties," he ventured, "and your sisters were all younger than tha . . ." He looked up and saw the venom in her eyes, and realized his error. "You know what? I'm going to let you figure this one out. You certainly know your body better than I do . . . although I do know it pretty well," he added with a sheepish grin. "And I *love* it . . . too . . . but I think I'm going to take my coffee," he said, getting up, "and wait for *this* storm to pass inside."

After he'd gone, Piper looked at the sky and wondered whether he was right. Maybe she was going through menopause. She certainly was due—her sisters had all been in their early fifties . . . *and* they couldn't believe she hadn't gone through it yet.

Suddenly, the sky grew black and the wind whipped around the house, sending a pile of beach chairs clattering across the porch. The oak trees her father had planted swayed violently, sending a whirlwind of leaves swirling into the dark sky, but then, just as quickly as it had come, the wind ceased, and an ethereal light filled the yard.

❧ Chapter 30 ☙

Birdie looked out the kitchen window to see whether David was on his way up from the barn yet, and when she didn't see him, she refilled her glass.

"Have you seen my car keys?" he said, coming up behind her.

She spun around, startled. "I thought you were outside."

"I was outside," he said, looking under a pile of papers, "but now I'm inside looking for my keys. I want to be on my way before the Quinn sisters converge on this house."

Birdie pushed her glass back behind the coffeemaker and continued chopping marinated artichokes for the dip she was making. "What time do you think you'll be home?" she asked, trying to sound nonchalant.

"Oh, probably late. It takes time to lure these men into thinking I don't know what I'm doing and then steal the pot out from under them."

"Mmm," Birdie murmured, knowing all too well her husband's poker skills. "I'm sure they're going to fall for your scheme."

David chuckled.

"Are the fledglings set for the evening?"

"They should be," he answered distractedly as he headed back up the stairs to look in his other pants' pockets.

Birdie sighed and sipped her wine—half of her problem was her guilty conscience. "All I need is more guilt," she muttered cynically, sliding the glass back behind the coffeemaker.

"What'd you say?" David said, coming back in with his keys in his hand.

"Talking to myself."

"Is that because you're the only one who understands?" he teased, kissing the back of her neck.

"Yep. It's not easy being me."

"I know," he said, wrapping his arms around her waist. "What are you making, by the way?" he asked, eyeing all the ingredients on the counter.

"Dip," she said, stiffening at his unexpected display of affection.

"What's the matter?" he asked, frowning.

"Nothing . . . just a little busy right now."

He let go. "Okay. I'll see you later then," he said, sounding wounded.

"Okay," Birdie said, pretending she hadn't noticed that her words stung. *Man up,* she thought cynically. *Don't start something you can't finish.* She and David had never talked about the lack of intimacy in their bedroom, and whenever he put his arms around her lately, it just made her bristle because he didn't seem to want to do anything about it. It had just become a sad, unmentionable fact, over which she had no control. "Good luck pulling the wool over their eyes," she said. "Oh! And let me know if you need a ride."

"Touché," he said with a sad smile. "But I'm sure by the time I'd need a ride, you shouldn't be driving, either," he added, nodding toward the coffeemaker. He leaned over and gave Bailey a kiss on the top of her head. "See you later, old pie." She thumped her tail and kissed his cheek in return, and as he went out the door, he called over his shoulder, "Say hi to your sisters for me."

"I will," she called back and then sighed, relieved to be alone. She pulled her glass out from behind the coffeemaker and took another sip. She loved baking and cooking, especially when she had a glass of wine nearby.

She scraped the artichokes into the bowl along with mayo and grated Parmesan, added a can of mild chopped chilies and then spread the mixture evenly in a pie plate and slipped it into the oven. She put the bowl in the sink, filled it with hot, sudsy water, dropped all the utensils in, and refilled her glass, finishing the bottle—which, she reminded herself, hadn't been full. She rinsed out the bottle and put it in the recycling bin, under the milk jugs and OJ bottles. Then she retrieved two more bottles from the cellar and put them on the counter. She turned on the radio, and set to work washing the dishes.

"Need to go out?" she asked, drying her hands on a dish towel and holding the door open. Bailey struggled to her feet and followed Birdie outside, and while she took care of business, Birdie cut several lush purple blooms off one of the lilac bushes next to the house. She put them in an old glass pitcher that had belonged to her mom, and as she set the pitcher on the table outside, she heard Bailey sounding the alarm. She looked up and saw Sailor's white MINI pulling into the driveway with Remy in the passenger seat.

"Hi, sweetie pie," Sailor said, leaning down to kiss the top of Bailey's head. "Hi, sweetie pie," she said again as she gave Birdie a hug and handed her a bottle of wine.

Birdie eyed the plate her sister was balancing in her other hand and frowned. "No dip?!"

"No dip," Sailor confirmed with a smile. "I thought you guys might be getting tired of it so I made a baked Brie with apricot instead."

"Mmm, that sounds yummy, too," Birdie said.

"I just need to stick it in the oven a minute."

Birdie nodded and then noticed the welts on her sister's face. "What the heck did you do?"

Sailor shook her head. "I know—nice, huh?" she said, lightly touching the poison ivy on her cheeks. "And this is looking *better*—you should've seen it before. Thankfully, I had an old prescription for prednisone."

"Don't you remember the saying Dad taught us when we were little?" Birdie said. "Leaves of . . ."

"I remember, but I didn't *see* any leaves of three."

"Well, they saw you, my dear," Birdie said.

She turned to give Remy a hug. "Blueberry pie?!" she asked, admiring the pie in Remy's hand.

Remy nodded as she handed her sister the pie

so she could reach into the backseat for *her* grape-infused offering, too—they all knew better than to show up at Birdie's house empty-handed!

"It's nice you two can share a ride now," Birdie said, gathering up the offerings in her arms.

"It *is* nice," Remy said. "Especially since I got to ride in a *cool* car."

"Don't you think Remy should get a MINI too?" Sailor said, coming around to join them.

"You should," Birdie agreed. "You deserve to *drive* a cool car."

Remy sighed. "I don't know. I think I'd have

trouble getting used to a new car—all those big gauges are a little confusing. In my car, I don't even have to think. It's like I'm *one* with Ol' Bess."

"Oh, you'd get used to it," Sailor assured her.

Remy smiled, thinking maybe she *did* deserve a new car. It would be nice to trade in her old Outback and get something a little sportier. "I think I'd get one like Birdie's, though," she said, looking over at the Clubman. She frowned. "What happened to your bumper?"

"Just a little fender bender," Birdie said. "I think someone bumped into it at Stop&Shop."

"That's a shame," Sailor said, walking over to take a closer look. "Are you going to have it fixed?"

"Maybe. We didn't report it, so if we do get it fixed, we'll have to pay for it ourselves."

"That's odd—it looks like something yellow hit you . . ."

"Let's go inside," Birdie said, ignoring the comment and walking toward the house, but just as she did, Piper pulled in in her old copper-colored Element—the back of which was covered with conservation bumper stickers. Bailey started barking again and Remy and Sailor smiled. Chloe was leaning so far out the window she looked like she might fall, and when Piper opened her door, she hopped out and practically knocked Bailey over with her greeting.

Piper reached across the seat for a covered plate. "I hope you guys don't mind bruschetta again," she said. "I've been so busy this week, I barely had time to shower . . . and I *didn't* get to stop at the package store," she said sheepishly, giving Birdie a hug. "Sorry." She sounded a little flustered and her face was bright red. She turned to give Remy and Sailor hugs, too, but when she saw Sailor's face she stopped. "Oh no! What'd you do?"

Sailor smiled. "I got naked and rolled in it!"

"Oh, I'm so sorry," Piper said sympathetically, hugging her.

"It's okay. I'm on prednisone—which has helped a lot. It even makes my other ache feel better. What about you? Your face and neck are bright red—did you forget your sunscreen?"

"No, I don't know what the heck's going on. It's the strangest thing—I just keep getting really hot and turning bright red for no reason."

Birdie laughed knowingly. "Well, it's about time!"

Piper shook her head. "I guess maybe it is. Nat had the nerve to call it *my* time. I almost killed him!"

Sailor nodded. "Men just can't say the words *menopause* or *menstruation*."

"I know," Piper said with a chuckle. "He even said I've been moody!"

"He'd better be careful," Birdie said with a

181

laugh, "if he wants to live through it! Let's go inside," she said, remembering her glass of wine waiting on the counter.

Five minutes later, they were all sitting on the back deck. "Look at these lilacs!" Remy exclaimed as she set Piper's bruschetta on the table.

Sailor—who was opening the wine—looked up. "They're beautiful, but I'm not touching *anything* green . . . no matter how harmless it looks."

They all laughed and Remy watched as she filled four glasses. "Are you supposed to drink alcohol if you're on prednisone?"

"I don't know," Sailor said, "but I'm not going to worry about it." She handed them each a glass.

Birdie took a sip and sat back like she was sinking into a comfortable old chair. "I wouldn't worry," she surmised contentedly. "Whatever you consume, as long as you do it in moderation, you'll be fine."

Sailor nodded in agreement, watching her oldest sister. Through the years, she'd sometimes wondered whether Birdie had a small drinking problem—*was there such a thing?* It wasn't because she'd seen Birdie drunk—she hadn't—at least not since college. And it wasn't the amount she drank—heck, Sailor drank just as much! It was the way she seemed to *need* to have a glass in her hand . . . and she was always obsessively possessive of the amount that was left in a bottle.

But even more than that, she always seemed so utterly content when she had a glass in her hand—it was as if she could handle anything as long as she had a glass of wine. It seemed to be her way of coping—her *only* way of coping.

Birdie felt Sailor's eyes on her and looked up. "What?"

"Nothing," Sailor said, her poison ivy–covered face blushing. "How's your ankle?"

"It aches a little, especially at night, but it's getting better."

"Is David playing poker?" Piper asked, dipping a cracker into the artichoke dip.

"He's trying," Birdie said with a chuckle. "He thinks he's going to win the pot."

They all chuckled, knowing David had a terrible poker face—he could never hide his emotions.

"Mmm, this dip is really good," Piper said, reaching for another cracker.

"It's easy, too. I'll give you the recipe."

"That reminds me!" Sailor said, jumping up to check on the Brie.

"It's nice the men still get together after all these years," Remy said, remembering how much Jim had enjoyed playing poker with David and John and the other men in their circle. "Was Dr. Sanders going tonight?"

"I imagine," Birdie said.

Remy nodded and looked down at her untouched glass of wine sparkling in the late day sunlight, trying to decide whether she should tell her sisters about her most recent conversation with John.

"Have you decided if you're going to your reunion?" Sailor asked, setting the baked Brie wrapped in a golden pastry shell on the table.

"Oh, my," Piper said admiringly. "I feel like such a schlep with my bruschetta and no wine."

"Don't be silly," Birdie teased. "It's *your time* . . . nothing should be expected of you!"

"Yes, you should be living in the red tent," Remy said, referring to the book by Anita Diamant.

"I think that was just when you had your period," Piper said.

"I bet they used it for menopause, too," Birdie countered. "Women should *live* in a red tent . . . and drink wine all the time. We should be pampered continuously just for putting up with men . . . never mind all the extra stuff we have to endure."

They all laughed, even Remy, although she didn't really agree. She had never minded putting up with Jim.

"I think you should definitely go," Piper said. "When is it?"

"Two weeks from tonight," Remy said.

"Is John still thinking of going?" Birdie asked.

"He is—he asked me the other day if I'd decided."

Birdie frowned. "I thought you went to see him

a couple of weeks ago," she said curiously, surprised that they'd spoken again.

"I did," Remy said, biting her lip and trying to decide how much to say—she didn't want to worry them for no reason. "I had to have some follow-up tests."

They all looked at her, waiting for her to continue.

Remy shook her head. "It's not a big deal. Ninety-nine percent of the time, it's nothing."

"What's nothing?" Birdie pressed.

Remy sighed. "I just had—*have*—a trace of blood in my urine, and I had to have an abdominal ultrasound—which came back normal. But now I have to go for another test to make sure there aren't any polyps in my urinary tract."

"That sounds fun," Sailor said sympathetically. "Who does that?"

"A urologist," Remy said resignedly. "I'm going Monday."

"Do you want me to go with you?" Piper asked.

"No, no," Remy said. "Don't be silly. I'm sure I can handle it." She smiled, even though she wasn't looking forward to it.

"Did John say what causes it?" Birdie asked.

"He said kidneys can sometimes leak a trace amount of blood cells—it's common in runners and people who do a lot of lifting."

Birdie nodded. "Well, you do a lot of walking, maybe it's that."

"Maybe," Remy agreed. She hadn't thought of that before, but now that Birdie said it, it probably *was* the reason! Suddenly, she felt as if the weight of the world had been lifted from her shoulders. "It's no big deal," she said again, reaching for her wine glass and a bit of Brie on a cracker. "Oh. My. Goodness! Sailor, this is amazing," she said with her mouth full.

Sailor smiled. "I'm glad you like it. Now, tell us you're going to go to your reunion."

Remy laughed. "Okay, okay, I'll go to my reunion."

"All right!" her sisters cheered, and the dogs—who'd been lying on the porch, waiting hopefully for tidbits to hit the floor—pulled themselves up and wiggled around happily, too.

⚜ Chapter 31 ⚜

Piper pulled off her running shoes, eyed the worn soles and tattered mesh tops, and decided she really needed to get new ones. She pushed them under the bench, leaned back, dripping with perspiration, and watched Chloe—lying on the cool tile floor—lapping up the last of her water. Wearily, she stood up to refill the bowl and immediately felt her socks soaking up water. "Great," she said, shaking her head. "You should try to keep your water in your bowl," she

186

scolded, and Chloe thumped her tail in agreement.

"Hey, Mom," Elias said, coming into the mud-room with his backpack over his shoulder.

"Hey," she said. "Watch where you're walking —the floor's wet."

"Nice," he said, eyeing Chloe. "Did you do that?" he teased, and she thumped her tail some more—*yes, it was me*.

"Where're you heading so early?" Piper asked.

"Flying lesson."

"Oh, right," she said, remembering. "Do you know where Dad is?"

"Running an errand."

"Will you be home for dinner?"

"I'm not sure. What are we having?"

"Spaghetti."

"I'll be home," he said with a grin.

"I knew that would work."

He laughed. "Okay. See you later."

"See you later. Text me when you're back on the ground."

"I will," he said, pushing the screen door open. "Love you."

"Love you, too."

She watched as he pulled away.

"Moving on!" she said, turning her attention back to the day. She looked at the old Seth Thomas clock hanging on the kitchen wall. "First, coffee. Then, shower." She walked over to put a pot on and was surprised to find one already waiting. She poured a cup and hurried up the stairs to shower.

She turned the temperature to cool, peeled off her running clothes, and looked at her reflection—her face, neck, and "bib"—the area below her neck that was permanently tan and freckled from a lifetime of wearing bathing suits and tank tops *and* getting too much sun—were even redder from running. She sighed, pulled back the shower curtain, climbed in, and let the cool water cascade over her head and shoulders. She quickly washed, and as she rinsed, she remembered reading how Katharine Hepburn had loved taking ice-cold baths and swimming| in the frigid Long Island Sound year-round. *Year-round! And* she'd lived to be ninety-six— there must be something to the idea of shocking the system! Piper turned the knob a little to the right and laughed as the chilly water rushed over her head, and then she braced herself and turned it all the way to the right. "Woo-hooo!" she squealed in delight.

She heard the bathroom door open, and a moment later, Nat peered around the curtain. "What the heck's going on in here?" he teased. "How come I didn't get invited to this party?"

"You're welcome to join," Piper said, laughing, "*if* you can handle the temperature!"

Nat put his hand under the icy stream of water and shook his head. "Ha!"

"Chicken!" she teased.

"I'm not chicken," he said, pulling off his T-shirt and dropping his shorts and boxers in a heap onto the floor. A moment later, he was shaking his wet head and pulling her against him.

"I was wrong. *You* are very brave," she said, laughing and feeling how aroused he was. He kissed her neck, and as she leaned back against the wall, he slid his hands down her back and they both watched as he teased her.

"Mmm," she murmured. "I'm going to start taking cold showers every day."

"Mmm, me too," he said, grinning.

They heard footsteps followed by clicking paws coming up the stairs, and in alarm, stopped talking. "I forgot my headset," Elias called.

"Okay," Piper called back, trying to sound normal. "Be careful!"

"I will," Elias said.

They heard him tromp back down the stairs and Nat smiled and pulled her closer, but a moment later, they heard paws clicking across the bathroom floor, and a moment later, a furry head pushed its way around the curtain and peered at them.

Piper laughed. "You stay out there!"

Chapter 32

Sailor sat down at her drawing table, switched on the light, and realized she hadn't replaced the fluorescent bulb yet. So much for working under pure light, she thought, scratching the poison ivy that still lingered between her fingers. She leafed through the sketches for her children's book, which had been sitting in a pile for three weeks, waiting for attention, and although she was anxious to have everything approved so she could start painting—she'd feel better once she had a paintbrush in her hand—she just couldn't seem to focus. Plus, she hadn't given any thought to the release of her new children's book—which was in just a couple of weeks! In fact, the only book signing she'd set up was at a bookstore in Chatham over the Fourth of July weekend. She hated when she had to shift gears to promote a book when she was in the middle of working on a new one. The two activities were as far apart as day and night—as was the required mind-set!

Frank's attorney had been in touch with hers that morning, and she'd learned that he'd begun making arrangements to put their house on the market—which meant he didn't want it, either. It was a shame they'd be selling when the housing market was still in the tank—they'd probably take a big hit. She also learned that their official divorce papers were being drawn up, and although she'd tried really hard to get out of it, her lawyer had pressed her for a meeting to work out the details of dividing up their assets. He'd actually used the word *imperative*.

With a sigh, she opened her laptop, checked her e-mail and the news—which was as gloomy as ever—and then clicked on her Facebook page. She hadn't been on since before Birdie's birthday and she wondered how many other birthdays she'd missed. Oh well, her close friends—who knew her life had been turned upside down— would understand.

In the beginning, when Facebook had been all the rage and her friends had constantly sent her invitations, she'd been reluctant to join. People didn't need to know her business, and she didn't know what she'd post anyway. But finally, at the prodding of her publisher, she'd set up a fan page for her children's books and was unexpectedly surprised by the number of people who "liked" it. Later, she discovered that her fan page didn't allow her to see or "like" other people's posts, so she set up a personal page, too, and for the first six months, she'd been addicted! When did she get to be such a busybody? Finally, a friend told her about *SelfControl*, an app for people (like her) who didn't have self-control; they could use it to block their own Internet access. You just logged in, set the amount of time you wanted to block, and then focused on your work. Of course, if you started to go through withdrawal, you could always go back and change the time. Sailor had found the app an indispensable tool in getting work done, and she also found it helped her gradually wean herself off the social media site—a feat she felt oddly proud to have achieved.

Now, as she scrolled through her friends' posts, watched some cute pet videos, and scrolled past a ridiculous number of political posts—no surprise, since it was the heat of the election season—she began to feel like she was wasting precious time, so she clicked off, closed her laptop, and then closed her eyes. She was already dreading going into Boston, especially on a Friday—traffic would be miserable, not to mention it was her turn to host girls' night and she wouldn't have any time to get ready. On top of that, the thought of sitting down across from Frank made her hands shake. She'd need a double dose of Prozac just to get herself there. She opened her eyes and looked down at the box of photographs still sitting on the floor.

Everything was *waiting*—the pictures were waiting, her book was waiting, Josiah was waiting for her to call back—and now, her divorce papers were waiting, and she didn't feel like dealing with any of it. She felt like she was in limbo—unable to function or accomplish anything. She'd moved to the Cape with so much gusto, and now she felt as if she'd lost all her steam.

She went into the kitchen, refilled her coffee cup, found a hammer and the bag of picture hangers she'd purchased the day before, and walked down the hall. She clicked on her old radio—the one she'd had since college—and heard Cat Stevens's unmistakable voice singing "Trouble." She smiled and started to sing along softly, remembering the famous scene from the classic film *Harold and Maude*—the one in which Harold, after learning of Maude's death, drives his Jaguar—which he's converted into a hearse— up a mountain road and off a cliff. In shock, moviegoers think that Harold—devastated by loss—has committed suicide, but a moment later, they see him standing on the edge of the cliff, playing the banjo Maude had given him. From loving Maude, Harold learned that life is too precious to waste, and because Maude charged him with going out and loving again, that was what he would do.

Sailor sighed. How many times in her life had she felt like Harold? Too many to count, she was sure, but as she laid the pictures across the floor, she knew Maude was right. Life was too precious to waste, and she, too, would find someone to love again. Just, maybe, not so soon. Maybe the fact that she'd started seeing

Josiah before the ink was even scrawled across her divorce papers—never mind dry—combined with everything else that was going on, had taken the wind out of her sails. Maybe her divorce bothered her more than she realized. After all, how could you be married to someone for thirty years and not be a little upset when it ended? "Ah, *trouble*," she murmured with a sad smile.

She gazed at the photos, trying to decide the best way to hang them. Finally, she determined it would be easiest to start in the center and work out. She picked up a photograph—one in which they all looked like they were in their late thirties—all except Piper, who never aged, and who, in the picture, was wearing a Red Sox cap. Funny, she'd never noticed her wearing that cap before. As she gazed at it, another photo—one of a much smaller Red Sox cap that had washed up on Nauset Light Beach—filled her mind. The photo had been in the newspaper after Easton had gone missing. The heartbreaking headline had read:

EIGHT-YEAR-OLD EASTHAM BOY
STILL MISSING—FEARED LOST

Sailor had found several copies of the clipping in her mom's Bible and she'd slipped one out and tucked it away, and although it had been years since she'd seen it, she could still picture it. Tragically, two days after that headline was in the

194

paper, the owner of the Beachcomber Inn had found a young boy's body washed up on Cahoon Hollow Beach—eight miles from where they'd been hiking.

Finding Easton's body had been both a blessing and a curse. It had given her family closure and a body to bury, but it had also made her brother's death *real*. Their sweet, fun-loving brother was never coming back. He would never again make them laugh or lift their spirits with his winsome smile. He would never again make their family whole.

Sailor found the center of the wall, tapped a nail through a hook, hung the picture, and stepped back. She reached for her coffee, took a sip, picked another picture, tapped in a nail, and hung a second picture beside it. As she hung each picture, she thought about where they'd been in their lives at the time, and as she continued to work, she began to feel the easy satisfaction of accomplishing something. Surely, she'd once again feel—as her father used to say—fair winds and a following sea. She just had to get through Friday—even if it took a double dose of Prozac!

She hung the last photo and stepped back. The pictures, hanging side by side, were an amazing collection. They belonged in an art show! She'd always had an eye for composition, but when she'd hung the last photo, she realized one spot looked a little empty. She sighed—she'd have to fix it later, because right now she was hungry!

She reached for her empty coffee cup, turned up the radio so she could hear it in the kitchen, and headed down the hall to see what there was for lunch. She filled her cup with sudsy water, turned off the tap, and heard Frank Sinatra's voice drifting down the hall. She leaned against the counter, picturing her parents dancing around the living room to "Summer Wind." The kids had stood watching and giggling as their handsome dad had swept their mom off her feet; even seven-year-old Easton had pulled five-year-old Piper out onto the middle of the rug, too. She smiled wistfully, remembering. Then she shook her head. After Easton died, they never saw their parents dance again, and suddenly, it dawned on her why there seemed to be an empty space on the wall of pictures.

❦ Chapter 33 ❦

Remy emerged from the doctor's office into the bright sunshine and blinked back tears. Everything was fine! She was fine!

Even though she'd felt reassured when Birdie suggested walking as a possible reason for the blood in her urine, by the time she'd gotten home, she was worrying again. And over the weekend, no matter how many times she murmured, "All will be well . . . all will be well . . . all will be well," she couldn't bring herself to believe it, and she felt guilty because her faith was so easily shaken. "I'm sorry I didn't trust You," she whispered. "Thank You for making everything okay."

With a much lighter heart, she walked to her car. She started it up and rolled down the windows—*it was hot!*—and for the millionth time, she wished that her air conditioner worked. Here it was, summer again, and she still hadn't taken it in to be fixed, and she dreaded the thought of going through another summer without it—especially since traffic on the Cape in the summer often slowed to a crawl, and you just sat there, sweltering. She sat in the parking lot, tapping her steering wheel and gazing at the odometer—the old car had 182,046 miles on it! How in the world had she racked up so many miles when she never went anywhere?

Finally, with beads of perspiration trickling down the sides of her face, she put it in gear and pulled out of the parking lot, but instead of turning left, toward home, she turned right, toward Hyannis, and forty-five minutes later, she pulled into the parking lot of BMW of Cape Cod. She parked her old Subaru, got out, and wandered over to a small group of MINI Coopers that were parked side by side at the end of the lot—they certainly were cute! In fact, that dark gray one on the end was really nice. She continued to look them over, wondering why some models had vents in their hoods while others didn't. Did Birdie's and Sailor's have vents? She couldn't remember. And why did the one with the 2008 sticker cost less than the one with the 2003 sticker? She didn't know a thing about cars—never mind buying one—and now, here she was, at a car dealership, wishing she'd brought someone with her. Birdie and Sailor would know what questions to ask, and they wouldn't let some sleazy salesman take advantage of them. What had she been thinking, coming all the way down here by herself? Why was she always so foolish?

She peered inside the one that looked like Birdie's, trying to remember what the model was called. Birdie's was light blue, but this one was orange.

"Good morning," a voice said, startling her.

Remy turned around and saw a tall gentleman with white hair walking toward her. "I'm just looking," she said, hoping he would walk on by.

"That's fine," he said. "It's always fun to look."

Remy smiled. The man's face—and voice—made her think of Jim. How funny, she thought, that God would send a car salesman out who looked—and sounded—like her husband.

He extended his hand. "James London."

Remy stared at him as if he had two heads, and then, remembering her manners, reached out to shake his hand.

"What's the matter?" he said, smiling. "You look like you've just seen a ghost."

"I . . . well . . . I feel like I am seeing a ghost! My late husband's name was Jim Landon . . . and if he hadn't died, he would've looked like you in his old age."

James laughed. "Do I look old?"

"Oh no," Remy said, flustered. "I didn't mean it that way! You *don't* look old . . . it's . . . it's just Jim died young . . . and it's hard for me to imagine how he would look now."

James nodded. "I understand . . . and I'm sorry for your loss."

"It's okay. It was a long time ago," Remy said awkwardly. "But thank you." She looked away, feeling herself slip into her social misfit mode— her natural state in almost every situation.

Remy had always felt she was a born social misfit—she was famous for starting to speak at the very same moment someone else started to . . . and when she did manage to contribute a thought to a conversation, she spent the rest of the evening —even the next day—ruminating and regretting what she'd said or how she'd worded it. Long ago, she'd decided it was better—and safer—to keep her mouth shut.

"Well, since you're only looking, I won't bother you, but if you have any questions, I'll be just inside that door—where it's air-conditioned," he said, smiling as he wiped his brow.

Remy nodded. "Thank you." She watched him walk away and then turned back to study the spec sheet of the 2013 Spice Orange MINI Cooper Clubman S.

She wondered what the *S* meant.

⊰{ Chapter 34 }⊱

Birdie listened to the fully fledged ruffed grouse banging its wings against the inside of the box. They were standing in the wooded area on the far side of Great Pond, well off Cahoon Hollow Road, the winding thoroughfare on which the injured juvenile had been found, and they'd just found evidence—pellet-shaped droppings—that other grouse were in the area. "She's going to reinjure her wing if she keeps banging around in there."

David knelt down, opened the box, and gently turned it on its side. The dappled, reddish-brown bird tumbled out, blinked at them, and flew away, its wings filling the silent woods with drumming. Birdie watched and prayed—as she always did—that the released bird would not only survive, but thrive.

"Want to go to the Beachcomber for steamers and drinks?" David asked as they walked back to his Volvo.

Birdie frowned. The Beachcomber was steeped in history . . . *and* it was one of David's favorite spots. The old building—currently the home of a popular restaurant and bar—had originally served as the Cahoon Hollow Lifesaving Station. Built in 1853, and rebuilt after a fire in 1897, it was the only lifesaving station, of nine—Monomoy Point, Chatham, Orleans, Nauset, Cahoon's Hollow, Pamet, Peaked Hill Bars, Highlands, and Race Point—that still stood on its original site.

Since well before the 1800s, the treacherous water along the Outer Cape had become the graveyard for over three thousand ships, and the men who'd manned the nine stations since the 1800s had saved over a hundred thousand lives. David had read every book on the subject, and when the Whydah Museum opened in Provincetown with a collection of artifacts and treasure from the famous *Whydah Galley*—a slave ship captured and captained in 1717 by the pirate Sam "Black" Bellamy, but shipwrecked two miles south of Wellfleet—they had been among the first to visit.

As much as David was drawn to the historic station, Birdie was repelled by it. Easton's body had washed ashore on Cahoon Hollow Beach—a fact David knew—so whenever they went to the Beachcomber—which wasn't often—it always brought back the vivid scene of her brother's body, covered by a sheet, being carried up the steep incline and placed in a waiting ambulance.

"If you want to," she said, trying to shrug off

the memory. Drinks and steamers sounded good—especially the drinks part.

They parked behind the old building, walked around to the entrance, went inside, and discovered there was already a line. David gave the hostess their name, took the beeper she handed him, and followed Birdie past the T-shirt stand out to the patio.

"What are you having?" he asked.

"My usual."

David walked over to the bar—which was really a window in the side of the building—and ordered a merlot and a beer, and while Birdie waited for him to come back, she watched a little boy run across the sandy parking lot toward a woman who'd just come up from the beach. "Look, Mom!" he shouted. "I found a heart stone!" The woman knelt down and he held his hand out. "You can have it," he said, his face beaming.

Birdie couldn't hear the woman's reply, but she could see the smile on her face as she pulled him into a hug.

"Hold him tightly," she whispered, hot tears stinging her eyes. "Never let him go."

"What'd you just say?" David asked, coming up behind her with their drinks.

Birdie blinked back tears. "Nothing," she said. "Just talking to myself."

"Again?" David teased, handing her a plastic cup, filled to the brim.

She nodded. "Yes. You know—because I'm the only one who understands."

"Yes, I know," he said with a wry smile. "Well, cheers!" he said, holding up his cup.

"Cheers," she said with a nod.

By the time a table became available, Birdie had finished a second glass, and when they were seated, she ordered her third.

"An order of steamers, too," David said, and then looked at Birdie. "Anything else?"

Birdie quickly scanned the menu. "Scallops?"

"Sure," David said agreeably.

The waitress nodded. Moments later she came back with Birdie's wine and a mountain of steamers with bowls of both broth and melted butter.

David reached for a clamshell, pried it open, and pulled out the clam. Then he pulled off the black membrane, dipped it in the broth and warm butter, and dropped it in his mouth. "Mmm-mm," he said with a grin as he wiped his lips with his napkin. "I can't remember the last time we had steamers."

"Probably last summer," Birdie mused, sipping her wine. She put down her glass and picked up a clam, but when she tried to open it, it slipped out of her hands and rocketed like a projectile over to the next table. Her face turned bright red. "I'm so sorry," she said, getting up to retrieve it, but when she did, she accidentally knocked over her drink. David quickly picked up the glass, but it was too late, the red wine had already streamed onto his white slacks.

"Damn it!" she muttered, plunking back down on her seat as the little girl from the next table brought the wayward clam back to its rightful owner. "Thank you, dear," Birdie said kindly, but after the little girl had returned to her table, she muttered, "I'm such a damn fool!"

Seeing the commotion, a waitress quickly appeared with a cloth and wiped down the table. "Can I get you another?" she asked.

"Please," Birdie said. Then she looked up and saw the look on David's face. "Oh, don't start," she said coolly.

"I didn't say a thing."

"You don't need to," Birdie said with a sigh. "You have no idea how much I hate coming here," she added bitterly.

David frowned. "You're right. I didn't know. If you'd said something, we wouldn't have come."

"I shouldn't have to say anything," Birdie said, her voice rising.

"We've been coming here for years."

"Not willingly."

"Honestly, Birdie, I didn't know it was a problem. I'm not a mind reader."

"It doesn't take a mind reader to put two and two together. I only come here because you like it."

David slumped back in his seat and stared at the clams and the basket of scallops. He'd suddenly lost his appetite.

Birdie shook her head. "How could you not know?"

"I don't know," David said with a resigned sigh, shaking his head. "I guess I should have. Shall we go then?"

"No, eat your food."

"I'm not hungry."

Birdie took a sip of her wine and then reached for the same clam and tried to open it again. When she still couldn't get it open, she threw it back in the bowl, unrolled her napkin, pulled out her plastic fork, and stabbed a scallop.

As they drove home from Wellfleet in silence, Birdie felt as if the end had finally come. They didn't know each other as well as they thought, and if they didn't by now, they never would. She sighed. It had finally happened—she'd lost all patience with David. He had been the only person left—besides her sisters—whom she could tolerate for more than ten minutes, but she guessed their relationship had run its course. She decided she'd be better off living alone, with no one to bother her.

❦ Chapter 35 ❦

"Has anyone heard from Sailor?" Remy asked as she sat down across from her sisters. It was Friday, and although it was Sailor's turn to host, her trip to Boston had resulted in a change of venue. The meeting with Frank and their lawyers was scheduled for two o'clock, but she had no idea how long it would take or how heavy traffic would be coming back. Sailor had suggested postponing but Remy had reminded her that she'd be in Vermont the following Friday—which would mean, if they postponed for her, as well, three weeks would go by. In the end, Remy offered to switch and Sailor happily agreed.

"I haven't," Piper said, looking over at Birdie—who shook her head. Piper shrugged and turned back to Remy.

"I can't believe you bought a new car! Are you feeling okay?"

Remy laughed as she scooped some of the dip she'd made. "Well, the salesman was so nice and helpful, and he reminded me of Jim," Remy said. "I know that makes me sound gullible, but with my trip to Vermont coming and no AC in my Subaru, I decided it was time."

"That is so unlike you," Birdie said, taking another sip of her wine.

"That's for sure!" Piper said. "I love the color. What did you call it?"

"Spice Orange."

"I guess we can't call you *vanilla* anymore," Piper teased.

Remy chuckled. "I guess you can't."

"Has Sailor seen it . . . or does she know about it?"

"Not yet. I was hoping she'd get home in time to see it tonight."

"She's going to fall off her chair," Piper said.

"Is Dr. Sanders still going to Vermont with you?" Birdie asked. It seemed utterly implausible to her that John Sanders, the doctor they'd been going to since they were young women, was suddenly going away for the weekend with Remy, of all people!

"He *is*," Remy said. "I stopped by to show him the car—which he loved—and he said he was really looking forward to it."

"When are you leaving?"

"Friday."

Birdie nodded. "Are we skipping next week?"

Remy shook her head. "Sailor and I switched."

"The week after that is the Fourth of July already!" Piper said. "I hope everyone's coming —it would be nice to get a head count." She eyed Remy, who frowned as if she suddenly remembered what she'd forgotten to do.

"I hope so, too," she said. "I'll have to ask the

kids again and let you know." In truth, she'd forgotten to ask Payton, Eliza, and Sam whether they were coming to the Cape for the family picnic at Piper's, but since they usually came—and should know to plan on it—she wasn't worried.

Piper refilled Birdie's glass. "What's got you so glum?" she asked, knowing to choose her words carefully. If she asked the same question in a slightly different way—*What's got you in such a mood?*—her sister could easily get annoyed. It didn't take much!

"Oh, the usual stuff. Same you-know-what, different day."

Piper frowned and glanced at Remy. They waited for her to continue, but she just took another sip of her wine and sank more deeply into her chair.

Just then, they heard a car pull into the driveway and Piper smiled. "Sailor," she said, getting up. If anyone would be able to get the bee out of Birdie's bonnet it was their outspoken sister. A moment later, Sailor came up the steps, looking puzzled. "Whose MINI is that in the driveway?" she asked, looking to see whether one of her sisters had come with a friend.

"Mine," Remy said.

"No way!" Sailor said incredulously.

"Way," Remy said with a slow smile.

"You retired Ol' Bess?!"

"I did," Remy said, feeling a pang of guilt. Ol'

Bess had been good to her, but she was rusty and old and she had to give her up sometime. "Ol' Bess has seen better days and her air conditioner hasn't worked in years. It was time."

Sailor nodded, still in shock. "I couldn't really see the color. Is it Spice Orange?"

Remy nodded.

"What year?"

"2013."

"How many miles?"

"Forty-eight thousand."

"Stick?"

"Of course."

"Is it an *S*? I didn't notice in the dark."

"If you mean supercharged, yes," Remy said authoritatively, remembering how James had explained what the vent—or scoop—was for.

"Where'd you get it?"

"Hyannis."

"By yourself?!"

"Yes, *by myself*—why does everyone think I'm not capable of doing things by myself?" she asked.

"Well, it's just . . ." Sailor said, trying to find the right words. "It's just . . ."

"It's just you never do," Birdie said, finishing her sentence for her.

"I do so," Remy countered, feeling stung. "I've lived all my life by myself and I've done *every-thing* on my own."

Birdie, Sailor, and Piper were suddenly quiet. Remy was right. They'd always thought of her as a bit of a church mouse, but their quiet sister had raised three children, maintained a lovely home, paid all her bills, and lived independently for most of her adult life.

"You're right," Sailor said. "You *have* done everything on your own. It was wrong of me to say that. I'm sorry."

"It's okay," Remy said, immediately forgiving her. "Now, tell us about your meeting."

Sailor laughed. "Oh, well, I'll need a drink first!"

Piper poured another glass of the chardonnay she'd brought and handed it to her, and Sailor scooped a tortilla chip into the dip and smiled at Remy. "You made my dip!"

Remy nodded. "I knew I'd get the chance."

Sailor took a sip from her glass and licked her lips. "Mmm, this is good," she said, looking at the bottle. "So, I got there right on time, and of course, Frank—who *just couldn't get out of work*—was forty-five minutes late. Same old story," she said, shaking her head and taking another sip. "Anyway, the house is going on the market and we had to agree on a price. We're asking a hundred thousand less than we paid for it, and the Realtor still thinks it's too much! She said, for the money we're asking, the kitchen and the bathrooms should be upgraded. She said people just aren't using granite anymore and the popular color for cabinets is white, not dark wood."

"Ha," Piper said. "I *knew* granite would go out of style. That's why I've kept our good old Formica."

Birdie chuckled. "If any kitchen needs upgrading, it's the kitchen at Whit's End!"

"Hey," Piper said defensively. "You should appreciate that I've kept everything original. That kitchen is full of memories—just think of all the family meals made on those counters. Not to mention the birthday cakes and science projects."

"And love . . . it's really all the love that's been made on those counters," Sailor teased with a grin.

"It was the table, not the counters," Piper said, laughing. "Except for maybe that one time . . ."

"TMI!" Birdie said, holding up her hand. "We don't need to know!"

"Oh, by the way," Sailor said, eyeing Birdie as she suddenly remembered how her morning had started. Birdie looked up. "This morning, before I got in the shower, I looked out the window and saw a little finch fluttering around under my bird feeder. At first, I couldn't tell if it was injured or a baby, but it definitely couldn't fly. Needless to say, because my sister, the well-known ornithologist, is always telling me that we shouldn't intervene in the lives of wildlife—I didn't. I just took my shower, figuring the little bird's parents were around. But when I got out of the shower and looked out the window again, the little finch was dead . . . and you'll never guess who murdered it."

"A hawk," Piper offered.

Sailor shook her head.

"A kestrel," Birdie said.

She shook her head again.

"That orange cat you've had hanging around," Remy said.

Sailor shook her head for the last time. "A chipmunk!"

Remy looked horrified. "A chipmunk?!"

"Yes."

Piper frowned. "I thought chipmunks ate seeds."

"Did *he* kill it?" Remy asked, finding this news implausible.

"I didn't witness the actual crime," Sailor said. "I don't have a security camera aimed at my bird feeder, but I think it was definitely him just by what he was doing to it."

"Don't say any more," Remy said, shaking her head. "That's awful."

"Geez, I will never look at a chipmunk the same way again," Piper added.

"I know!" Sailor said. "I wouldn't have believed it myself if I didn't see it with my own eyes, but I looked online to see if it was just one deranged chipmunk, but other people have seen it, too. So even if the parents *are* around"—Sailor eyed Birdie—"it doesn't mean the fledglings are safe."

"It certainly doesn't," Birdie said. "They're most vulnerable when they're young, but there's nothing that can be done about it."

Sailor looked in her sister's eyes, wondering if she realized what she'd just said. "There's nothing that can be done about it," she repeated, but Birdie just looked away and took another sip of her wine.

"So, other than putting the house on the market, what other decisions did you have to make?" Piper asked, anxious to change the subject.

Sailor shook her head. "It was pretty straightforward. He gets *his* car; I get mine; the contents of the house will be sold and the proceeds will be split evenly. It was a total waste of time. I could've easily made these decisions over the phone."

"Did Frank say anything to you?" Remy asked.

"He tried to apologize, but I just didn't want to hear it."

Birdie, Remy, and Piper heard the sadness in their sister's voice and raised their eyebrows.

"What?" Sailor said. "It's over. It's just over . . . and I need to *get* over it." She felt tears sting her eyes, but there was no way in hell she was going to let Frank make her cry, especially in front of her sisters. She took a sip of her wine and looked at Birdie. "Enough about my boring divorce. You don't seem your usual chipper self, either."

Birdie chuckled. "Chipper? I don't think that's a word *anyone* associates with me."

"Maybe not *anyone,*" Sailor said, "but those who know you *best* do. We know your *chipper* scale barely registers in the sunny range, but tonight it's in the gloom-and-doom range. What's up? Trouble in paradise?"

"Ha," Birdie said, her voice edged with sarcasm. "Paradise has dried up and blown away."

Sailor frowned. "How come? Are you and David not getting along?" She found this hard to believe since David was so easygoing . . . *and* he was a saint for putting up with Birdie's moods.

"We're not," Birdie said, "and while I steam like a pressure cooker, he avoids the steam."

"Hmm," Sailor said. "That doesn't sound good. He must've done *something* to make you upset."

Birdie shook her head. "It's not any one thing. It's all the little things, added up . . . and me, losing my patience with everything he does. I honestly think I'd be happier living alone."

"No, you wouldn't," Remy countered. "David is a love and you're lucky to have him. Living alone is no fun at all. There's no one to snuggle up against when you get a chill at night. There's no one to have a cup of coffee with over the morning paper. There's no one to hold you when you're afraid and tell you everything's going to be okay. You don't know what it's like, Birdie, and for you to say such a thing is callous. If David could hear you, he'd be heartbroken."

Birdie shrugged. "You speak from *your* experience, Remy, and I speak from mine. Being married isn't all it's cracked up to be."

Remy stood up, overwhelmed by her emotions and blinking back tears. "Who wants rice pudding?"

Piper looked up in surprise. "You made *rice pudding?*"

Remy nodded.

"Where'd you get the recipe?"

"Mom's cookbook."

"Her *Good Housekeeping* cookbook?"

Remy nodded.

"I've been looking all over for that cookbook."

"I have it."

"I can't believe you made rice pudding—that's why I was looking for it! Nat had a craving and . . ."

"That was weeks ago," Sailor said. "You haven't made that poor boy rice pudding yet?"

"No," Piper admitted sheepishly. "I wanted to make Mom's recipe."

"I told you to ask Remy."

"I know but I kept forgetting."

Remy mustered a smile. "I know all about forgetting," she said sympathetically.

Piper stood up. "I'll help you."

She followed Remy inside, and as soon as the screen door closed behind them, Sailor turned to Birdie. "That was a little harsh."

Birdie sighed. "I didn't mean to be harsh, but

honestly, I don't need Remy—or anyone else—telling me how hard their life is."

Sailor shook her head. "You know, Birdie, I think it's time you let go of the past. Whether you realize it or not, you've let Easton's death color all of your days, and in doing so, you're ruining your own life."

"There is more to what has shaped my life than Easton's death," Birdie countered, sounding annoyed. "You seem to have forgotten all the miscarriages I had."

Sailor was quiet. "I haven't forgotten, Birdie. It's just that life goes on . . . and at the end of the day, what's most important is the lives you've touched and how you've—" But before she could finish, the screen door swung open again and Piper came out carrying four bowls of warm rice pudding topped with cool, melting whipped cream.

"This is going to bring back memories," she said with a smile.

❧ Chapter 36 ❧

Piper and Nat stood in the driveway, looking up. Piper focused her phone on the tops of the trees and they both waited. Moments later, they heard the sound of an engine. "Here he comes," Nat said. Piper pushed the Record button and a second later, a small plane buzzed the tops of the trees, wagging its wings. "There he is!" Nat said, smiling and waving, even though he knew Elias probably couldn't see them.

When the plane was out of sight, Piper pushed the button again and looked down at her phone. "That was so cool!" She started to watch the video but heard the sound of the engine growing louder again and refocused her phone on the sky above the house.

"Here he comes," Nat said and Piper pushed the button just as the plane buzzed the roof of the house before soaring back out over the Bay. "What a lucky kid," Nat said with a hint of envy in his voice. "I always wanted to learn to fly."

"You still could," Piper said.

"Nah," Nat said. "I'm too old."

"No, you're not," she countered as she watched the new video.

Nat heard the sound of the engine coming from her phone and looked over her shoulder. "I can't believe he's up there all by himself."

Piper looked up in alarm. "He's by himself?"

"Didn't he tell you?" Nat said. "He's soloing today."

"Noo . . . he didn't tell me!"

Nat chuckled. "He probably didn't want you to worry."

Piper knew Elias had been taking flying lessons since the previous summer and he'd had countless hours in the sky with his instructor, but to find out he was a thousand feet above the earth in the metal contraption *alone* was unsettling. "How did he text us to tell us to come outside? There's no texting and flying."

"I don't know," Nat said. "He probably typed the message before he left and hit Send when he got close."

"I hope so," she said skeptically.

Nat put his arms around her and pulled her close. "Now *we* have just enough time before he gets home," he murmured.

"Time for what?" Piper asked, frowning, although she knew very well *what* he meant.

"You know what . . ."

"Oh, I don't think so," Piper said with a groan. "Not while he's up in that plane *alone*. I can't think about anything else when I'm on alert."

Nat looked puzzled. " 'On alert'?"

"Yes, that's what moms do when their only child might plummet to the ground at any moment."

"That's not going to happen."

"Maybe not," Piper said—she didn't think she'd ever felt less in the mood. "But I'd just be going through the motions . . . and it definitely wouldn't be fun."

"Elias wasn't flying last night," Nat pressed, "and you didn't want to then, either."

"That's because he was home," Piper said, as if the reason should be obvious.

"So?"

"So . . . he might hear us."

"He's never heard us before. He never hears *anything*."

"It's different now . . . he's older. Besides, we have stuff to do," she added, putting her hands on his chest and gently pushing him away. She was suddenly feeling very warm and his body was making her downright hot.

"Whatever," Nat said, backing off.

"Don't be mad," she said—she hated that word—*"whatever."*

"I'm not mad."

"Yes, you are."

"No, I'm not."

Piper shook her head and turned to walk to the house, but when she heard Nat's truck starting, she looked back. "I thought we were going to get some things done around here," she called, "like weeding and painting and cleaning out the garage. The picnic is in a week and a half."

"I have things to do at the sanctuary, too," he said, putting his truck in gear.

"Whatever," she muttered. She didn't even look up as he pulled away. Maybe Birdie was right—maybe living alone *would* be easier! She leaned down to tug on a huge dandelion that was flourishing in the walkway. "I think I've tried to pull you out before," she said, kneeling on the warm slate and digging her fingers into the dirt, but when she pulled on it, it snapped off at the ground.

"Damn it!" she muttered, standing up and walking stiffly toward the shed. She returned with a long metal-pronged tool and a sturdy wooden bushel—both of which had belonged to her grandmother. She could still see her Gram's hunched figure, kneeling in her yard, painstakingly digging up dandelions, one by one. "This one's for you, Gram," she said, stabbing the sandy ground around the dandelion. She pried and pulled and dug, and after a fierce struggle, the foot-long carrot-shaped root released its stubborn grasp on the earth and was promptly and unceremoniously tossed into her grandmother's old bushel.

Piper moved on to the next dandelion, pushed the weeder into the ground, pried the sandy dirt, and pulled again. As she worked, she thought about her grandmother.

Gram—her mom's mom—had been the most fiercely independent woman Piper had ever met, especially after her husband died. Gram had been only fifty-two when Gramp died, living just long enough to hold his newest little granddaughter in his lap. Two weeks later, he succumbed to Lou Gehrig's disease, and after he died, Gram had soldiered on, alone. "It was for the best," family members said, believing Gram would be more at peace now that Gramp—an alcoholic—wasn't causing her so much heartache and misery.

Gram had always been set in her ways, though, so her outlook on life didn't change much. She had survived the Depression with a husband who squandered the little income they had on booze and, as a result, she'd learned to get by on next to nothing—a lesson she never forgot. Even after she started to earn her own income—which had been more than enough for one person to live on—she continued to be thrifty. She often mixed her cereals, having a bowl of a new cereal mixed with whatever needed to be finished. They could be as different as Rice Krispies and Corn Flakes, but she always insisted they tasted good together. She also kept her refrigerator neat and bare—only the essentials—and the shelves always sparkled. She wrapped her bread tightly in several plastic bags to keep it fresh, and she always had a piece of hard candy in her pocketbook, but what Piper remembered most about Gram was how much she loved having her granddaughters stop by for a visit, and how she always had on hand the makings for her famous ice-cream sodas—ginger ale and sherbet.

The only time Piper had ever seen her grandmother cry was when Easton died, and even then, her tears had been silent and her grief, solitary.

"Why did God take Easton up to heaven?" she asked her one time when they were playing rummy.

"Oh, I think He must've needed a good pitcher

on his Little League team," Gram said, studying her cards. Piper sat across from her, considering this while she sipped her frosty, creamy ginger ale through a straw, and finally, she decided Gram was probably right—Easton had been a really good pitcher.

Piper wiped her brow now—which was drenched in perspiration—and realized she'd lost track of time *and* forgotten to put on sunscreen. She heard crickets chirping, wiped her hands on her shorts, and reached into her pocket for her phone. She had two messages—one was from Elias, telling her he was back on the ground— which he'd sent a half hour ago! And the other— just now—was from Nat: Sorry. Be home for lunch. She stood up and typed back: Sorry too. She looked over at Chloe stretched out in the shade and then added: Would u mind picking up some ginger ale and sherbet?

❧ Chapter 37 ❧

"That's great," Sailor said as Josiah opened the bottle of wine they'd just bought. "Should I say 'Congratulations'?" she asked uncertainly. What *did* you say to someone whose divorce had just been finalized? Was that what people would say to her when she was finally free of Frank?

"Thanks," Josiah said, pouring two glasses and putting the bottle in the bucket of ice the waitress had brought. "You don't need to say congratulations, though. Some of my friends have—because I'm finally free—but I have mixed feelings. It's not like it's some great achievement . . . it actually feels more like failure."

Sailor nodded, knowing just how he felt. She looked out the breezy window of Moby Dick's Restaurant—they'd found a great table upstairs—and all of a sudden, she felt like she wanted to go home. When Josiah had originally asked her to dinner, she'd declined, but when he texted her again later and said he was going to be in Truro to show a house, she'd relented. But now, she wished she'd stuck with her original answer. Ever since she'd met with Frank, she hadn't had much of an appetite, and now, sitting across from Josiah, she felt even less hungry. *What is wrong with me? It's a simple date with a nice man—why can't I just enjoy it?*

"A penny for your thoughts?" Josiah said, taking her hand.

"Ha!" Sailor said, shaking her head and pulling her hand away. "You would ask me that now."

Josiah raised his eyebrows curiously. "Why?"

Sailor sighed. "How long did it take for your divorce to go through?"

"Oh, I don't know," he said, thinking back. "I guess everything started to fall apart last fall—

when I began to suspect she was fooling around
. . . and then I confronted her on Thanksgiving at
her brother's house—it was pretty poor timing
on my part." He smiled and shook his head,
remembering the discussion that had evolved into
an all-out scene. "She was sitting on the couch
before dinner, sipping her wine, and everyone
was chatting, but she kept looking at her phone
and smiling, and since everyone we knew was
there, I wondered who she could be texting that
would make her smile like that."

"I know just what you mean," Sailor said. "It's
like they're in their own little world and they
think no one is noticing their stupid, goofy
grins." She shook her head. "Frank used to do the
same thing. It's insulting because they're sitting
there, having a private little party on their phone,
and they think we don't know!"

Josiah nodded. "The whole cell phone thing
is insulting—which is why I lost it in front of
everyone. Talk about ruining everyone's holiday!
Anyway, we filed for divorce before Christmas,
and now it's the end of June, so I guess it
took"—he calculated—"almost seven months."

Sailor shook her head. "So, we *just* filed. I'll be
lucky if mine's *wrapped up* by next Christmas,
and so much of it depends on how long it takes
to sell the house. I'm dreading the next several
months. I just want it to be over."

As she said this, a waitress came up the stairs

and called Josiah's name. He waved his hand and she brought over their order. "Do you need anything else?" she asked and they looked over the tray, shook their heads, and thanked her.

Josiah immediately dug into his Moby Burger. "Sorry," he murmured. "I'm starving!" Sailor, on the other hand, just picked at her broiled scallops and shrimp. "It's really good," she said apologetically. "I'm just not that hungry."

Josiah wiped his mouth and eyed her scallops. "Go ahead," she said, pushing the basket toward him.

He popped a large, golden brown scallop in his mouth. "Mmm . . . better than sex," he said, laughing.

Sailor raised her eyebrows. *"Really?!"*

Josiah's cheeks turned bright red. "I'm just kidding," he said, grinning sheepishly.

Sailor looked down.

"What's the matter?" he asked. "I really *was* kidding . . ."

"I know," she said. "It's not anything you said." She looked up, searching his eyes. "And it's not you—I think you're wonderful, Josiah. It's just . . ."

He frowned, waiting for her to continue.

Sailor took a deep breath. "It's just, as much as I like you, I don't think I'm ready to jump into another relationship just yet."

He nodded slowly. "I had a feeling you might

say that," he said softly. "I remember how I felt—lost and confused and sad all at once."

Sailor nodded. "I'm really sorry, Josiah. Maybe down the road, when this is all behind me . . . I'll be ready, but right now . . ."

"You don't need to explain," he said, smiling.

Sailor nodded and took a sip of wine.

"Need a refill?"

"*Do* I?" she said with a sad smile.

Josiah pulled the bottle out of the bucket and refilled her glass and Sailor pushed her plate toward him. "I hope you won't let this seafood go to waste. . . ."

"No worries there," he said, grinning. "Especially since they're better than sex . . . and there's none of that in my near future."

Sailor laughed. "Nor mine."

❄️ Chapter 38 ❄️

Remy stepped out onto the porch with a cup of green tea in her hand—which she'd recently read was the rock star of antioxidant and nutrient-rich beverages—and her book, *Gift from the Sea*, under her arm. She was determined to focus her tired, old brain on reading again, but as soon as she sat down, Edison appeared from around the corner, padded softly across the porch, and hopped onto her lap.

"How'm I going to read with you sitting there?" she asked, stroking his soft fur, but he just curled up, pretended not to hear her, and started to purr. Remy shook her head, took a sip of her tea, and propped the little book on the far side of him. She opened to where her bookmark was tucked and smiled—she was on one of her favorite chapters —the one in which the author compared the lovely moon shell to an island, and then went on to muse about the solitude of man and the idea that all men were essentially alone—that all men were islands in a common sea. The chapter celebrated solitude . . . and whenever she read it, it made her feel less alone.

With renewed determination, she started to read, but before she was halfway down the second page, her mind wandered off and latched on to her worries about the upcoming weekend. She looked up at the sun-dappled leaves dancing in the breeze and tried to quell her anxiety, but it was hopeless. She wished, with all her heart, that she'd never said yes to going to the reunion . . . and worse, that she'd never mentioned it to John—*what* in the world had she been thinking?!

She closed her eyes and let out a long sigh. She'd spent all of the previous day trying to find something to wear. She'd even gone down to Chatham to look in the shops. Finally, she'd settled on a blue and white linen sundress that, when she'd tried it on, the saleslady had said looked *fabulous*—but that was her job so she obviously couldn't be trusted. And then, she'd found matching shoes at the Shoe Salon—but she still wasn't convinced the dress was right for the occasion . . . or that it even looked good on her. She shook her head—*I trust a car salesman, but I don't trust the lady at the dress shop.*

She'd already tried the outfit on three times since she'd brought it home, and each time, she'd studied her reflection from every angle and then carefully slipped it off, hung it back on its hanger, draped the garment bag back over it, and hung it up, wondering if she could still return it. Oh, if she could only get out of the whole thing and just stay home! She'd rather spend the weekend under a rock than drive all the way to Vermont to see people she couldn't give two figs about! And then there was John—what in the world were they going to talk about for five and a half hours in the car, never mind all weekend, which would include at least a half a dozen meals? Maybe she should just call him and tell him she wasn't feeling well. She could assure him that it was nothing that required a doctor's appointment— she just wasn't herself and had no energy. She groaned. Why did the one person she'd unintentionally invited to her college reunion have to be her doctor? When she'd asked him, she'd really just been kidding—she'd never expected him to say yes. And then to find out he loved Vermont!

And what if she did end up going? What kind of questions would her classmates ask? *And* how would she answer them? Yes, she and John were old friends; yes, he was single; no, he'd never married; yes, he was a doctor; no, they'd never dated; yes, he was good-looking; no, she wasn't attracted to him . . . *Or was she?* Lord, help her! Was she attracted to him?!

Remy looked up at the sunlight filtering through the trees and decided right then and there she was *not* going. She picked up her phone and started to dial Sailor's number but then stopped and wondered if she should tell Piper instead. Which sister would give her the least grief? Birdie probably couldn't care less, although she had seemed a little curious about the whole affair—wrong word!—and she was probably expecting her to bail out anyway. She was still staring at her phone, trying to decide, and berating herself for being so indecisive, when the phone suddenly started to ring, startling her.

"Hello? . . . Oh, hi, Dr. Sanders! Yes," she said, laughing. "I guess I will have to call you John. My classmates *will* think it's odd if I introduce you as Dr. Sanders." She paused, listening. "Well, I was thinking we should leave fairly early and plan to stop and have lunch somewhere along the way. I think registration starts around two and then there's a reception and cocktail hour, so we should allow time to check in to our hotel."

She hesitated, then took a deep breath. "Are you sure you still want to go?" She nodded. "Okay. Yes, I'm really looking forward to it, too. . . . That sounds good. I'll expect to see you here around eight, then." She smiled, but after she hung up she let out a loud "Ahhh!" startling Edison—who looked up in alarm and then hopped off her lap and scooted around the corner of the house. "So much for staying home!"

❧ Chapter 39 ❧

Birdie was staring stonily out the kitchen window when David came back into the house. "Are you sure you don't want to come along?" he asked.

"Yes," she answered coolly.

"I thought you wanted to see her being set free. . . . and I thought we could go to that French restaurant in Mashpee that you like. What's the name of it?"

"Bleu."

"Yes, Bleu—they have that scallop dish you're always raving about."

Birdie shook her head indifferently. "No, thanks."

He shrugged. "Do you want me to pick up something for dinner, then?"

"No."

"Do you have something you're planning to make?"

"I don't know."

He sighed. "All right. I'll see you later, then."

"See you later."

Birdie listened as his car pulled away and felt her shoulders relax. It had been a long week—staying mad at someone took a lot of energy. Ordinarily, she would've *loved* watching the young barred owl fly back to freedom . . . and she would've *loved* going to her favorite French restaurant. The scallop dish with the yummy maple grapefruit glaze was to die for—her mouth watered just thinking about it—and they could've ordered a bottle of Château de Candale. It could've been a really nice evening . . . *if* David hadn't ruined everything.

She stared glumly out the window. She just couldn't seem to put the last couple of weeks behind her—David's insensitivity at the Beachcomber; his implication that she drank too much; his habit of tallying the wine bottles in the recycling bin; and his unwillingness to do anything about the lack of intimacy in their bedroom. It was all more than she could take. She'd had it with being married . . . and everything that went along with it . . . like figuring out what to make for dinner. And she definitely didn't need him looking over her shoulder for the rest of her life!

She opened a bottle of wine and poured a glass. "C'mon, Bay," she said, "let's go outside." The old black Lab pulled herself up, followed Birdie outside, and sank down in the last rays of the late-day sunshine.

Birdie set the bottle on the table, settled into her favorite chair, and took a long sip. She leaned back to watch a pair of cardinals fluttering back and forth to the feeder and took another sip. *After all these years, you'd think David would understand. Every year, he takes that damn picture of us . . . and he doesn't even realize that someone's missing. It will never be complete. There will always be an empty space . . . a face that should've grown old beside us.* She took another sip, realized her glass was almost empty, refilled it, and tried to imagine how Easton would look now. *He would be handsome,* she thought wistfully, *with those sparkling blue eyes of his . . . and he'd probably have silver hair . . . just like the rest of us.* She took another sip of her wine, studied the amount that was left in the bottle, and wondered whether it would fit in her glass. She poured it slowly until it reached the very top, and then brought the bottle to her lips and finished it. She leaned over, took a sip from her glass so it wouldn't spill, glanced at the time on her phone, and tried to remember what time David had left. Her mind seemed a little foggy as she tried to calculate how long it would take him to get to Mashpee, free the owl, and drive back home. She stood up, swaying slightly, and carried the empty bottle inside. She carefully rinsed it, took it out to the garage, and slid it gingerly under the orange juice bottles and milk jugs. Then she went back inside, reached for another bottle, and focused intently on making her hands and mind work together to screw the corkscrew in straight.

This is perfect, she thought as she pulled out the cork. *David will never know.*

She carried the bottle outside, along with her laptop, and sank into her chair, feeling decidedly lusty . . . or lushy . . . whichever. Forgetting Sailor's warning to avoid going on Facebook when you'd been drinking, she clicked on her page and began to scroll through her newsfeed, suddenly feeling very fond of her "Friends" and liking almost every post—from a college acquaintance's daughter's engagement photo—even though they hadn't been in touch in years— "Good for her!"—to a sweet story about two old dogs who'd been missing for five days, and when they were finally found, it was determined that one of the dogs had fallen into a shallow well and the other one had stayed right by his friend's side, keeping watch. It was such a good story, she even shared it, typing the comment: "Dogs are more loyal than humans!"

She swirled the burgundy liquid in her glass and watched it catch the sunlight. Entranced by the sparkle, she swirled it again—with a little more vigor this time—and a wave of red sloshed over the top and splashed onto her white slacks. "Craparooni," she muttered, brushing the stain with her hand and taking another sip.

She looked back at her laptop and noticed that the edges of the screen seemed a little blurry and dark. She tapped the brightening button on the keyboard but the screen was already on the brightest setting. "What the hell?" she muttered. "I better not have to take this damn thing back to Apple again." She stared at it, suddenly remembered something she'd been meaning to look up, and typed *"Viagra side effects"* in the search box. She clicked the Enter button, and a bazillion drug-related websites popped up. She clicked on the top one and saw everything from bladder pain to chest pain. "Geez-freakin'-Louise," she muttered. "How in the world do so many men take it, then? The company must list all these side effects because they have to cover their bloody arses." She sighed. "Whatever. People take it anyway—the sex lives of old people is a freaking million-dollar industry."

David wouldn't take it, though—he didn't take any pills, not even a vitamin—which she could certainly understand—she didn't like taking pills, either, but you'd think, once a month . . . or even once every *two* months, he could take it just to keep their love life interesting. She shook her head. There was a time in their marriage when she would've loved being left alone, but now that she didn't have a freaking choice in the matter, it left her feeling neglected, unattractive *and* unloved. David still reached for her hand at night and he still wrapped his arms around her . . . but it just wasn't the same.

Birdie set her laptop on the table, drained her glass, and refilled it. "Whatever," she mumbled. "Life sucksanthen yadie, right, Bay?" The old Lab, hearing her name, pulled herself up, moseyed over to rest her head on Birdie's lap, and gazed at her with worried eyes. "Donworry, sweeie," Birdie said, stroking her head. "Mommysfine. No bigdeal." She lightly touched the white fur around Bailey's muzzle, and as she looked into her cloudy eyes, she was suddenly overwhelmed by the realization that her beloved dog was getting old. "Idon knowha I'llmanagwithow ya," she whispered, tears filling her eyes. She leaned down to rest her cheek on Bailey's head. "Promismeyouwoneverleeme."

Bailey swished her tail tentatively and anxiously licked Birdie's salty cheeks. "Iloveyootoo," she whispered, wiping her eyes and suddenly realizing her nose was running. "Ineetagetatishoo," she said, lurching forward as she tried to stand. She grabbed the table to get her balance, bumped it, and then watched in horror as her wine glass rocked back and forth. Finally, in seemingly slow motion, it tipped over, splashing its contents across her laptop. "Damn!" she blurted, trying to reach for the glass, but for some reason, her hand seemed to have a mind of its own, and at the very same moment, Bailey, startled by Birdie's sudden outburst and odd behavior, scrambled to her feet, bumped the table again, and sent the bottle flying, spilling more precious wine just as the glass hit the floor and shattered. "FUDGE!" Birdie shouted, causing poor Bailey to scamper off the porch with her tail between her legs.

Birdie stood up straighter, trying to focus on the mess. Then she closed her eyes and tried to stop swaying. She held on to the back of the chair for support and then walked slowly and purposefully toward the house. Moments later, she came back with a dustpan and a towel. She knelt down, picked up the wine bottle, and holding it up to the light, saw there was a little left. She wiped off the outside of the bottle, set it aside, and began picking up the shards from the broken wine glass. There were hundreds of pieces, though—all swimming in the puddle of wine—and she couldn't decide what the best way was to pick them up—sweep through the wine with the broom or wipe up the puddle with the towel? She sat down on the porch, considering her two options, and then got on her knees and started sopping up the mess with the towel. The towel, however, quickly became heavy with the red liquid, and when she folded it over and started to wipe again, a piece of glass sliced into her palm. She cried out in pain and tried to stand up, but she couldn't seem to get her balance so she crawled across the wooden floor and when she got to the door, tried again. This time she was able to stand, but as she walked across the kitchen, she had to hold on to the counter to keep from falling.

She rinsed out the cut, made sure the glass wasn't embedded in her palm, and stuck a Band-Aid on it. Then, remembering she needed a garbage bag, she reached under the sink. She went back outside, finished wiping up the puddle, and dropped the glass-filled towel into the garbage bag. She placed the rest of the broken glass on top of it, looked down and realized the knees of her white slacks were now burgundy and gray— not to mention there were burgundy splatters *every-where*. She unbuttoned them—they were getting too tight anyway—and clumsily stepped out of them, almost falling over in the process, and then dropped them into the bag, too.

Now, what to do with the bag? She heard a car pull onto the road and, in a sudden, sobering panic, picked up the wine bottle, dumped the remaining liquid over the railing, dropped the bottle into the bag, grabbed her laptop, and hurried into the house. She heaved herself up the stairs, stuffed the bag and her laptop in the back of her closet, and pulled on a pair of old shorts, almost falling over again. Then she blinked at her flushed reflection in the mirror, and hearing footfalls on the porch, headed back down the stairs, holding tightly to the railing, but when she walked in the kitchen, she immediately sensed that something was wrong. Did David know? Had she missed something?

"What's the matter?" she asked, her heart pounding.

He gave her a puzzled look. "Where's Bailey?"

She swallowed, her heart pounding even faster. "She was just outside. . . ."

⊰ Chapter 40 ⊱

Sailor climbed into Piper's Honda Element and pulled several more flyers out of the folder she'd tucked between the seat and the console. She looked at the picture centered in the middle of the page—it was an old photo of Bailey so her face wasn't white, and she was wearing felt Christmas antlers. It wasn't the best picture of her, but it was the only one she had. "Want to hang some over there?" she asked, motioning to the parking lot of the Salt Pond Visitor Center.

"Sure," Piper said. She turned onto Nauset Road and immediately turned right into the parking lot. "You should've brought your bike so we could put some up along the bike trail."

"I should've," Sailor agreed. "Want to do that this afternoon?"

Piper nodded. They got out and stapled lost dog posters on every available post. They even put some on the windshields of cars. Then they climbed back in and continued driving around, scanning yards and driveways and stopping at almost every telephone pole so Sailor could put up another poster. "I only have one left," she said, looking in the folder. "I'll have to print more when I go home to get my bike."

"Print a ton," Piper said.

Sailor nodded and reached into her pocket for her phone. She called Birdie's cell phone but when her sister didn't answer, she tried her at home. Finally, she tried David's cell, but it just rang, too.

"She said she'd call if they found her," Piper said, looking over.

"I know, but their number is on the poster and if they're not answering, how are we going to know if someone calls?"

"You should've put *our* numbers on the posters."

"Maybe I'll change it on the next batch."

"Good idea. Why don't you try calling Nat and see if he and Elias need more, too."

Sailor pressed Nat's number, and even before it rang on her end, he answered. Piper listened as Sailor talked to him, gathering from her sister's end of the conversation that he and Elias had plastered downtown Orleans with posters, they needed more, and they hadn't seen any sign of Bailey. Finally, she heard her sister make arrangements to meet at Birdie's in an hour with sandwiches from Box Lunch.

Sailor ended the call and looked at the time. "This is going to take more than an hour," she said with a sigh.

Piper pulled into the Eastham Superette. "Put the last one up in there and then we won't even bother getting your car—I'll just go with you. I already have my bike on the back anyway."

Sailor climbed out, hung the flyer where everyone could see it, and came back out. "The cashier said she saw a black Lab near the elementary school this morning."

"We were just there."

"Do you think we should go back and look again? It's on the way."

Piper pulled up to the light and nodded, tapping her fingers impatiently. "C'mon! This light takes forever," she grumbled.

When it changed to green, she turned left and headed up Route 6 again, and just past the visitor center, turned right and then left toward the elementary school. She slowed down, turned into the deserted school parking lot, and they got out and walked behind the building and around the playground, but there was still no sign of Bailey. Piper shook her head. "Where the heck can she be?"

"I don't know," Sailor said, "but we better keep

moving or we won't be back to Birdie's in an hour."

They drove slowly through the neighborhood, still looking and calling, and then finally turned onto Route 6 again.

"Did Birdie ever say why she thought Bailey took off?" Piper asked. "She's so old—I just don't get how she could get lost."

"I know," Sailor said, shaking her head. "You'd think she'd know her way home by now, and Birdie didn't really say what happened. She said she was sitting on the porch and knocked over a glass of water—which broke and startled Bailey—and after she cleaned it up, she realized Bailey wasn't in the yard."

Piper frowned. "Birdie was drinking a glass of *water*?"

Sailor chuckled. "I know, right?"

"Where was David?"

"He'd gone to Mashpee to release an owl. . . ."

"And Birdie didn't go?"

"No, she said she didn't want to go."

"This is all just so odd. Bailey wouldn't have just taken off unless something really upset her."

"It *is* odd," Sailor agreed, "and when I talked to Birdie, she was absolutely beside herself. She said she will never forgive herself if something happened to Bailey."

"Oh my goodness! Can you imagine if we don't find her?"

Sailor nodded. "Just keep praying!"

"I am!" Piper said.

Without realizing it, they both started looking along the side of the road, praying they wouldn't see a lump of black fur.

An hour later, they pulled into Birdie's driveway and found Nat and Elias walking around the yard, calling Bailey's name, but no big black Lab came trotting out of the woods, wagging her tail. It made the yard seem very lonely. Sailor and Piper climbed the steps to the porch, carrying sandwiches, wraps, and drinks, and set everything on the table. "Come and eat!" Piper called while Sailor tried to reach Birdie again. This time, she answered.

"Where are you?" Sailor asked and then nodded. "We're back at your house with lunch. Can you stop here? . . . I know you're not hungry, but you should have something to eat and then we'll keep looking. . . . Okay, well, David's probably hungry. . . ."

She frowned and looked at her phone. "She hung up on me."

"Just eat," Piper said, unwrapping sandwiches and setting them on paper plates. Suddenly, a napkin blew off the table, and when she reached to pick it up, she felt something sharp cut into her finger. She cried out in pain and surprise, and looked down to see blood spurting from her finger. She wrapped a napkin around the cut and held it tightly while she looked down at the wooden floorboards. "Don't walk over here," she warned. "There's glass everywhere . . . *and* that stain doesn't look like water," she said, pointing.

"Maybe it's old," Sailor suggested.

"Yeah, right," Piper said. "I need a Band-Aid." She walked over to the door and turned the knob. "Geez-Louise, she locked the house! I knew we should've met at Whit's End."

"I have a Band-Aid," Nat said, digging out his wallet and pulling out a Band-Aid.

Piper eyed the faded wrapper skeptically. "Is it sanitary?"

"Why wouldn't it be sanitary?" he asked. "It's been in my wallet."

"Exactly."

"Do you want it or not?" he asked.

"I want it," she said, holding out her finger.

Nat wrapped the Band-Aid around her bloody finger. "It looks like you might need stitches. . . ."

"I don't have time for stitches," she said, reaching for a bottle of iced tea and popping it open.

"Did you get a Caesar salad wrap?" Elias asked, coming up onto the porch.

"We did," Sailor said, smiling, "but you can only have it after you give your favorite aunt a hug."

"Hi, Aunt Sail," Elias said, dwarfing her as he wrapped his arms around her. "Where's Aunt Remy?"

"She's on her way to Vermont for a class reunion."

"Oh," he said, looking puzzled.

"She doesn't know about Bailey. We were afraid she wouldn't go."

He nodded and Sailor held him at arm's length. "You look like you grew six inches since the last time I saw you!"

He smiled sheepishly.

"How's flying?" she asked, handing him his wrap.

"Good."

"School?"

"Good."

"The women in your life?"

He laughed as he took a bite. "Fine," he said with his mouth full.

"You're about as talkative as your old dad," she teased.

"Hey!" Nat said, coming up the steps with a broom. "You can drop the *old* part."

"I was just teasing," Sailor said, popping open her coffee and taking a sip.

Piper watched Nat sweep up the glass with the broom. "Was there a dustpan in the shed?"

"No, but there's probably a piece of cardboard in the truck."

Piper went to look and came back with a piece of thin cardboard and a paper bag. She handed it to him and opened the bag. "It looks like a wine glass to me," she said. "The shards are very fine."

Nat didn't say anything. He'd never been one to

judge, but he did raise his eyebrows and press his lips together—which was a statement in itself. His facial expressions always spoke volumes.

Piper sighed, knowing exactly what he was thinking—Birdie wasn't being entirely forthcoming about what had happened last night.

They finished their lunch, threw all the trash in the bag, and while Nat lifted their bikes off the back of Piper's Honda, Sailor divided up the new flyers.

"Do you have something we could carry these in?" she asked.

"I have a backpack," Elias offered, "but it's full of stuff."

"Would you mind emptying it?" Piper asked.

Elias went around to the passenger side of the truck and pulled all his pilot gear—headset, charts, and his iPad—out of his backpack.

"Sorry 'bout that," Piper said, looking over his shoulder at everything on the seat.

"No big deal," he said, handing her his empty backpack.

She handed him half of the posters and slipped the other half into the backpack, along with the staple guns and tape, and then slung it over her shoulder and took her bike from Nat. "Okay, so, we're gonna ride toward Coast Guard Beach since a woman saw a black Lab over by the elementary school this morning and it's pretty much the only lead we have."

Nat nodded. "I guess we'll head toward Skaket again. I just find it so hard to believe she's across Route 6."

They pushed off on their bikes, waved, and realized the sky was getting dark and the wind had picked up. "I bet we get caught in the rain," Piper called.

"I bet you're right," Sailor called back.

An hour later, Piper was hanging a poster outside the ladies' room at the Coast Guard Beach while Sailor was *using* the ladies' room. "I shouldn't have had that coffee," she said as she came out, drying her hands on her shorts.

Piper chuckled as they walked down the boardwalk. "I know what you mean. Coffee goes right through me—I don't think it even bothers entering my bloodstream."

Sailor laughed, too, glad that she wasn't the only one with the problem.

They stopped at the information board, which was regularly updated by the lifeguards with the water temperature, the times of high and low tides, and any rip current—or shark—warnings. "Do you think the lifeguards would mind if I put a poster up here?" Sailor mused.

"Go for it," Piper said, reaching into Elias's backpack. "The worst they can do is take it down."

Sailor taped it to the board and it fluttered in the wind.

"You better staple it, too."

Sailor stapled all four corners. "It'll probably *still* blow away."

They stood there looking at the picture of Bailey with her ears back and her eyes worried. "She didn't like wearing those antlers," Piper said.

"No. She tolerated it just long enough for me to take the picture."

Piper sighed. "She is such a sweetie pie. I hope that we find her."

They walked down to the beach and stood looking out at the waves. Every once in a while, a shiny black head popped up out of the dark water and peered at them curiously for a few minutes before disappearing under the surf again.

"I don't remember there being so many seals when we were kids."

"I don't, either."

They heard barking and both their hearts skipped a beat. They looked down the beach and saw a young boy picking up a tennis ball while a big black Lab bounced up and down on the sand, waiting for him to throw it. The boy leaned back and threw it as far as he could, and then, the Lab charged after it.

"That dog has too much energy to be Bailey," Piper said, sounding disappointed.

They both felt raindrops on their arms, and Sailor shivered in the wind. "I guess we'd better head back."

"I guess so," Piper agreed.

⊰ Chapter 41 ⊱

"This is beautiful," Remy said as John pulled into the parking lot of the Lilac Inn. Earlier in the week, Remy had called to book two rooms at the Middlebury Inn, but because she'd waited so long, there weren't *any* rooms left—never mind two. She'd hung up and called John, hoping he'd agree that it would be best if they just stayed home, but he assured her he knew of a place in nearby Brandon.

They climbed out of Remy's car—which she'd happily let John drive—and he lifted out their luggage and set it on the ground. Remy, accustomed to doing everything herself, reached for her bag, but John picked it up first. "I've got this, miss," he said with a smile that made her heart skip a beat.

"Well, if you insist," she teased.

"I do."

The drive to Vermont had been more than pleasant. Remy's fear that they wouldn't have anything to talk about was quickly forgotten— they'd talked about everything from their favorite local Cape Cod artisans to their shared love of reading. They also discovered they were both Red Sox fans—Remy admitting that she really only watched because Jim had loved the Red Sox.

John was also very interested in hearing all about the goings-on in the lives of Remy's children, Payton, Eliza, and Sam, and Remy found herself chatting away cheerfully while John laughed at all of the anecdotes and funny antics of her grandchildren. More than once, she started off by saying, "This probably won't be of any interest to you. . . ." but John always assured her that it would be.

In Hanover, New Hampshire, they stopped for lunch, and over soup and salad, John regaled her with stories of his time at Dartmouth.

"To think you were right here while Jim and I were in Middlebury is just so . . . unbelievable," Remy said.

"It *is* a small world," John agreed, smiling.

They'd been quiet for the rest of the ride, each lost in their own thoughts, but the silence hadn't been awkward—it had felt like the easy, comfortable silence of two old friends.

They walked up the front steps into the elegant lobby of the inn and were immediately greeted by a big black Lab, who, Remy thought, looked just like Bailey. As the innkeeper showed them to their rooms, he told them about all of the local attractions, but John explained that they were there just for a college reunion.

"Reunions are fun," the innkeeper said, "but if you find you've had enough socializing, there are plenty of other things to do. It would be a shame to come all the way up here and not see *some* of the sights, and if you like hiking, the Robert Frost Trail is one of Vermont's best-kept secrets."

"I hiked the Robert Frost Trail a long time ago," Remy said, remembering a hike she'd taken with Jim.

The owner unlocked the doors to their rooms and left them talking in the hall.

"You sound like you'd rather go hiking," John teased.

"I actually would like to try to do some other things while we're here," Remy admitted. "You won't know anyone at the reunion and I'm worried you'll be bored . . . and me . . . well . . ." She smiled. "I've been a social misfit all my life—I always say the wrong thing at the wrong time—so the less time I spend at the reunion, the less of a fool I'll make of myself."

"You're not a fool," John said, frowning, "and I don't think I've ever heard you say the wrong thing at the wrong time . . . or any other time, for that matter. I think your stories are wonderful and funny, and I don't think you realize what a lovely, warm personality you have."

"Hmm," Remy said, eyeing him, "you must be thinking of someone else."

"I'm *not* thinking of someone else *and* I am looking forward to having you on my arm at the reception in"—he looked at his watch—"an hour."

Remy raised her eyebrows in alarm. "An hour?" She felt her heart pound. "I have to get ready!"

John watched as she turned around and bustled into her room, letting the door *click* behind her. A second later, she reappeared, smiling sheepishly. "Meet you back here in an hour?"

John laughed and nodded.

❦ Chapter 42 ❧

Birdie stood at the kitchen window, watching the rain trickle down the glass. She pictured Bailey—wet and frightened and hungry—somewhere out there in the darkness.

"Oh, please let me see her again," she murmured, tears filling her eyes. "Oh, Lord, please keep her safe. Please let her find her way home. I'll do anything to have her back home." She felt as if her heart would break if she never saw her sweet dog again, and she blamed herself. She blamed her foolishness . . . her selfishness . . . and her complete lack of self-control. What in the world was wrong with her? If she'd just gone with David, or stayed home and behaved like a normal person—making dinner or taking Bailey for a walk—it wouldn't have happened. Now, she'd give anything to be able to take her dog for a long, meandering walk again. They'd walk slowly and she wouldn't be impatient . . .

and she'd let Bailey stop to sniff every lovely scent she could find along their quiet road.

"Hey," David said softly, coming into the kitchen. "Do you want some supper—some scrambled eggs, maybe?"

Birdie wiped her eyes and shook her head.

"How about a cup of tea?"

She shook her head again. "No . . . no, thanks," she whispered.

David put his arms around her. "We'll find her," he said softly. "I'm sure she's fine—she's probably curled up in someone's warm kitchen right now."

Birdie shook her head. "If someone has found her, they would've called—she has her collar on . . . she has a chip. They would've found our number and called to tell us she's okay."

David was quiet. Birdie was right—if someone good and caring had found Bailey, they *would* have called. They would have known she belonged to someone who was missing her very much, and they would've wanted that person to know she was safe.

Birdie looked at the empty dog bed and the untouched bowls. "I just want to see her again," she cried. "I just want to hold her in my arms and tell her everything's okay. I can't bear the thought of not finding her . . . of never holding her head in my hands and looking into her sweet eyes. . . ."

David pulled her closer, his own eyes filling with tears. Birdie was right—the thought of never again seeing Bailey's sweet brown eyes gazing up at him with all the love in the world was unbearable. "We'll find her," he whispered.

❧ Chapter 43 ❧

Piper knelt down next to the wet, orange tiger cat that had followed them into Sailor's kitchen. "Who is this?" she asked in surprise. The cat pushed his head into Piper's hand and closed his eyes in contentment.

"I don't know who he is, but he keeps showing up and sauntering in here like he owns the place. I've been meaning to make posters for him, too. I even took his picture, but I haven't gotten around to printing flyers. His family is probably worried sick."

"He doesn't have a collar so maybe he doesn't have a family."

Sailor shook her head. "I think he has a home."

"He thinks he has a home, too," Piper teased, "and it's right here, isn't it, sweetie?" The cat stretched out on the floor, purring loudly, loving all the attention.

"Don't get too comfortable," Sailor warned as she unwrapped the takeout dinner they'd picked up at Arnold's. She pulled a little piece of lobster out of one of the rolls, knelt down, and offered it to him—and he sniffed it curiously and then gulped it down. "I guess you *are* hungry," she said, standing up to get him another piece.

"Do you really think you're going to get him to leave when you're feeding him lobster?! And, by the way, he told me he likes it dipped in butter."

Sailor chuckled and stood up. "Would you like a glass of wine?"

"Nah, I better not," Piper said. "Mike filled our glasses to the brim when we were waiting for our food, and now I can hardly stay awake."

Sailor took a bottle out of the fridge and poured herself a glass. "Iced tea?" she asked, surveying the contents of the fridge.

"No, that'll keep me awake."

"Water?"

"You want me to have to get up in the middle of the night, don't you?"

"My goodness, you *do* have problems," Sailor teased. "Don't worry," she added, laughing. "I have all the same problems myself."

Piper laughed as she poured melted butter over her lobster. "Like Mom used to say, 'It's no fun getting old.' "

"It definitely isn't," Sailor agreed. She took a sip of her wine. "How do you think Remy's doing?" she asked.

"I'm sure she's fine," Piper said, taking a bite

of her lobster roll. "I'm so glad she went. I kept expecting her to back out, didn't you?"

Sailor nodded. "I thought for sure she'd call on Thursday and tell me she'd changed her mind."

"Well, I'm glad she didn't. It's good that she's getting out of the house and doing something fun . . . and I'm glad John went, too. That whole thing is such a hoot!"

"It *is* a hoot!" Sailor agreed, leaning down to give the cat the last bite of her lobster. "I *never* saw it coming!"

Piper shook her head. "Me, neither!"

Sailor took another sip of her wine. "Oh!" she said, motioning for Piper to follow her. "I want to show you something."

Piper and the cat followed her into her studio and Sailor turned on the light over her desk. "Ta-da!" she said, motioning to the pictures.

"Wow!" Piper said, crossing her arms. "Wow! Wow! Wow!" She stepped back, taking in the entire wall, and then stepped closer to study each photo. "It's so cool to see them all hung together . . . *and* to see how we've changed—it's like having your whole life in front of you." She pointed to the very first photo David had taken. "Look how young we were," she said, smiling. "Do you remember how young and handsome David was when we first met him? When he and Birdie first started dating? I had such a crush on him." She paused. "It's funny—he isn't in any of the pictures . . . but seeing them conjures up images of how he looked when he took them."

Sailor nodded. "You're right. I never thought of that before, but in every one of these pictures, we were looking at him." She smiled. "He was . . . and still is . . . very handsome. And he has captured us all growing old through the lens of his camera."

Piper studied each photo. "Look at this one," she said, pointing to one in which they all looked like they were in their thirties. "Birdie looks like she might even smile."

Sailor nodded. "That was right before her last miscarriage. She was about eight weeks along."

"That's right," Piper said, remembering how devastated her sister and David had been after losing their fourth baby. She shook her head sadly. "I hope they find Bailey. I can't stop thinking about her being out in the rain and the dark—she must be so scared and hungry. . . ."

Piper's words hung in the air as "Smoke Gets in Your Eyes" started playing in Sailor's pocket. She pulled her phone out, looked at the screen, and frowned. "I don't recognize this number. I don't even recognize the two-oh-three area code. . . ." She shook her head and started to slip her phone back into her pocket.

"What are you *doing?*" Piper asked. "You need to answer it!"

"Oh, right!" Sailor said, suddenly remembering

that her number was on some of the posters now. "Hello?"

Piper listened, her heart pounding as her sister spoke. "You did?! Is she okay? Where? Oh my goodness, thank you," she murmured, tears of relief spilling down her cheeks. Piper continued to listen wide-eyed, her own eyes filling with tears. "She was limping? . . . Is she okay?" Sailor nodded. "Well, thank goodness your sons were out running." She nodded again. "We're in Truro. . . . No, she's not from Truro, but we . . . we'll be right down. What's the address?" She reached for a pen and scribbled down the address on a scrap of paper. "Five Bridge Road. I know where that is. Yes, we'll be there in twenty minutes. Thank you so much!" She hung up the phone, smiling and crying all at the same time.

"Where is she?" Piper asked, her heart pounding.

"Right in Orleans," Sailor said. "A family that is renting a house on Bridge Road found her. The man said his sons were out running and saw her limping along the side of the road. They'd just passed a poster on a telephone pole and they couldn't believe it was the same dog."

"I can't believe it, either!" Piper exclaimed, following Sailor back to the kitchen. She looked down at the cat curled up on the new chair in the living room. "I think your new pal plans to spend the night."

Sailor looked over. "Okay," she said to him, "but only because it's raining."

"Don't worry," Piper whispered as she stroked his ears. "I'm sure she'll let you stay as long as you like."

Sailor eyed her sister suspiciously. "What did you tell him?"

"Oh, nothing," Piper teased as she closed the door.

⊰ Chapter 44 ⊱

Remy took one last look at herself in the mirror. She was wearing the blue and white linen dress and matching shoes she'd bought in Chatham—*and* she'd finally taken off the tags. She sighed resignedly. "Oh well, it's the best I can do," she said, picking up her purse and opening the door.

John—who'd knocked a moment earlier—looked up and smiled. "Wow! You look lovely!"

Remy raised her eyebrows. "I won't believe you if you overdo it."

"You should believe me because you do."

"Thank you," she said, hearing her mother's admonishing voice: *"Always accept a compliment graciously."* He offered her his arm and she took it, too, leaning lightly on it as he escorted her down the stairs and through the lobby.

"You kids look great," the innkeeper said.

"You're going to *wow* your old classmates," he added with a grin. "Have fun!"

"Thank you," Remy said, feeling her heart start to race at the mention of her classmates.

A half an hour later, John parked near Gifford Hall and walked around to help her out of the car. "We *have* arrived," she murmured nervously, looking up at the stately stone building.

"Indeed, we have," John said, smiling, "*and* it's a beautiful night. I heard it's raining back home."

"It is?" Remy frowned, picturing the rain on Cape Cod—which suddenly seemed very far away. She pictured Route 6, wet with puddles; she pictured the cars traveling with their wiper blades splashing back and forth; she imagine the rain on her stone steps and gardens, and suddenly, she missed it very much. "Let's go home," she said, pulling John to a halt.

"Go home?" he said, looking at her in surprise.

"Yes, I'm suddenly very homesick . . . and I don't really want to see any of these people anyway."

"Let's just go in and have a drink," John encouraged. "And afterward, if you still want to leave, we will."

Remy nodded, gripping his arm for support— moral and emotional—and went inside.

"Remy Landon!" a woman called from across the room, waving her hand. She swooped toward them like a hawk, and gave Remy a hug and a peck on both cheeks. "I would've known you anywhere! You haven't changed one iota!"

Remy smiled, trying to place the woman, and then noticed her name tag. "Paula Peck," she said, "you haven't changed a bit, either."

"It's incredible," Paula said conspiratorially, "our children have all grown up, but we've stayed the same age!"

Remy laughed in polite agreement.

"And who is this handsome fella on your arm?"

"Oh, I'm sorry," Remy said, feeling flustered. "This is John Sanders."

Paula held out her hand in greeting. "You're a doctor, I see," she gushed.

Remy frowned. *How did she know* that?

John nodded, lightly touched his lapel pin— the one Remy hadn't noticed—and shook her hand. "Yes . . . yes, I am. It's a pleasure to meet you."

"Oh, trust me, the pleasure's all mine," Paula swooned.

John smiled politely.

"Well," Paula said, turning back to Remy. "We're so glad you came. We haven't seen you since the first time you came . . . you know, after Jim died . . . and we were wondering if we would ever see you again!"

Remy wondered why Paula kept using the word *we*—was she speaking for herself and her husband or was she speaking on behalf of the whole class? "Well, here I am," she said awkwardly.

Paula nodded and motioned in the direction of the bar. "The real party's getting started over there . . . and the name tag table is over there," she said, pointing, "but I don't think you need a name tag because everyone will know who you are!" She gave her another kiss and swept off in the direction of the bar.

"Wow," John said, laughing. "I didn't think they made 'em like that anymore."

Remy shook her head. "Yes, and now I remember why I didn't want to come."

"Well, let's get a drink before you really decide. What's your poison?"

She smiled—John was definitely making it more fun. In fact, she was certain, if she'd come alone, she wouldn't have made it this far. "Just a glass of white wine."

"Chardonnay or pinot?"

"Pinot."

John turned to the bartender, asked for two glasses of pinot grigio, and returned a moment later, holding a glass out to her. "Cheers!" he said softly.

"Cheers," she said, smiling and clinking his glass.

Remy looked around the room and saw Paula standing with a group of people, nodding in their direction, but she didn't mind. They could talk all they wanted. She was a proud alumna of an old New England college. She'd graduated with honors and married a wonderful man. She'd survived his loss and soldiered on alone. She'd raised three amazing children and kept current with the times by reading and continuing to learn. And now, years later, she was here again and she'd brought an old friend who thought she had a wonderful, warm personality. And she wasn't going to be intimidated by the sideways glances of former classmates—who were probably just curious, friendly old people—like herself.

⊰ Chapter 45 ⊱

Birdie was lying in bed—her pillow soaked with tears—when she heard a knock on the kitchen door downstairs. She sat up and listened as David—who was in the kitchen—put down his newspaper and started to get up, but whoever it was that knocked hadn't waited for someone to answer; they'd just come right in! "Hellooo . . ." a voice called. "Anybody home?" A moment later, she heard a commotion that included paws clicking on wood followed by exclamations— the sounds of joy!

"David?" she called, getting up and pulling on her robe. "David? Who's here?"

"Why don't you come and *see* who's here!"

Birdie hurried down the stairs, tying her robe, saw her sisters standing in the kitchen with their raincoats on . . . and then she saw Bailey standing between them. Tears streamed down Birdie's cheeks as the dog limped over into her arms, wagging her whole hind end. Her fur was wet and her paws were muddy, but Birdie didn't care. She just buried her face in her neck and sobbed. "Oh, Bailey, where have you been? I missed you so much."

Piper and Sailor and David all watched as Birdie wrapped her arms around her sweet dog. Finally, she let go and Bailey hurried back over to David and back again to her, as if saying, *"Where, oh, where have you been? I've been looking all over for you!"*

Birdie stood up and wiped her eyes. "Where did you find her?"

Sailor smiled. "A family from Connecticut is renting a house on Bridge Road and their two boys were out running. They saw a poster and then they saw Bailey limping along the road. They called her name and she came right up to them. Her paw was bleeding so the older boy stayed with her while the younger one ran home to get the car."

"I wonder how she hurt her paw."

"I think one of her pads is cut—nothing serious."

"Oh, you poor thing," Birdie said, kneeling down to examine her pads.

"Did they say how she was when they got her back to the house?"

Sailor nodded. "She drank a whole bowl of

water, devoured the food they offered, and then curled up near the door and promptly fell asleep."

"She must've been exhausted," David said, kneeling down next to her. "You've had quite an adventure, haven't you, ol' girl? I bet you're glad to be home," he added softly and Bailey licked his chin and thumped her tail.

Birdie gave each of her sisters a hug. "I can't thank you and Nat and Elias enough for all your help—taking time off from work, making posters, putting them up everywhere, and spending the whole day looking. I don't think we would've ever found her without you."

"Oh, I don't know," Sailor said. "She was still right here in Orleans—I think you would've found her."

"Did you thank the family?" David asked.

"Of course," Piper said. "They said they were happy to help."

"We should give them a reward," Birdie said.

"I think, if they haven't left already, then they're leaving first thing in the morning. Their car was packed and they were loading their bikes."

"Then, we'll just have to send blessings," David said.

"Very big blessings!" Birdie said, kneeling down to give Bailey another hug.

❈{ Chapter 46 }❈

"The secret to rice pudding is adding the sugar at just the right time, and then, adding a little warm milk to the egg before adding the egg to the milk or it will scramble." Piper read the directions out loud as she stirred. "This better be good," she murmured, glancing at the clock, "because it's taking forever." Ten minutes later, she was still stirring when Nat came into the kitchen. "What's for supper?" he asked, looking over her shoulder.

"I don't know because I'm too busy making dessert."

"Is that what I think it is?!" Nat asked, raising his eyebrows.

"That depends on what you think it is," Piper said.

"Why don't we just have that for supper?"

"Because you'd be missing out on several other major food groups."

"How about pizza? Does that cover the other food groups?"

"Not really."

"Why not?" he asked, sounding indignant. "There's tomato for the vegetable group, sausage for the meat group, cheese for the dairy group, and crust for the grain group—it sounds pretty balanced to me." He opened the fridge and reached for a beer. "*And* we could have beer just to throw in some additional grain for the base of the pyramid."

"Beer is in your grain group?"

"Yes—it has oats and barley," he said as if it should be obvious. "Not to mention what you're making—rice is a grain and milk is a dairy . . . *and,* if you add raisins, that's a fruit. It doesn't get any more balanced than that."

She shook her head. "You *do* know that the food pyramid from our childhood has been completely debunked?"

"It has?" Nat frowned. "And to think, all these years I've been making sure I had an abundant supply of grain in my diet."

"Yeah, and you're still skinny as a rail," she said with a hint of envy.

"That's because I have a great metabolism."

"I know," Piper said. "Elias has the same metabolism."

"Speaking of Elias . . . where is *our* boy?" Nat said, wrapping his arms around her.

"He went camping with the guys."

"That's right! I forgot. How do you know he's camping with just guys?"

"Because that's what he said," Piper said, slipping out of his arms.

"Where're you going?" he asked, sounding wounded.

"I have to add sugar," she said, reaching for

her measuring cup. "Could you keep stirring?"

Nat picked up the spoon and stirred while Piper measured a third of a cup of sugar and poured it into the hot milk and rice. "Keep stirring," she said.

"I'm only too happy to stir in your sugar," he teased with a grin.

"Very funny," she said, rolling her eyes as she consulted her laptop. She spooned some of the hot milk and rice into the beaten egg and then added it, too.

Nat glanced at her laptop. "I thought you wanted to make the rice pudding from your mom's cookbook."

"I did, but I keep forgetting to borrow it from Remy, and now she's away, so I thought I'd give this recipe a try—it has over three thousand reviews."

"Is that a lot?"

"It's a ridiculous amount," she said, turning the burner off and adding a teaspoon of vanilla, a tablespoon of butter, and a quarter cup of golden raisins.

Nat stepped back, watching as she took over. "Well, anyway, would you like to order a pizza since it's just the two of us?"

"That's fine," Piper said. "The Fourth is next weekend and we really need to start getting ready."

"It's next weekend?"

"It is," Piper said, looking up. "Why?"

"Because the aquarium called and said the female loggerhead we rescued is doing much better and will probably be ready to be released by next weekend."

"Not on the holiday, though. . . ."

"Well, it's up to us, but we'll have her back out here by then. They said they'll call when she's ready to be picked up."

Piper nodded. "All the more reason we need to get this place straightened up—in case I don't have your help next week." She held out a spoonful of rice pudding and he tasted it. "Mmm, it's still hot, though."

Piper finished the spoonful and nodded. "It *is* hot!"

"I told you," he said. "Didn't you believe me?"

"I believed you," she said, taking a sip of his beer. "I just wasn't sure if your idea of hot was the same as mine . . . and I think I burned my tongue."

"Let me see," he said, motioning for her to stick out her tongue. "Hmm, it's a little red. Oh, by the way," he said, frowning. "I keep meaning to ask you what that sex manual is doing on my bureau."

"It was on the cookbook shelf."

"I didn't know we had a copy."

"Yes, you did."

"No, I didn't."

"Don't you remember the time we drank a

whole bottle of Boone's Farm and I showed it to you . . . and you wanted to try . . ."

Nat's face lit up and he laughed. "I *do* remember," he said, sipping his beer. "Why don't we go see if we can find that page again?"

"What about pizza? I thought you were hungry."

"I *am* hungry. . . ." he murmured, handing her his beer and pulling her toward him.

"I really have a lot to do," she murmured in protest.

"It can wait," he whispered. "And I will help you."

"Yeah, right," she said skeptically, taking a sip of his beer.

"I *will* . . . Promise."

He led her toward the stairs and as she passed the newel post, she reached for it. "I really think we should get started now."

"I'm already started," Nat said with a grin.

"I don't mean *that*."

"Elias isn't here so we should take advantage of the moment."

"What if he forgot something and comes home?"

"He didn't forget anything."

"Where's Chloe?"

"Asleep on the couch."

Piper realized she was running out of excuses and reluctantly let go of the post. "You know," she said, as he led her up the stairs, "if I lie down, I'm going to fall asleep."

"No, you're not," he said, retrieving the book from the top of his bureau.

"Yes, I am." She lay across the bed and pretended to start snoring.

Nat sat next to her and started to leaf through the pages. "What page was it on? Do you remember?"

"I don't remember, hon, it was like forty years ago," she said sleepily.

"Hmm," Nat said. "Look at this one. . . ."

Piper rolled to her side, wishing she'd left the book on the cookbook shelf, then looked at the page. "Interesting," she said, smiling and sliding her hand along his thigh. "What's wrong with the good old missionary position?"

"Nothing's wrong with it," Nat said, pretending to study the page.

"You should be happy to be getting any action at all," she said, sliding her hand up his thigh.

"I *am* happy," he said, trying to suppress a grin.

"Well, if you don't hurry up, I'm going to fall asleep."

Nat closed the book and tossed it to the floor. "The missionary position it is," he said, laughing and rolling on top of her.

⊰ Chapter 47 ⊱

Sailor took a sip of her coffee, knowing—since it was after eight o'clock *in the evening*—she'd probably regret it, but she really needed to get some work done. When she was in college, she'd lived on coffee. "Those were the good old days," she murmured with a smile. Burning the midnight oil had been the norm back then. She and her roommates had stayed up until all hours of the night painting and drawing and lost in their own worlds. It had been a long time since she'd been so caught up in a drawing that she'd lost track of time.

She picked up her paintbrush, dipped it into the smooth paint, and felt her shoulders start to relax. She looked at the sketch she'd lightly traced onto the gessoed board and started to paint. This was what was missing. Almost immediately, she felt the strain of the last month drain from her body. She turned her radio to a classical station and swirled the paint, meticulously blending the colors. The lovely first notes of "Pachelbel's Canon" began to play and she stopped to sip her coffee—*life is good,* she thought, smiling. Suddenly her cell phone started to ring and she looked at the clock. It was after eight on a Saturday night—who could be calling? *Maybe it is Merry,* she thought hopefully, but when she looked at the screen, her hopes were dashed. She hesitated and then tapped the Accept button. "Yes?" she said and listened as Frank spoke. "My signing is at Where the Sidewalk Ends in Chatham on Saturday. . . . Yes, everything's fine. . . . You?" She nodded, absentmindedly swirling her paintbrush into the red and blue paint and watching the pattern it made. "No, I'm working on them, though. I should have them soon." She paused. "Maine? But they always come here on the Fourth. . . . No, I'm not going to be too busy. I thought Merry would bring the kids to the signing . . . she always does." She shook her head. "Whatever, Frank . . . honestly, I don't think anything is sacred to you." She ended the call and turned off her phone. Then she looked down at her palette smeared with purple paint and sighed—so much for working. She carried the gloppy paintbrush and her coffee mug out to the kitchen, dumped the coffee, cleaned and dried her brush, and went back into her studio. She changed the radio back to Ocean 104.7 and turned it up so she could hear it in the kitchen.

She heard a meow on the back porch and opened the door. The orange tiger cat sauntered in, bringing with him the cool summer breeze. "Hello there, mister," she said. "Are you hungry?" she asked, opening the cabinet. "I don't have lobster . . . but I *do* have tuna." She opened a can and scooped it into a bowl. "I promise I'll get more cat food this week," she said, setting it in front of him and jotting *cat food* on a scrap of paper.

She opened the fridge, pulled out a slice of leftover pizza, and poured herself a glass of wine. She turned on the oven, put the pizza in, and went into the living room. Without turning on the light, she sank into her new chair, leaned back against the pillow, and took a sip of her wine. She couldn't believe Frank had invited their kids to Maine for the Fourth. He *knew* they always came to the Cape—it was tradition! Piper always had a big picnic and they all helped out. It was the *one* holiday when they were all together, and just because he wasn't invited—he should've thought of that before he started fooling around—that didn't mean the kids weren't . . . and the kids knew it, too—at least they should've known! She couldn't believe they'd accepted his invitation.

Didn't they know how disappointed she'd be? It was bad enough she had to share them with their in-laws, but now she had to share them with Frank, too. God help her—she'd never see them! Suddenly the ramifications of being a divorced parent hit her like a Mack truck—nothing would be simple again when it came to the kids. Even though they were adults, Frank was still their father and they would still want to spend time with him. Life just wasn't fair!

She took another sip of her wine and listened to the haunting sound of Stevie Nicks singing "Gold Dust Woman" and tears welled up in her eyes. She knew the song was about drug use, but at that moment, the lyrics seemed to have been written for her. "I can't believe it," she whispered, shaking her head. She wiped her eyes, but more tears just kept spilling down her cheeks . . . tears of grief and sorrow for her broken family *and* for all the broken pieces of her life. She'd thought she'd been strong, moving out here alone. She'd told herself it didn't matter, but now, she realized —it was thirty years of her life and it *did* matter because . . . what else was there?

She felt something brush against her legs, and in the next moment, the nameless, homeless orange cat hopped lightly onto her lap and leaned against her, brushing his soft fur against her wet cheeks. "Hello there, mister," she said softly. "You know, you really need a name," she said, smiling as she listened to the last line of the song that was playing, "Call Me the Breeze." "How about Mister Breeze? What do you think?" she asked. The cat curled up on her lap, pushed his head into her hand, and purred loudly. "Consider yourself named," she said, taking a sip of her wine, "Mister Breeze."

✤ Chapter 48 ✤

Remy stood in the late afternoon sunshine, reading "The Secret Sits"—one of several poems posted along the Robert Frost Trail.

"What do you think he means?" John asked, slipping his hand into Remy's.

Remy felt the warmth of his skin and felt her heart race. "I think," she said, trying to focus, "he means that we humans are too busy running in circles and thinking we know everything . . . but if we slowed down long enough to reflect and look inward, we'd have a better chance of understanding ourselves and the world."

John nodded. "So he's saying we should slow down, let go of what we think we know, and just let things unfold."

"Yes," Remy agreed, daring to look at him.

John searched her eyes. "Do you think that's what *we* should do?"

"Hmm?" she murmured, her heart beating out of her chest.

"You know, let go of what we think we know . . . and let things unfold?"

She swallowed. "Is that what *you* think we should do?"

"I do," he said, smiling the smile that was stealing her heart.

"If you think so . . ." she said softly.

"Do *you* think so?" he asked again.

She nodded and he held her face in his hands and softly kissed her.

Remy felt her mind racing like a horse that had just been released from the gate. *Oh my, oh my . . . oh my!*

John leaned back and searched her eyes again. "What do you think?" he asked.

She smiled. "Oh my!"

"Oh my, too," he said, his eyes sparkling . . . and then he pulled her close and kissed her again. "I think I'm falling for you, Remy Landon," he whispered.

"I think I'm falling for you, too, John Sanders," she murmured, gently pushing away all the memories she'd been clinging to like a lifeline—for a lifetime.

"I know I'm not Jim. . . ." he said softly, as if reading her mind.

"I don't want you to be Jim," she whispered.

"We'll just let things unfold. . . ."

She nodded and he took her hand. "How long is this trail?" he asked.

"It's as long as it takes," she said, smiling.

"You're so right," he said, chuckling.

They walked across streams, through meadows and forest, stopping to read the other Frost poems posted along the way, and debated their meaning.

"I always thought 'Stopping by Woods on a

Snowy Evening' was a contemplation of suicide," John said, "and Frost's use of the word *sleep* really means death."

"I've heard that, too," Remy said, "but I think it's an awfully dark interpretation. I think the poem is simply about taking the time to enjoy the beauty of the snow in the silent woods before rushing back to the responsibilities of this world."

"Maybe . . . but why, then, does he repeat that last line, ' . . . and miles to go before I sleep'?"

" 'Miles to go' simply means he has plenty of life ahead of him."

"And what about the 'sleep' part?"

Remy smiled. "Before he goes to bed, silly," she said, refusing to believe that her favorite poet hid anything ominous in the lovely poem.

"Ever the optimist," John teased.

"I try to be," Remy said with a smile. "Life's hard enough without being downtrodden all the time."

"How come your good nature doesn't rub off on your sister?"

Remy smiled, knowing immediately which sister he meant. "I don't know," she said with a sad smile. "Birdie has had a lot of heartache and disappointment in her life."

"So have you . . ."

"I guess we deal with it our own way. It's true I lost my husband, but I was also blessed with three wonderful children."

"And Birdie's been blessed with a wonderful husband her whole life."

"Birdie wanted children more than anything, and she's never been able to let go of what happened to Easton. The past haunts her."

"It's a shame," John said. "Life is too short—you only get one wonderful, amazing, precious life. . . ."

"I couldn't agree more," Remy said as they reached the trailhead.

They walked back to her car. "What's next?"

"Hmm . . . it's getting late. Are you hungry?"

"I *am* a little hungry . . . and I'm sort of craving pizza."

Remy laughed. "Actually, pizza sounds good."

"Do you want to go back to the reunion?"

Remy shook her head. "No, I've had enough. I'm pretty sure it's the last one I'll attend."

"Why's that?" John asked, turning the key.

"Oh, it was fun to see everyone, but that time in my life and the people I knew then— it's just not the same." She searched for the right words. "It's not that they're not important. It's just that they're not relevant to my life now. A reunion is like traveling back in time for a brief recap, but I think, instead of telling your story over and over to everyone who asks, each person should take a turn at a podium and give a brief update of their life—it would be so much easier."

"I can just see you standing at a podium," John teased.

Remy laughed. "Ha! That right there would be a reason to *not* go!"

❦ Chapter 49 ❧

As soon as Birdie pulled in, Bailey limped over to the car, wiggling her whole hind end. Birdie looked up to see if David was on the porch. The night before, they'd talked about making sure someone was always outside with Bailey—no more unsupervised freedom. Birdie opened the door and the old dog put her front paws on her lap and licked her cheek. "Hello, old pie," Birdie whispered, her voice still choked with emotion. Bailey kissed her again and then sniffed the air and realized her favorite food was in the car.

Birdie held her close for a minute, smiling. "What do you smell?" she whispered and Bailey wagged her tail even faster. Birdie gently lifted her down and then climbed out and pulled several shopping bags out of her trunk.

"Need help?" David called.

"Want to grab the pizza?" she said, trudging toward the house.

"You said you were going to the mall," David teased, eyeing all the bags as they passed each other. "But you didn't say you were bringing the mall home with you."

"Very funny," Birdie said, smiling as she went into the house and straight up the stairs.

Earlier that afternoon, David had announced he was going to the library, and Birdie had reminded him to take his house key because she might go to the mall. He'd reminded her it was Saturday—knowing she hated to go anywhere on a Saturday in the summertime, never mind all the way to Hyannis—but she'd told him she just wanted to look around a bit.

As soon as he'd pulled away, she'd hustled up the stairs, pulled the garbage bag and her laptop out of the back of her closet, and thrown them in the car. She'd let Bailey out to get busy, called her back inside, given her a treat, and locked the house. On the way to the mall, she'd stopped and thrown the garbage bag with her slacks, wine-soaked towel, bottle, and broken glass in the Dumpster behind Stop&Shop, and then opened her laptop. The keyboard was splattered with red wine—dry now, for the most part—but when she tapped her finger on the touch pad, nothing happened. She'd closed it, shaking her head, and as she'd driven to the mall, she'd tried to think of how she might explain buying a new one.

Back home and upstairs now, though, she quickly cut the tags off the white slacks she'd bought at Chico's—a store she'd never been in before, but when she'd inquired about the slacks in the window, the store clerk had handed her a size two . . . and she'd just about fallen over. When she'd tried them on, she was swimming in them. A size two was too big? This had never happened before—even when she was a teenager! She'd decided, right then and there—as she purchased a size one and a half—that Chico's was her favorite new store, and she couldn't wait to tell Remy about it. She'd also decided that all the other stores—L.L.Bean especially—whose size sixteen jeans cut her in half—could really take some lessons in resizing from Chico's. It would only be good for their business.

She hung the pants in her closet alongside two new blouses, and then pulled the box containing her new laptop out of the second bag. As she opened it, she wondered whether David would even notice. She'd had no choice—when she'd opened her old laptop to show the tech support fellow behind the genius bar, he'd just shaken his head. He'd plugged it in, tapped some keys to prove it was dead, and she'd nodded resignedly, and then she'd told him she didn't want it back. He'd summoned someone in sales, and a half hour later, she'd seamlessly slipped back onto the grid with a new laptop . . . paid for with cash. She leaned the laptop next to her bedside table— where she'd often left her old one—and tucked the box in the back of her closet. She looked around the room, turned off the light, and went downstairs.

"Wine?" David asked, holding out a glass.

She shook her head. "No, no thanks."

He raised his eyebrows, watching as she ran the tap and filled a glass with cold water. "Are you feeling okay?"

"I just think wine's been the reason I've been getting so many headaches lately," she said, trying to sound nonchalant and knowing full well that this part of her elaborate cover-up would be the hardest part to pull off. "I also think it makes my face puffy," she added for good measure. She didn't mention her nose, though, which she'd begun to think—to her horror—was looking a little purple.

David nodded and put the glass near his place at the table. "Pepperoni or cheese?"

"Cheese, please," she said with a smile.

He slid a slice of pizza onto a plate and set it in front of her, and then served his own. "Lie down, Bay," he said softly and the old Lab clunked to the floor between them.

"She's too funny," Birdie said as she took a bite and nodded in the old dog's direction.

"She is," David agreed. "I think she must've been really dehydrated—I've filled her water bowl three times today."

"She's probably still hungry, too."

"She probably is—Labs are always hungry. If

you left her food bag open, she'd eat the whole thing!"

Birdie laughed, knowing it was true. She took a sip of her water and felt oddly at peace—it was as if someone had given her a drug curbing her desire for alcohol. She took another sip and was amazed by how good and refreshing the water tasted.

David cleared his throat and she looked up, expecting him to say he knew the real reason she wasn't having wine, but instead, he announced, "I have a little surprise."

Birdie tried to swallow the bite she'd just taken, but it seemed to be blocked by the lump in her throat. "What?" she croaked.

He reached into his pocket, pulled a small bottle of pills out, and put them on the table. "John gave me these to try."

Birdie looked at the bottle and frowned, and David cleared his throat again. "It's Cialis."

"It's . . . oh!" Birdie said.

"I've had it for a while, but the timing has never seemed right."

Birdie bit her lip, not knowing what to say. "I'm sorry. I'm sorry the timing never seemed right. I guess I've just had a lot on my mind."

"Birdie, I know it's been a while since we've . . . been intimate," he said awkwardly, "and it's all my fault . . . but I wondered if you might like to give it a try."

"Of course," she said, trying to muster some enthusiasm for his unexpected invitation . . . because now—now that the prospect of having sex with her husband again was very much in her future, her desire—much like her desire for alcohol—was very much waning. "When do you want to try?"

"Tonight," David said, smiling.

"Tonight?" she repeated, trying not to sound alarmed. "Are you sure? Aren't you a little tired from all the excitement we've had this weekend?"

"Oh, I think I could handle a little more excitement," he said, smiling.

"Well, how soon beforehand should you take it?"

"I already took it."

"You did? And?" she asked uncertainly.

"Well, it's my understanding that it doesn't automatically happen. There is some physical stimulation involved."

"Oh," Birdie said, feeling her face turn red. She looked away, broke off a piece of pizza crust, and held it out to Bailey, who took it ever so politely.

"Want another slice?" David asked.

"No, no, thanks," Birdie said, finishing her water.

"They say high-fat foods might slow things down a little," he said, taking a bite of his second slice, "and I'm sorry about that—but I'm starving."

Birdie smiled and looked out the window at

the late day sunlight streaming across the yard, wondering how—after nearly forty-five years of marriage—talking about sex with her husband could still feel so awkward. She stood up to clear her plate, and as she washed the few dishes that were in the sink, she felt David come up behind her. He reached around her to put his plate in the sink, and then he wrapped his arms around her. "I've missed you," he murmured softly. "And I've missed making love to you."

Birdie turned off the water and turned to face him. "I've missed you, too," she said softly. She felt him press against her and smiled. "I think it's working."

"I think so, too," he said, grinning like a schoolboy. He leaned down and softly kissed her, but just as their lips touched, he pulled back, frowning.

"What's the matter?" she asked.

"I don't know . . . all of a sudden, I have this weird sensation," he said, pressing his fist against his chest.

Birdie's eyes grew wide as she watched him wincing with pain. "David, are you okay?" she asked in alarm.

"I do . . . don't know," he stammered, his face turning white. "I don't feel very well."

"Do you think we should go to the hospital?"

He looked at her, trying to focus. "I don't know . . . maybe . . ."

"Okay," she said, trying to not panic as she

reached for his arm. "Can you make it to the car?"

David leaned against the counter and put his hand on his chest, and then, grimacing, collapsed.

"David!" Birdie cried. She knelt next to him and Bailey pulled herself up and nudged his hand. When he didn't respond, the big Lab lay down right next to him and put her head on his chest. "Oh, David!" Birdie cried again. "I don't want to be alone." Her heart pounded as she tried to dial her cell phone, but her hands were shaking so hard she couldn't even slide her finger across the screen. She threw it on the counter, picked up the home phone, and dialed 911 and then waited for what felt like an eternity for someone to answer.

She heard a distant voice. "Nine-one-one. What is your emergency?"

"My husband's having a heart attack," she cried. "Please send someone right away." She gave them the address and David's age and then listened to the calm voice on the other end asking her if she knew CPR.

She shook her head. "No . . . not well—I mean, I've never had to use it."

"Well, you're going to use it now," the voice said calmly and clearly, "so put your phone on speaker."

"Please send help," Birdie pleaded, trying to find the button. "I really don't think I can do this."

"You can do it. Help is on the way."

Birdie knelt down next to David, tears streaming down her cheeks as she tried to focus on the dispatcher's calm voice. "Tilt your husband's head back, make sure his airway is clear, and then give him two quick breaths."

Birdie gently tilted David's head back and tried to see inside his mouth. "Oh God," she cried. "I think it's clear."

"Give him two quick breaths."

Birdie leaned forward and put her mouth over the lips she'd just kissed and breathed out, suddenly wondering how exhaled breath—carbon dioxide—could possibly help. "Okay," she said.

"Now find the vee under his sternum, and with the heel of your palm, give his chest thirty compressions."

"You have to move your head, Bay," she sobbed, gently pushing Bailey's head off his chest. She found the sternum and counted as she pressed down thirty times, all the time praying she wasn't doing more harm than good. "Okay," she said breathlessly, wiping the perspiration and tears from her face.

"Give him two more breaths."

Birdie leaned forward, gave David two more breaths, and when she lifted her head, she heard the sound of sirens wailing in the distance. "Oh, hurry," she cried. "Please hurry!"

"Ma'am, are you still there?"

"Yes," Birdie cried.

"Give his chest thirty compressions."

Birdie leaned over her husband and with tears streaming down her cheeks, pumped his chest thirty more times.

Suddenly, there was banging on the door. "Come in! Come in!" she called and two EMTs rushed in and took over, asking her a myriad of questions as they worked, but the one that made her heart stop was: "Has he taken any new medications?"

"No . . . I mean, yes."

"What was it?" the EMT asked, looking up.

"Cialis?"

"Do you know when?"

"About an hour ago?"

"Does he take anything for angina?"

"No," Birdie said, feeling a wave of nausea wash over her. Could this be all *her* fault, too? Did David have a heart attack because he'd sensed she was unhappy about their lack of intimacy?

Five minutes later, Birdie watched the EMTs load David's eerily still body into the back of the ambulance. One of the EMTs climbed in beside the stretcher while the other one closed the door. "Ma'am, are you able to drive or have someone bring you to the hospital?"

Birdie looked utterly confused and then realized she was being left alone. "Yes, my sister . . ." she said.

"Are you sure?"

"Yes, go!"

He nodded, climbed into the driver's seat, and pulled away.

Birdie listened to the haunting sound of the siren and watched as the lights filled the heavens. "Oh, Lord, You've let me down so many times when I've prayed, but I'm trusting You again *now*. Please don't take David . . . please don't take my husband!"

She hurried back into the house and found Bailey curled up in the spot where David had just been lying, the poor Lab's eyes filled with sadness. "Oh, Bay," she said, sitting down next to her. "It's going to be okay," she whispered tearfully. She lifted the dog's head onto her lap. "We've been through so much these last few days, but everything's going to be okay." The comforting words she spoke were as much for herself as they were for her sweet, old dog.

❧ Chapter 50 ❧

John and Remy were sitting on the inn's front porch, watching the fireflies blinking in the darkness. Remy smiled wistfully. "When I was a girl, my sisters and brother and I used to love catching fireflies and putting them in mason jars. We tried to use them as lanterns."

"Did it work?"

"Not very well," she said, "because they were always blinking."

John chuckled, trying to picture Remy as a girl.

"That's what we were doing the night Easton died—we were catching fireflies. It was the night before his birthday, and my mom was trying to get ready—making his cake and wrapping his presents—but then Sailor broke her jar and took Piper's. I remember it all so clearly, as if it happened yesterday."

"That happens sometimes when something tragic or traumatic happens—we either block it out or we remember it vividly."

She shook her head. "I think we all remember it with vivid clarity—at least I do—but we've never once talked about it."

John nodded. "Maybe that's why Birdie has had so much trouble healing. Maybe you *should* talk about it."

A firefly landed on Remy's pants and rested there, blinking. "You're probably right," Remy said.

"What happened after that?"

"After Sailor—who must've been around eleven at the time—took Piper's jar, Piper—who had to be about six—took her complaints straight tothe boss, who, as I mentioned, was busy in the kitchen." She paused. "Anyway, Sailor—ever prepared to defend herself—followed Piper inside, and Easton, who must've already been *in* the kitchen, heard Piper's complaint and immediately found a jar in the refrigerator . . . but it was full of homemade pickles."

"Oh no," John said, shaking his head. "I can see where this is going."

Remy nodded. "By this time, my mom had asked Sailor to call Birdie and me inside, too, so she could remind us that she had a lot to do. We were just getting ready to herd everyone back outside when our dad came home with the ice cream for Easton's birthday."

"You *do* remember it vividly!"

"I do because we never had black raspberry ice cream again."

"Oh no . . ."

She nodded. "Anyway, Easton, who was still holding the jar of pickles in his arms, asked if he could put them into something else, and as he took off the top and reached in to have one, he asked us if we wanted one . . . and of course, Sailor and Piper both tried to reach into the jar at the same time. That was when it slipped out of his arms. And spilled sticky pickle juice—and pickles—all over the floor."

John shook his head. "This would be remembered as funny if it hadn't ended so tragically."

"True," Remy said, nodding. "It would be one of those memories that we'd laugh about now."

"So, I imagine, this is where your mom asked your dad to get you guys out of the house."

"It is, and he took us up to Nauset Light to go for a hike on the beach, but it was getting dark so my dad told Easton to hold Birdie's hand. Easton said he didn't need to, but Birdie told him she'd help him find the best heart stone. . . ."

"Heart stone?" John asked, looking puzzled.

"You know, a smooth stone in the shape of a heart."

"I've never heard that term before."

Remy nodded. "We loved to look for heart stones, and Easton was especially determined to find one because he wanted to give one to our mom after the mess he'd made." She watched the fireflies dancing in the darkness and seemed lost in thought. "I've never talked about this with anyone," she said softly, "except Jim, and even with him, that's as far as I got."

John nodded and reached for her hand. "I'm glad you're talking to me," he said softly, "and if you don't want to tell me the rest, it's okay."

Remy's eyes glistened. "I *do* want to tell you the rest, it's just so . . . hard."

John put his arm around her and gently kissed the top of her head. "It's okay," he whispered, and as he pulled her close, the sound of an old-fashioned phone broke the silence. John pulled his arm away and reached into his pocket. "My phone," he said apologetically. He glanced at the screen. "It's Birdie," he said in surprise.

"She has your cell number?"

"She does—she's wanted to be able to reach me if something happened . . ." He frowned, wondering if something *had* happened. He slid the phone on. "Hello?"

Remy listened as he spoke. "Hi, Birdie, what's wrong? . . . Oh no! Is he okay?" Remy sat up, searching his face, and leaned closer so she could hear what her sister was saying. "It's David," John whispered. "The Cialis? I don't know . . . it's not likely. . . . Oh, Birdie, I would meet you in a heartbeat if I was there, but I'm still in Vermont. I will call Josh, though, and have him go right to the hospital. . . . Josh—Dr. Hart—my new associate . . . Yes, he knows what he's doing. . . . Of course, she's right here . . . ?" He handed the phone to Remy.

"Is David okay? . . . Yes, please call us back. . . . We'll be there as soon as we can," she said, nodding. "Yes, we're praying and we'll leave right away. . . . Love you." Remy handed the phone back to him. "She's so upset. I told her we'd head right home."

"Of course," John said, looking at his watch. "But it's nine o'clock, and even if we were leaving right this second, we wouldn't get there until two or three in the morning."

"I know, but what if David . . ." She couldn't even say the words.

"You're right," he said, standing up. "I'll call

Josh, and then just knock on my door when you're ready."

Remy nodded. "I'm so sorry."

"There's *nothing* to be sorry about. David's my oldest friend."

❧ Chapter 51 ❧

When Nat and Piper pulled into the driveway, Birdie was waiting on the porch. "Thank you for coming," she said tearfully. "I'm sorry to be so needy lately."

"Don't be silly, Birdie," Piper said. "What in the world happened?!"

"We were having a pizza and he suddenly started to have chest pains and I asked him if he wanted to go to the hospital, but before we could even get outside, he had collapsed."

"I didn't know David had heart problems," Nat said.

"I didn't, either. His blood pressure is always spot-on—unlike mine—and he's never had high cholesterol."

"Has he been feeling okay?"

"As far as I know. He was really upset when Bailey was missing, but we both were . . ."

"Does he take any medicine?"

"You sound like the EMTs," Birdie said, shaking her head and looking out the window, her tears blurring her vision. She'd mentioned the Cialis to John, but he'd said he thought it was unlikely to have caused any harm . . . but, somehow, she still believed it had to be related. David was in perfect health, and it was the only thing that was different.

"I tried to call Sailor, but she didn't answer her phone," Birdie said, changing the subject.

"I'll text her," Piper said, reaching for her phone.

"I called John, too."

"In Vermont?!"

"I forgot they were in Vermont."

"What did he say?"

"They said they'd leave right away."

Piper shook her head—it was a shame all this was happening the one time Remy had gotten up the courage to get away.

"I probably shouldn't have called him, but I did honestly forget," Birdie said regretfully.

"No, no," Piper assured her. "You absolutely did the right thing."

"I hope so. I just thought John would want to know and be here—he's been David's doctor . . . and friend forever."

⊰ Chapter 52 ⊱

Piper offered Birdie her arm, and Birdie took it as they hurried through the emergency room doors. "David Snow?" Birdie said in a voice choked with emotion.

The receptionist looked up. "I'm sorry . . . what was the name?"

"David Snow," Piper said more slowly and clearly.

The receptionist looked at her computer screen. "Hmm . . . Snow . . . here he is. He just came in—cardiac arrest, right?" She looked up for confirmation and Birdie nodded. "It looks like he's having some tests done. If you'd like to wait in the waiting room," she said, pointing over their shoulders, "someone will come out and talk to you."

"So, he's still . . . alive?" Birdie asked in thankful disbelief.

The receptionist nodded and smiled. "Yes, he's still alive."

"Thank the Lord," Birdie said, leaning heavily on Piper.

Piper guided Birdie to the waiting room, and moments later, Nat came in from parking the car and sat down next to them. "Any news?" he asked.

"They're running some tests," Piper said.

Nat nodded and squeezed her hand. "I called Elias but his phone went right to voice mail, so he must have it turned off to save the battery."

"Probably," Piper murmured. She watched Birdie pull a tissue out of her purse and dab her eyes, and for the first time in her life, she saw her sister as a stranger might see her. Usually, Birdie was very pulled together *and* classy, but tonight she looked like an old woman—worn and weary, as if life had gotten the best of her . . . as if the burden of another ounce of heartache would crush her. Piper put her arm around her sister and kissed the top of her head. "He's going to be okay."

Birdie nodded, mustering a feeble smile, and then looked out the window into the darkness. It was all her fault. She had, once again, brought tragedy upon them with her selfishness and lack of humility. To think she'd decided she'd had enough of being married . . . enough of David. Now she'd give anything just to have him back. A new hand had been dealt, she thought miserably, and all she could do was wait and pray.

It was almost eleven when Sailor peered around the doorway of the waiting room. "Oh my goodness. I've been trying to call you! How come you didn't answer?"

Piper pulled her phone out of her pocket and

looked at it. "Because there's no service in here," she said, standing to give her sister a hug.

Sailor looked around. "Is David okay? Where's Birdie?"

"She just went to the ladies' room. He's alive—that's all we know—we haven't had an update. They were doing some tests but that was hours ago. We were hoping to hear something by now, but it's been so busy—I think an ambulance pulls in every ten minutes!"

"Did Nat come, too?"

"He did but we never had supper so he just went out to get something."

"I wish I'd known. I could've brought you something."

"That's okay. He's bringing food back."

She looked around again. "Do they have coffee here?"

Piper eyed her sister and frowned. "Have you been drinking?"

"Why?" she whispered. "Can you smell it?"

"Well, ye-ah . . . you smell like a winery."

"Damn," Sailor murmured. "Do you have a mint?"

"No, I ran out of the house with just my phone. Why were you drinking alone? Is Birdie rubbing off on you?"

"I always drink alone, but tonight I had a little more than usual because I talked to Frank."

"You talked to Frank?"

"Yes. What a mistake that was."

"Why? What happened?"

"He has invited the kids to Maine for the weekend."

"This weekend?"

"No, next."

"The Fourth?!"

"Yes . . . and I can't believe they said yes. They *know* we always get together at your house."

"Did you call Merry?"

"No, but I will. I just hate the idea of having to split up all the holidays now."

Birdie emerged from the ladies' room and when Sailor turned to give her a hug, she frowned. "Have you been drinking?"

"Yes, which is why I need a cup of coffee."

"There's a Keurig," Birdie said, pointing to a small countertop with a coffeemaker and some cups.

"Perfect," Sailor said and then turned back to search her sister's face. "How are you holding up?"

"I'm holding, but I wish we'd hear something." As she said this, there was a commotion in the lobby and two EMTs rushed through with a little boy on a stretcher. "Seven-year-old. Male. Near-drowning," one of the EMTs called.

"Oh no," Birdie whispered, catching her breath.

Sailor squeezed her hand reassuringly. "He will be okay," she said, but Birdie didn't seem to hear. "Birdie, look at me," she said and Birdie turned from watching the stretcher that had just whisked by. "That boy will be okay," Sailor repeated softly, nodding toward the now closed doors.

Birdie searched her sister's eyes. "How do you *know?*"

"Because they said *near*-drowning."

Birdie nodded, and although she was still shaking, she sat down, her thoughts returning to David.

It was midnight before the young doctor walked into the waiting room and looked around, his eyes stopping on Birdie. "Mrs. Snow?" he asked.

"Yes?" Birdie said, her heart suddenly pounding.

"I'm Dr. Hart," he said, walking over to extend his hand.

"That's a good name for a doctor," Birdie said, standing up to shake his hand.

He smiled. "It's not spelled the same way, but it serves me well."

Birdie eyed the handsome young doctor's smooth cheeks. "You don't look old enough to shave, never mind be a doctor." She felt a sudden jab in her side and looked over at Piper. "What? Does he look old enough to you?"

"How's David?" Piper asked. "I'm Piper—his sister-in-law," she said, extending her hand. "And this is Sailor—one of his other sisters-in-law."

Dr. Hart shook both their hands and then turned back to Birdie. "Your husband has had a major coronary event caused by myocardial infarction

. . . which, in layman's terms, means he suffered a heart attack because he has blockage in one of the arteries and it's preventing blood from flowing easily to his heart."

"Will he be okay?" Birdie asked anxiously.

"He's being prepped for surgery right now and the surgeon will be out to explain the procedure which will clear the blockage and insert a stent in the artery. It's a very common procedure, and I expect your husband will come through it without any problems. Do you know if he has any allergies?"

Birdie shook her head. "I don't think so."

He nodded, jotting it on his chart.

"Any medications?"

"No," Birdie said, hesitating. "But he did take something earlier this evening that he's never taken before."

The doctor looked up. "What was that?"

"Cialis," Birdie said softly, hoping no one else would hear, but immediately, Piper raised her eyebrows and looked over Birdie's head at Sailor.

The doctor nodded and jotted it on his chart.

"Do you think it's related?" Birdie asked hesitantly.

"It's hard to say. Cialis does increase blood flow, so it may've gotten things moving a little more in there, but sometimes a blockage is so imperceptible it goes undiagnosed for years, so finding it now because of the increased blood flow—although frightening—is actually a blessing. Especially since *you* were there." He looked up. "Are you the one who gave him CPR?"

She nodded. "I tried."

"You did a great job," he said with a smile. "You probably saved his life."

⚜ Chapter 53 ⚛

At 4 a.m. Remy and John hurried into the emergency room and found Piper, Nat, and Sailor all dozing and Birdie watching *Casablanca* on the waiting room TV. When she saw them, she got up and gave them both hugs. "I'm sorry I ruined your weekend."

"Don't be silly," Remy said.

"He just came out of surgery," Birdie said, quickly updating them. "I didn't call you back yet because there's no service in here."

Their conversation roused Piper and Sailor, who smiled sleepily and stood up to give hugs, too, but Nat seemed dead to the world.

"How was the reunion?" Sailor asked.

Remy looked at John and smiled. "It was fun."

"That's it?! 'Fun'?" Sailor teased. "That's all we get?"

"For now," Remy said.

"Well, I'm going back to see how David's

doing," John said, looking at Birdie, "and to see if we can't get you back there, too."

"Thank you," Birdie said, "and thank you for coming home."

He put his arm around her shoulder and smiled. "Anything for you."

They all settled back into their chairs to wait, and Remy turned to Birdie. "So, what happened? What was David doing?"

"He was eating pizza," Birdie said, "and he just started having chest pains."

"And Birdie gave him CPR," Sailor announced proudly.

"You did?! I would never be able to give CPR," Remy said, shaking her head. "I would panic and just sit there and cry."

"That's pretty much what I did," Birdie said, "but the emergency dispatcher guided me through it."

"And the doctor said she probably saved his life," Sailor added.

Remy smiled and gave her sister a hug. "That *is* truly something, Birdie."

Birdie smiled. "I just did what I was told . . . for once."

They laughed and then all eyes turned to Remy. "Well?" Sailor pressed. "Was it as awful as you expected?"

"Not at all," Remy said. "We had a good time."

"How was the reunion?" Piper asked.

"We only ended up going to one event—the dinner reception on Friday. There were other events on Thursday—which I didn't realize because I didn't read the packet, but as it turned out, one event was enough."

"What did you do yesterday, then?" Birdie asked.

"We had breakfast at the inn—which was lovely—they have a dog that reminded me of Bailey." When she said this, Sailor and Piper looked at each other but didn't say anything. "And then, we went to a brewery for lunch, a winery, and hiking on the Robert Frost Trail."

"What did you do for dinner?"

"We went out for pizza . . . because John had a craving," she added, smiling at Piper. "And last night," she added, turning to Birdie, "we were just sitting on the porch talking when you called."

"It *does* sound like you had a good time," Sailor said. "Especially the winery and the brewery."

"Well, we had some excitement here, too," Piper said, looking at Birdie.

"You mean more than David?" Remy asked.

Piper nodded. "Bailey took off Thursday night and got lost, and we spent all day Friday putting up posters and looking for her. We didn't find her until Friday night."

"Oh no! Poor thing!" Remy said, and then she frowned. "Hold on! If she took off on Thursday, how come no one told me? I was still home."

"Because we thought you wouldn't go," Sailor said.

"I would've gone."

"No, you wouldn't have," Nat murmured, opening one eye.

Piper elbowed him. "Have you been listening this whole time?!"

"Do you really think a person could sleep through all this?" he asked, and then grinned at Remy. "Hi, Remy."

"Hi, Nat."

Just then, John appeared and motioned for Birdie to follow him. Birdie walked down the hall beside him, her heart pounding, and when she stood in the doorway of the ICU and saw all the tubes and monitors crisscrossing her husband's body, she caught her breath. "Oh, dear Lord," she murmured as tears filled her eyes, "please take care of him."

"He's going to be fine," John assured her, "but he probably won't wake up for a while. He needs rest." He squeezed her shoulder. "I'll leave you alone."

Birdie nodded and walked tearfully over to sit next to David's bed. She watched his heartbeat steadily blipping up and down on the monitor, and she listened to it beep every few minutes, checking his blood pressure and pulse. "Oh, David," she whispered, "I'm sorry I've been such an old shrew. I can't remember the last time I was actually cheerful around you—or anyone else, for that matter." She shook her head. "I don't know what's wrong with me. I have so much to be thankful for and yet I go around being unkind and intolerant to everyone . . . but especially you."

She reached for his hand—the strong hand she knew and loved so much—the hand that held tiny birds with the gentleness of a whisper; the hand that stroked Bailey's head so lovingly; the hand that knew how to fix anything . . . *and* how to give wonderful back rubs. "Oh, David, if anything happens to you, I don't know what I'll do," she said, her eyes blurry with tears. "I'm so sorry this happened, and I don't care if we never make love again. I just need you by my side. We've been through so much together and you're always the strong one, you're always the one holding me up when I feel like I can't go on." She brought his hand to her lips and then rested it against her cheek. "Please get better so you can come home . . . because if you don't," she whispered in a voice choked with emotion, "Bailey will die of a broken heart . . . and so will I."

Part III

She is clothed with strength and dignity;
she can laugh at the days to come.

—Proverbs 31:25

July 3, 1964

At the bottom of the steep wooden steps to the beach, they kicked off their sneakers and sandals and threw them in a pile. "Just like home," Whitney said, shaking his head.

"I'm going to find a heart stone for Mom," Sailor announced.

"Me too," Piper added.

"Me, three," Easton said with a grin. "I need to make up for dropping the pickle jar."

Whitney listened to their voices calling back and forth over the sound of the thundering surf and looked down the beach. People were still walking along the water, playing Frisbee, and fishing; there was even a small group sitting around a campfire, but it was definitely getting dark.

"Dad, can we build a campfire again some-time?" Easton asked.

"Yeah, that was fun," Remy added.

"Sometime," Whitney replied.

"Can we make s'mores, too?" Piper asked.

He nodded and switched on his flashlight. "Okay, so the rule is: Everyone stays away from the water," he commanded, shining his flashlight onto each child's face to confirm they understood. They all nodded, but as they walked toward the sound of the crashing waves, Whitney reached for Piper's hand and felt an odd shadow fall across his heart. "East, I want you to hold Birdie's hand."

"Oh, Dad," he protested. "I don't need to hold hands."

"Yes, you do."

"How'm I going to hold my flashlight *and* my pail?"

"Birdie will hold your pail."

Easton groaned. "I'm not a little kid any-more."

"I know you're not," Whitney said.

"Don't worry," Birdie consoled her little brother. "We'll work together and find the best heart stone."

"Okay," Easton said, his face brightening. He handed his pail to his sister, switched on his flashlight, and reached for her hand, and as the small group trooped along the water's edge, their bobbing flashlights looked like fireflies blinking in the darkness.

They walked in silence. The only sounds were the wind and the waves and the faint *click* of smooth stones and shells dropping into their pails. Twenty minutes later, Whitney looked back. The campfire was just a dancing flicker of gold, and the lighthouse looked as if it was miles away. "Time to head back," he announced.

"Nooo," Sailor protested.

"I haven't found a heart stone yet," Easton moaned.

"Five more minutes," implored Remy.

"C'mon, Daddy, just a little farther," Piper pleaded, pulling him along.

Whitney relented. "Okay. Five more minutes, but then we turn around. We still have to walk all the way back . . . and the tide's coming in."

Piper pulled him to a stop and bent down to examine a tiny gray stone that had been worn into the shape of a heart. "Look at this one!" she exclaimed. "It's perfect!"

"Let me see," Easton said, shining his flashlight onto her palm. He nodded and then lingered, searching the sand, hoping there might be another.

"C'mon, East," Birdie said as the rest of the family's flashlights bobbed away.

"Just a minute," Easton said, pulling his hand free. He stepped closer to the water, and as he shone his flashlight onto a line of stones that had just washed in, a gentle wave circled his ankles and drifted out, pocketing his feet in cold, wet sand.

"Dad said to stay out of the water," Birdie scolded.

"I'm fine," he said, shining his flashlight onto another line of stones.

"C'mon, East. It's dark and you're too close to the waves."

"Hang on," he said, spying an aqua green stone glistening under the clear water. "I found one!" he shouted, but as he bent to pick it up, it tumbled away.

"Easton, let's go," Birdie commanded.

"Just a minute. I have to find it again," he said, crouching down to search the swirling water.

Birdie started to walk away, but hearing a loud thundering sound, turned back. A huge wave was rumbling out of the darkness. "Easton, look out!" she shouted.

Easton looked up, saw a wall of water churning toward him, and started to stand, but before he reached his full height, the rogue wave crashed over him, pulling him under.

"Easton!" Birdie shouted, rushing into the surf, plunging her arms into the frigid, frothy water, and looking around wildly, frantically searching . . . searching . . . praying for him to reappear . . . but there was no sign of him anywhere. She felt a powerful undertow wrap around her legs and try to pull her out to sea as swirling sand rushed from beneath her feet.

"Easton, where are you?" she screamed again and again, the icy fingers of terror gripping her heart. "Da-ad!" she cried, looking down the dark beach, but her voice was drowned by the wind and the crashing waves.

"Oh, God, help me!" she pleaded, tears streaming down her cheeks.

❦ Chapter 54 ❦

Piper climbed onto the stepladder she'd just carried up two flights of stairs and, feeling slightly winded, reached up to unscrew the bulb in the rafters. "Oh my goodness! I'm more out of shape than I thought!" She screwed in the new bulb and discovered that having her arms over her head made her feel even more out of breath. "We need to get out running again," she told Chloe—who had followed her up the stairs and was now nosing around the dusty, cluttered attic. She climbed down and pulled on the string, and the new bulb flickered to life. "And there was light!" Piper said, smiling.

She set the dead bulb on a table near the door and made her way through the maze of boxes to her mom's hope chest. She lifted the top and the familiar scent of cedar drifted out. She carefully removed the tray of beads and the stack of letters tied together with faded red ribbon, picked up the stack of sweaters, and lifted out the old photo album. When she opened it, the photo of the five of them in front of Nauset Light—the one in which they had their arms around each other—was on top. She gazed at it and then put it on her dad's old mission chair. She closed the album and started to put it back, but then a small white and blue baseball cap tucked down between the sweaters caught her eye. She pulled it out and ran her fingers lightly over the faded red felt *B* stitched on the front.

"Mom? Are you up here?"

In the back of her mind, Piper heard Elias coming up the stairs. "Hey," he said, standing in the doorway. "Do you know where the . . . Sheesh! There's a lot of stuff up here." He started to pick his way through the boxes. "Mom?" he said softly. "What's the matter?" He came up behind her and looked over her shoulder. "Hey, that's a cool cap. Whose was it?"

Piper swallowed. "It was Easton's."

Elias frowned. "Your brother's? He was a Red Sox fan?"

She nodded, pressing her lips together. "He was. He loved baseball . . . and he was wearing it that night. . . ."

"The night he died?" Elias asked.

Piper nodded again, the memory of the long-ago night rushing back to her as if it were yesterday . . . the memory of standing on the beach, shivering and crying and feeling utterly lost while her father and sister screamed in anguish.

"Did you know it was up here?"

Piper shook her head, fighting back tears.

Elias picked up the old photo she'd put on the chair and studied it. "Is this you?"

"Yes, that's me."

"Look how cute you were," he teased, trying to get her to smile.

She laughed and brushed back her tears.

"And is this Easton?" he asked.

"It is. I always thought you looked like him when you were little."

Elias nodded. "It's such a great picture. I love how Aunt Sailor is making bunny ears behind Aunt Remy's head—that is so typical," he said, laughing.

"It *is* typical," Piper agreed with a chuckle. "*So* Sailor."

"What are you going to do with the cap?"

"Put it back," she said, tucking it back in her mom's hope chest.

Elias watched as she piled sweaters and letters and trays of beads on top of it and then shook his head. "My psychology professor would call that a classic example of literally burying a memory."

"I'm not burying a memory," Piper said defensively. "I just don't have time right now. We have a lot of people coming this weekend."

"Which reminds me—I came up here to see if you know where the trimmer is?"

"It should be in the shed or in the garage. Did you ask Dad?"

"He's not here—he had to run up to the sanctuary."

"He did? Doesn't he know I need help *here,* especially since you guys are going to Boston tomorrow."

"He said he'd be right back," Elias said, picking up the album that was still sitting on a box. He slowly turned the pages. "Are these pictures of Grandma and Grandpa?"

Piper looked over his arm and nodded.

"How come you never showed them to me?"

"I don't know . . . because I avoid coming up here."

"I thought I got my height from Dad, but look at Grandpa—he was pretty tall."

"Six-foot-two," Piper said, nodding.

"Where'd they get married?" he asked, studying the beautiful, old wedding photos.

"In Boston."

Elias looked at her thoughtfully. "Mom . . . how come you and Dad never got married?"

Piper smiled. "I was wondering if you were ever going to ask that question."

"I've always wondered—it's kind of odd to have parents who love each other and who've lived together but never married. All of my friends think you *are* married."

"And how come you never told them we weren't?"

"They never asked."

"They never asked . . . and you never volunteered the information because you didn't want them to know."

"Maybe," he said with a shrug.

Piper nodded. "Well, my dear, life is complicated . . . as are relationships—as I'm sure you're figuring out. Your dad did ask me to marry him . . . on a couple of occasions, in fact, but I wasn't ready. I guess I found the idea of being wholly committed to one person a bit frightening because . . . what if something happened? What if I lost him?

"But then, when I was pregnant with you, something changed—I felt that I *was* ready. I was so full of love for you . . . and he was part of you, and as I felt you growing inside me and my love growing for both of you, I began to think I was ready to take a chance, but then, your dad never asked again—I guess he was tired of being turned down."

"How come you didn't ask him?"

"That's a good question," she said, smiling, "and I don't know the answer. Why don't we go see if we can find that trimmer?"

Elias nodded, still holding the album. "Is it all right if I bring this downstairs so I can look at it some more?"

"Of course," she said, tucking the black-and-white photo under her arm to take down, too.

❧ Chapter 55 ❧

Sailor took a sip of her coffee and typed the word *"all"* into her search box. Before she'd even finished, though, Google had offered her several options. "Google, you know me better than I know myself," she murmured, clicking on her favorite recipe site. She typed *"summer salads"* and then tapped the Enter button and began scrolling through a list of recipes, trying to find something fun to make besides her layered dip—which was a given—and the traditional tossed salad she always made with the maple dressing everyone loved. She glanced over at Mister Breeze, who was sunning himself in an adjacent chair. "What do you think, Breeze, potato or pasta?" He blinked indifferently and she smiled. "That's okay. I'm just glad to have someone to talk to besides myself."

Out of the corner of her eye, she noticed something move, and when she looked up, she realized the chipmunk was sitting perfectly still on the edge of the new birdbath she'd bought after she'd finished weeding and pruning the garden. "Hmm, what sinister plan are *you* plotting, mister?" she asked, eyeing him suspiciously. "Another murder, perhaps? It's hard to forget the taste of blood once you've had it, isn't it?" She watched him for a few moments and then realized there was a mourning dove stretched out in the sun. Her eyes grew wide. "Oh no, you don't!" she shouted, getting up and startling the chipmunk—who scurried away, and the mourning dove—who flew up, its wings whistling, warning the other birds to *Flee! Flee!* Within seconds, there was a mass exodus of flapping wings.

Mister Breeze sat up to see what all the commotion was about and she eyed him, too. "Don't get any ideas," she said warningly.

She looked back down at her screen and continued scrolling. "I'm thinking pasta," she murmured, narrowing her search, "since I'm pretty sure Birdie will make potato salad." Just as she said this, the Platters started playing on her phone and she looked down at the screen. "Speak of the devil," she said, accepting the call. "Hey, Birdie," she answered. "How's David?" She nodded, listening. "Well, he better take it easy or he'll end up back in the hospital. Mm-hmm . . . By the way, are you making Mom's potato salad for the Fourth?" She nodded again. "I was just wondering because I know you have your hands full, and if you don't have time, I'd be happy to make it. . . . Is he going to be able to come? . . . Okay, good . . . I'm glad . . . and make sure you bring Bailey, too. . . . Yes, I'll talk to you soon." She paused, listening, and then raised her eyebrows in surprise. "I love you, too," she said, and as she ended the call, she tried to remember whether she'd ever heard Birdie say "I love you" to *anyone* before. "Maybe Bailey or Chloe," she mused, smiling.

She returned to her search and finally settled on an old-fashioned macaroni salad that looked —and sounded—like the one her mom used to make. She took a sip of her coffee, reached for her pencil, and jotted down the ingredients she'd need for the weekend, and ten minutes later—after a trip to the bathroom—she slipped on her flip-flops. "Be back soon," she called, thankful to have someone—even if it was just Mister Breeze—to say it to. She was almost out the door when she decided to hit the bathroom one last time, just in case. "I'm really leaving this time!" she called.

As Sailor turned onto Route 6, she heard the wail of sirens and looked in her rearview mirror but didn't see any emergency vehicles. There were always so many sirens on the Cape—a day didn't go by in the summer when she didn't hear the haunting sound. She turned down her radio, realized the sirens were getting louder, and looked in her mirror again. This time, she saw flashing lights. She pulled over, waited for the ambulance out of Provincetown to speed by, and then pulled back onto the road, whispering a prayer—as she always did—for whoever needed help.

She turned the radio back on and heard the unmistakable beginning chords of "Don't Let the

Sun Catch You Crying" drift into her car. She shook her head and reached for the knob but then stopped. It had been a long time—fifty-two years, to be exact—since she'd listened to the melancholy lyrics of the song that had been a hit the summer she'd turned eleven. The song had been on the radio constantly that summer, and it had made her heart ache even more . . . because all she could *do* was cry.

She gazed out the window, listening to the lyrics, and allowing the memory of a long-ago summer night to fill her mind. She was back in her father's wood-paneled Country Squire station wagon, and with the evening breeze drifting through the open windows, she and her siblings were singing along with Gerry & The Pacemakers at the top of their lungs . . . and even though she and her sisters couldn't carry a tune, Easton had the voice of an angel—which was fitting, she thought sadly.

She looked out the window, remembering the events that had followed—walking along the beach looking for heart stones and her father looking back and realizing that Birdie and Easton weren't with them. "We have to go back," he'd said, picking up Piper and starting to run. "Remy," he'd shouted, "hold Sailor's hand!" And they'd run as fast as they could. She'd fallen twice, scraping her knees, and when they'd found Birdie, her father had pulled her up off the sand and shaken her, shouting, "Where is Easton? Why did you let go of his hand?" She could still hear the terror in his voice and she could still see Birdie motioning tearfully to the dark, pounding waves, and then Remy had pulled her younger sisters back from the water and squeezed their hands . . . and Piper had cried out, "Ouch, Remy, you're hurting me. Where is Easton?"

Sailor bit her lip now and realized she could barely see the road through her tears. She pulled over and turned off the radio. It was still too much to bear. . . .

❧ Chapter 56 ❧

Early on Friday morning Nat and Elias loaded the sanctuary truck with supplies and drove to Boston to bring home the loggerhead turtle they'd rescued. She'd been treated with anti-biotics and nutrient-rich foods, and although she would always have scars on her shell, the open wounds had healed. Piper went to the sanctuary with them and saw them off. Then she finished up some long-overdue reports she'd been putting off and headed to Stop&Shop to finish her food shopping for the weekend. She was in the deli section, perusing the pre-sliced deli meat and waiting for her number to be called, when she heard a familiar voice behind her. "Hey, girl! Fancy meeting you here!" She looked up and saw Sailor holding out a hot Starbucks coffee from the bakery section.

Piper gratefully took it and gave her sister a hug. "Oh my goodness, you're a godsend! I wanted to get a coffee, but when I came in, the line was too long."

"And you obviously didn't see me *in* the long line," Sailor teased, "but I saw *you* coming in all bleary-eyed!"

Piper laughed. "I *am* bleary-eyed! Nat and Elias left at four a.m. to go get the turtle, and I went in with them to help them get the truck ready to transport her."

"When is the big day?"

"I'm not sure. Have you heard the forecast?"

"Yeah, it doesn't sound good."

Piper nodded. "That's what I heard, too, although I think it's supposed to clear by Sunday afternoon and Monday is supposed to be gor=geous . . . so maybe early Monday morning. Are you going to come?"

"I want to . . ."

"Oh, by the way, happy pub day . . . a little late! How's the book doing?"

"Thanks. I won't really know for a while."

"When's your signing in Chatham?"

"Saturday from two till three thirty—so it'll actually be good if it's raining because people will be out shopping instead of going to the beach."

"Saturday is tomorrow, you know."

Sailor frowned, realizing her sister was right. "I don't know why I keep thinking today is Thursday."

"Well, if I were to come down around three tomorrow, do you want to go to Chatham Squires for a drink?"

Sailor smiled. "That would be great!"

Piper searched her sister's face. "If I didn't know better, I'd think you'd been crying."

Sailor chuckled and reached up under her eyes. "Why? Is my mascara making me look like a raccoon?"

"Maybe a little," Piper said, handing her a tissue. "Why were you crying?"

"I just heard that old song by Gerry and The Pacemakers. . . ."

"Oh," Piper said, nodding in understanding.

"Anyway," Sailor said, changing the subject, "I'm planning to bring my layered dip, a tossed salad, and a macaroni salad on Sunday. Do you need anything else?"

"Are you sure you have time to make all that? Don't forget, you're going to be busy."

"I'm sure. They're all easy. Anything else?"

Piper frowned. "I don't think so. Nat and Elias are picking up corn, I'm picking up the hamburgers and hot dogs right now, Birdie's making potato salad and an hors d'oeuvre, and Remy is making dessert."

"What's she making?" Sailor asked.

"I don't know—she said it was a surprise."

"Hmm," Sailor said. "Well, I'm sure it'll be good."

Piper nodded. "Oh! And guess what else!"

"What?!"

"She asked me if it would be okay if John came."

"No way!"

Piper nodded.

"Wow . . ." Sailor said, raising her eyebrows. "I think she's withholding information."

"I think you're right," Piper said and they both laughed.

"Last call—number fifty-six!" a voice from behind the deli counter called for the third time.

Piper looked down at her number. "Oops, that's me," she said, waving her hand to let him know she was there. "Thanks for the coffee," she said, giving her sister another hug. "You're the best!"

"You're welcome."

"I'll see you tomorrow in Chatham . . . *if* I don't see you again in this store!"

"Okay! I'm looking forward to it!"

They parted ways, each consulting their list and only passed each other one more time—in front of the ice-cream case. "It's for Elias," Piper said, grinning.

"Yeah, right," Sailor said, laughing.

≈{ Chapter 57 }≈

As promised, the only appearance the sun made on Saturday was when it peeked over the watery horizon at dawn. Dark clouds rolled in from the west, right along with lines of cars crossing over the bridges from the mainland for the long holiday weekend.

Remy looked out the kitchen window, trying to decide whether or not she had enough time to get in her walk before it started raining, and then she turned on the TV to watch the forecast. There was an ominous line of thunderstorms marching across Connecticut, but it looked like it wouldn't reach the Cape for a couple more hours, so she *should* have time. She might even have time to go to the market.

She tied her sneakers, stopped at the bathroom, and then walked over to turn the TV off, but just as she reached for the remote, the TV started beeping and an emergency warning scrolled across the bottom of the screen, warning residents that the impending storm could bring hurricane-force winds, driving rain, and golf ball–size hail! She turned off the TV and made a mental note to put her new car in the garage. The last thing she needed was golf ball–size hail hitting it!

She opened the back door and Edison scooted

in. "Is it that bad out?" she asked, but he'd already disappeared up the stairs. The weatherman had promised that the storm would usher in cooler air and she hoped he was right. The last several days had been oppressively hot and humid . . . much too hot for June . . . but as she closed the door, she suddenly realized it was July. What had happened to June?!

The last week had been a whirlwind of activity. From helping Birdie get David home and settled, to walking Bailey so Birdie could stay by his side. And from going out to dinner with John two of the last four nights, to going out for breakfast yesterday, she couldn't remember when she'd been so busy. Not since all her kids were home, she decided, and that reminded her—Payton and her family were all due to arrive that night, in the middle of the storm! She wondered if she should tell her to wait and come in the morning when Eliza and Sam and their families were coming. She'd been looking forward to having a chance to visit with her oldest daughter alone for a few hours but there was no sense in taking chances. She picked up her pace, her mind racing with all the things she still needed to do, and she almost tripped on a root. "There's *definitely* no time for that," she murmured.

When she finally got home, the first fat raindrops were splashing on her bare arms. She hurried into the house, used the bathroom again, grabbed her purse and keys, and headed to the market. She was happy to find a spot right in front and hurried inside with her jacket over her head to grab the two things she needed: a pint of whipping cream and a half gallon of black raspberry ice cream. But when she passed by the coffee and tea display, she decided to treat her-|self to a warm chocolate croissant and a cup of Earl Grey tea—it was that kind of day!

She drove home, pulled into the garage, gathered her things, and just as she pushed open the mudroom door, the skies opened up. "That was close!" she said, putting the ice cream in the freezer and looking out at the sheets of rain racing across the white-capped bay. She listened to the wind howl around the house and then heard a loud clattering and knew the porch furniture was blowing over. The kitchen lights flickered and she looked up anxiously. "Please don't let the power go out," she said, reaching for her tea. "I still have a cake to bake!"

❧ Chapter 58 ❧

Piper felt like the Tasmanian devil as she rushed around the house, tucking away papers, washing windows, scrubbing floors, wiping down the counters, cleaning out the fridge to make room for all the food, and vacuuming up several weeks of wispy golden retriever hair that had congregated in the corners. All the while, Chloe followed her around, happily carrying new Zoe in her mouth and wagging her tail because she knew—from past experience—that cleaning meant company was coming!

While Piper worked inside, Nat and Elias worked outside—mowing and trimming the lawn, weeding all the flower beds and the vegetable garden, and *finally* spreading the huge pile of mulch that had been sitting in the driveway for a month. Piper went out to see how they were doing and realized the sky was slate gray. *So much for setting up the picnic tables and chairs,* she thought glumly. "You guys better head in," she called as a gust of wind sent leaves spiraling into the sky.

She opened the fridge, pulled out the cold cuts she'd bought the day before, and opened up a new bag of grinder rolls. Chloe settled strategically at her feet to watch her every move. "You're silly, you know that?" she said, breaking off a piece of cheese and offering it to her. Chloe took it politely, and in the very next moment, a bright light flashed outside, followed by a loud *clap* of thunder that made the lights flicker. Piper looked outside again and saw Nat and Elias scrambling to put their tools away, and just as the skies opened up, they tumbled through the door, laughing. "Don't you two know you shouldn't be carrying metal tools around during a thunderstorm?"

"Yes, we know," Elias said, reaching around her for a piece of cheese and then breaking off a small piece for Chloe.

"I just gave her a piece," Piper scolded.

"Oh well," he said, kissing the top of the golden's head. "She got two pieces!"

Chloe licked his cheek and thumped her tail. "I think she said she wants a piece of ham," he said, trying to reach around his mom again, but this time, Piper slapped his hand. "Hey!" he said, laughing. "Sorry, Chlo . . . I tried."

Piper handed him a plate and saw him reaching for a large unopened bag of Cape Cod waffle chips. "Those are for tomorrow."

Elias looked wounded. "They are?"

"Oh, go ahead," she said, rolling her eyes. "But don't eat 'em all."

Thunder rumbled across the heavens, and then they heard *patter*ing and *click*ing on the roof and they all stood up and looked outside. "It's hailing," Nat said in surprise.

"Holy cow! Look at the size of it!" Elias pushed open the door and picked up several pieces of the frozen water and held them in his palm. As they looked at them, they heard a loud *crack* followed by the sound of splitting of wood. Piper looked out and saw a long, heavy branch of one of the oak trees spear the ground. She went out on the porch to see the damage and watched as the wind rushed through the remaining branches of the old oaks, swaying them violently. Her heart pounded. "Please don't let any of those old trees come down," she whispered. Almost immediately, she heard her father's reassuring voice from her child-hood telling her that the roots of the trees he'd planted when they were each born would intertwine as they grew and would be able to with-stand any storm. "They will never fall," he'd said.

Piper pictured the roots of the old trees deep below the earth's surface, wrapping around each other like the long tendrils of life, weaving and growing . . . ever deeper . . . ever stronger . . . able to withstand any of life's storms.

Piper smiled and then looked down at her wet clothes and sighed. She went back inside and glanced at the clock—it was already two o'clock! Where had the day gone?! She hadn't even showered yet, and she was supposed to be in Chatham in an hour! "I have to go," she said, rewrapping the cold cuts and putting them back in the fridge.

"Where are you going?" Nat asked in surprise.

"Sailor's book signing."

"You're driving to Chatham in this?"

"I am. I told her I'd come and then we're going to the Squires after."

"I thought we had stuff to do."

"I did all *my* stuff," she said.

"Nice," Elias said with his mouth full of grinder. "How come you didn't invite us?"

"Because I didn't think you'd want to go, and besides, you have to go to the sanctuary to check on the old lady."

"That's right!" Nat said. "Thanks for reminding me." He looked at Elias. "Want to come along?"

"I'd love to," Elias said. "Thank you for inviting me."

"Okay, you two," Piper said, laughing as she wiped the crumbs off the counter. "I honestly didn't think you'd want to go to a children's book signing, and since I'll probably grab something to eat with Sailor—"

"And drink," Nat said, winking at Elias.

Piper shook her head. "Well, anyway, you two should probably plan on stopping for pizza or something on your way home."

"Sure," Nat teased, nodding to Elias. "She goes from telling us she's going to a book signing to now telling us she's going out for dinner and drinks."

"And she didn't invite us," Elias added.

"*I* didn't say anything about drinks," Piper countered.

"I don't think the Quinn sisters can get together *without* drinking," Nat teased.

"Oh yes, we can, and now, I'm heading upstairs to take my shower."

"Mom, don't you know you're not supposed to take a shower during a thunderstorm?"

"I'll have to take my chances," Piper said, "and by the way, you two spend a lot of time ganging up on me when you're together." She eyed Elias. "So I might just have to send *you* back to school early."

"No, we don't," they said in unison. "Do we, Chlo?" Nat added, rubbing the golden's ears. She wagged her tail in happy agreement.

❄{ Chapter 59 }❄

Sunday morning dawned cool and crisp. Birdie poured two mugs of coffee while thinking about the day ahead. She and David were supposed to be at Piper's around two and she still had her potato salad to make—which wouldn't take long, but she wanted to make something else, too . . . and she hadn't decided what yet.

She set one of the mugs down in front of David, who was looking at the paper. "Would you like some scrambled eggs?"

"Sounds good," he answered. "Want help?"

"No, you stay put."

She opened the fridge and took out the ingredients she'd need: four eggs, milk, and just enough butter for the pan. Ever since they'd retired, David had been in charge of breakfast, but ever since his heart attack, Birdie had been in charge of everything . . . and she took David's new low-fat, low-salt diet very seriously. They'd always eaten plenty of fruits and vegetables, but now, Birdie had decided to make a conscientious effort to minimize their fat and salt intake, too. The thought of David dying had scared *her* more than it had scared him!

"Toast?" she asked.

"Half a slice," he said, watching her bustle around the kitchen, making the eggs and opening the bread bag. He watched her turn on the front burner and drop a dab of butter into the frying pan, and the simple act made him smile. The last week had been a whirlwind for both of them, but mostly for Birdie. She'd brought him home from the hospital and helped him get settled; she'd coordinated with Remy to stop by and walk Bailey; she'd made sure he had everything he needed and waited on him hand and foot. She'd given him her undivided attention and assumed all the responsibilities around the house that had been his; in fact, her willingness to do everything had started to make him feel guilty. Especially yesterday, when the power had gone out for over an hour and she'd been in the middle of cooking an Oven Stuffer. She'd kept her cool while they waited for the power to come back on . . . and the chicken had turned out to be one of the tastiest they'd ever had.

"It must be that low-temp, slow-cooking method people are always talking about," she'd said, chuckling, when he commented on how moist it was.

David was astounded by the change that had come over her—she was no longer in a brooding, dark place . . . and he hadn't seen her take even a sip of wine—in fact, there were no wine bottles around at all!

"What're you making for the picnic?" he asked.

"Potato salad and maybe fruit salad, but if I make a fruit salad, I have to run to the store," she said, scraping the scrambled eggs onto two plates.

"That's fine. I'm sure I'll be okay. Bailey will look after me, won't you, girl?" He stroked her head—which had been on his lap every time he sat down since he'd gotten home from the hospital. "I'm lucky to have *two* girls looking out for me."

Birdie chuckled and reached for her coffee. "It will be nice to see everyone. I can't remember the last time we saw Remy's grandkids."

"Probably last summer," David surmised, taking a bite of his toast. He frowned. "Isn't Sailor's family coming, too?"

"Noo . . ." Birdie said, shaking her head, "and she's *not* happy about it."

"Why aren't they?"

"Because Frank invited them to Maine."

"Had she invited them here?"

"She hadn't—she just assumed they knew they were invited because we always get together on the Fourth, but now, everything's different. She's discovering she's going to have to get used to sharing the kids on the holidays."

David shook his head and took a bite of his eggs. "You're going to have to give me a refresher on Remy's grandkids because I don't remember their names."

Birdie smiled, swallowing the bite she'd just taken. "I couldn't remember, either," she said, reaching for the index card that was propped up between the salt and pepper shakers and the napkin holder. "That's why I asked Remy to write it down." She put on her glasses and studied the card. "Okay . . . so Payton and Tom have two girls, Hunter and Parker—who are ten and eight."

"Oh, right," David said, his memory jogged. "The girls with the boys' names."

"Right," Birdie said.

"I think odd names run in your family."

"I think you're right," Birdie said, laughing. "Shall I continue?"

"Yes," he said as he sipped his coffee.

"Sam and Tess have a boy and a girl. Elliot is seven and Maya is five."

David nodded. "That's a little better. Sam always had a good head on his shoulders."

"Eliza and Tim have three boys now—she just had the third one in March. Their names are Mason, Cayden, and Logan—they are three, two . . . and the new little one is almost four months."

"What is it with people giving their children

names that all sound the same?" he asked, sounding perplexed.

"I have no idea," Birdie said. "Maybe it's to make it easier for their elderly aunts and uncles to remember."

"Or harder," David said. "Thank goodness Sailor's grandkids *aren't* coming because I would never remember everyone. I'm lucky if I can keep the first generation straight."

Birdie smiled. "I'm sure you'll do fine, and if you forget, you can always resort to *'Hey, you!'*"

"I might just have to," he said, chuckling, and then he looked at her with a puzzled expression. "What's your name again?"

Birdie laughed and shook her head.

⁕ Chapter 60 ⁕

Sailor hurriedly packed the food she'd made into the new cooler she'd bought and then carried it out and loaded it in the back of her car. The food would be fine—she only had one stop to make along the way—but she worried that Piper wouldn't have enough room in her fridge for everything, and having an extra cooler around would only be helpful. She went back into the kitchen and looked around one last time as Mister Breeze sauntered in from the bedroom.

"What's it going to be, sir, in or out?" she asked, holding the door open for him. "I'm going to be gone *all day*." He swished between her legs and stood on the threshold, peering outside and blinking at the sunshine. "That's all right. Take your time," she said. "I'm not in any hurry." The orange cat—who had put on a little weight and whose coat was getting shiny—stretched his front legs with his butt in the air and then stepped gingerly outside. "Good choice," she said, slipping her bag over her shoulder and stepping out behind him. She closed the door and knelt down to stroke his head. "I'll be back tonight." He pushed his head up into her hand, purring, and then hopped up into one of the chairs and stretched out in the sunshine.

Twenty minutes later, Sailor was perusing the shelves of Birdie's favorite package store when Alec—the young new owner with the French accent that Birdie thought was cute—came up behind her. "Where is your sister?" he asked with concerned eyes. "I haven't seen her in long time."

"Birdie?" Sailor asked, frowning.

"*Oui*, she looks like you but older—long, silvery hair," he said, motioning with his hands. "Pretty face"—he circled his own face as he said this—"I miss her."

Sailor laughed. "I don't know where she's been."

"She is my best customer. She buys wine by the case!"

Sailor shook her head. "I'll be seeing her this afternoon and I'll tell her you miss her."

Alec nodded. "*Merci*. Now, may I help you find somezing?"

"Oh, I'm looking for something picnicky. . . ."

He nodded and showed her a sauvignon blanc that was very popular and he picked out a new malbec for Birdie. "This is for your sister—she favors red. It is on the house—you tell her it is a gift from me."

Sailor laughed. "Okay, thank you, Alec. I will definitely tell her."

He nodded and turned to another customer ho was waiting to ask a question. Sailor turned away at the same time to look at the beers and promptly bumped into another customer. "Oops, I'm sorry," she said, almost dropping the wine bottles. She clutched them to her chest and looked up. "Oh, hi!" she said, her face lighting up.

"Hi," Josiah said, smiling. "Fancy meeting you here."

"I was going to say the same thing," she said, laughing. She looked down and saw he already had a six-pack in his hand. "I don't know much about beer . . . is that any good?"

Josiah held up the six-pack of Naughty Nurse and shrugged. "I don't know—this is my first Naughty Nurse," he said, smiling, "but it sounds good."

"I'm looking for something to take to a picnic for my brother-in-law—who just got out of the hospital . . . although I'm not sure if he can have beer yet." She looked at the come-hither look of the nurse on the label and smiled. "That would be perfect! Where'd you find it?"

Josiah motioned to a beer case, and Sailor pulled out two more six-packs while still juggling the wine. "So, what are you doing for the holiday? Anything fun?"

"Not really. Just me and my nurses," he said, gesturing to his six-pack.

Sailor frowned. "No family picnic?"

"No, before my divorce my wife and I always used to go to her family's picnic in the Berkshires and then to a concert at Tanglewood, but not anymore."

Sailor suddenly felt bad. "I know just how you feel," she said sympathetically. "My sister always has a big family picnic around the Fourth—it's been a tradition forever—and my kids and grandkids always come, but this year, my ex invited them to Maine. I still can't believe they're not coming."

"I'm sorry to hear that."

"I'm sorry, too." She paused. "Hey, if you're not doing anything, why don't you come to our picnic —I'm sure there will be more than enough food."

Josiah shook his head. "Thank you, but I don't

want you to invite me just because you feel sorry for me."

"That's not why I'm inviting you," Sailor said. "I'm inviting you because I *want* you to come. I know I said I'm not ready to jump into another relationship, but that doesn't mean we can't be friends."

Josiah hesitated and looked down at his six-pack.

"Just come," she pressed. "I'm going there right now and you can follow me, or you can leave your car here and ride with me. It's not far."

Josiah pressed his lips together, considering. "I don't have anything to bring."

"You're bringing beer."

"Are you sure?"

"I'm positive."

Josiah smiled and finally relented. "Okay."

"Great!" Sailor said, beaming. "It'll be fun! My sisters have been asking to meet you." She paused and looked at him again. "Maybe I should warn you about my sisters first. . . ."

He laughed. "I already met one of them."

Sailor frowned. "When?"

"When you first bought the cottage, I dropped off some Munchkins and sunflowers, and she was there . . . Piper, I think."

"Oh, right! I forgot. Well, there you go! I'm sure she'll love seeing you again."

❧ Chapter 61 ❧

"They're here!" Elias called, pushing open the screen door.

Hearing his words, Chloe hurried to the kitchen with Zoe in her mouth and wiggled her way outside, bumping the door out of his hand and making it *bang* against the house.

"Nat, you really need to fix the door," Piper called as she dried her hands on a dish towel. Remy and John were just climbing out of her car when an entire caravan pulled in after them. A collection of small people emerged shyly from the three out-of-state vehicles, and Chloe—who was absolutely beside herself—hurried over to welcome them, wiggling all around them and proudly showing off Zoe. "Hi, Aunt Piper," Elliot said, giving his great-aunt a hug at the very same time he put his hand on Chloe's head. "Did Chloe get a *new* Zoe?!"

"She did," Piper said, laughing, "and I can't believe you remember that, Elliot."

"I remember," he said, holding Chloe's head in his hands, "because last year, you wouldn't let her bring her old Zoe inside."

"That was because she smelled."

"I know," Elliot said, laughing. "But now you have a new Zoe, don't you, girl?"

Chloe wiggled around him and then hurried off to say hello to Parker and Hunter and Maya and Mason and Cayden . . . and give a sniff to Logan's trailing blanket.

Nat and Piper and Elias shook hands and gave hugs to all the cousins and aunts and uncles. There were *oohs* and *aahs* over the new baby and exclamations concerning growth spurts. Sam looked up at Elias as they shook hands. "You definitely didn't get your height from the Quinn side of the family," he said, laughing.

Elias laughed. "You might be surprised. I have to show you a picture I just found."

Moments later, Birdie and David pulled in, and as soon as Chloe saw Bailey, she dropped Zoe like last week's news and hurried over to say hello. Seven-year-old Elliot watched the two dogs greeting each other, nose to nose, tails wagging, and then he picked up Zoe and brought her into the house so the stuffed dog wouldn't accidentally get left out in the rain again.

Everyone else gathered around David and Birdie, giving more hugs and asking David how he was feeling. "Oh, I'm just a little tired," he answered, smiling, "but, really, much better."

Finally, Sailor pulled in with her passenger and waved, and Nat turned to Piper. "Who's that?"

"That's Josiah—the Realtor who found the cottage for her," Piper said. "They went out a few times, but she said she decided she wasn't ready to jump into another relationship." She paused. "I wonder what changed."

Sailor lifted the cooler out of the back of her car and Josiah immediately stepped forward to take it from her. Sailor hesitated, shaking her head, but he insisted and then Sailor looked up and saw everyone watching them. "Hi!" she called, relinquishing the cooler and waving. She reached back into the car, piled the three six-packs of Naughty Nurseon top of the cooler, grabbed the two bottles of wine, and walked over with Josiah. "Everyone, this is Josiah," she said. "And, Josiah"—she motioned with her hand—"this is every-one!" She quickly went around the circle, introducing each family member while giving them each a hug, and Josiah set down the cooler and shook hands.

When she was finished, he smiled. "I hope you're all planning to wear name tags!"

David laughed. "I heartily agree!"

Nat reached for the six-packs while Elias picked up the cooler. "Okay to put these on ice?" Nat asked and Josiah nodded.

Elias turned to Sailor. "Cooler in the kitchen?"

She nodded and then looked at Piper. "Unless we're having snacks out here?"

"We have everything set up on the porch," Piper said. "We were going to set the tables up in the yard but we didn't know if it might rain again, so we decided the porch was a better option . . . and easier on our old legs."

John turned to Remy. "Do you want me to get the cake?"

"Oh yes!" she said, suddenly remembering. "*And* the ice cream—which is probably melting!"

"I'm sure the ice cream's fine," he reassured. "It's in a cooler, too."

"Oh, good! Otherwise we'd have soup."

Birdie motioned for Hunter and Parker to follow her and then noticed Maya hugging her father's leg and beckoned her to come, too. Moments later, the two older girls, grinning from ear to ear, carried the salad bowls past everyone, and Maya followed, carrying a paper bag with dog treats in it. Bailey and Chloe sniffed the air and followed the girls inside—from where all the yummy smells were coming!

"I guess *they* know where to go," David said, laughing. "Shall we follow?"

They started to walk toward the house, but when they heard more cars turning into the driveway, they stopped and Sailor smiled in surprise—it was Merry and Sawyer, and their family, and in the second car were Thatcher and Elle!

"I thought you were going to Maine!" she cried.

"We wouldn't miss the Quinn family picnic, Mom," Merry said, climbing out to give her a long hug. "Especially this year."

"Hi, Mom," Thatcher said, hugging her, too.

"Hi, Grandma," Lily and Frances called, running around the car and jumping into her arms.

⊰ Chapter 62 ⊱

The afternoon drifted by lazily. The children raced around the yard, laughing and calling to one another, their happy voices filling the summer air. The men congregated around the grill, eating Sailor's dip and Remy's guacamole, talking about baseball, drinking beer, and watching Nat masterfully flip burgers. Finally, Nat dispatched Elias to find out how many people wanted cheese, and the women began uncovering salads and setting them on tables. They laughed as they worked, caught up on each other's news, and sipped wine—all except Eliza, who was nursing, and Birdie, who opted for sun tea instead—a request that raised several sets of eyebrows.

"So, Mom," Merry teased as they waited in the kitchen, "who's that cute guy out there?"

"Josiah?" Sailor asked casually. "He's just a friend. I ran into him at the package store o my way here, and since he didn't have anywhere to go this weekend—because of his divorce—I invited him."

"He's divorced?" Merry pressed.

"Mm-hmm," Sailor said, stirring the maple salad dressing she'd made.

"How'd you meet him?"

"He's the Realtor who found the cottage for

me," she said, tossing the salad. Then she looked up and eyed Birdie. "By the way, Alec asked me to tell you he misses you. He sent that bottle of malbec over, on the house," she said, nodding to the unopened bottle of red wine on the counter.

"Alec?" Birdie asked quizzically.

"You know, the cute French guy who owns the package store."

"Oh!" Birdie said, laughing as she uncovered her potato salad and sprinkled paprika on it. "Well, the next time you see him, tell him I miss *him*, too . . . and thank him for me."

Payton smiled and looked at her mom. "Since we're on the topic of men . . . Mom? Do you have anything to share?"

"Me?" Remy shrugged, smiling. "I don't think so."

"That's not what I heard," Piper teased. "I heard you guys went out to dinner twice this week . . . and out to breakfast, too!"

"Who told you that?" Remy asked, sounding suspicious.

"Are you kidding?" Piper teased. "You are the talk of the town! It's not every day that Cape Cod's most eligible bachelor is seen in the company of the same woman several times in one week."

"The real question," Sailor said with a grin, "is, was there a good-bye between dinner and breakfast . . . or just, *'Hello, love'*?"

They all laughed and Remy shook her head, trying to suppress her smile.

"Did you go to your reunion?" Eliza asked.

"She did," Payton said. "*And* Dr. Sanders went with her."

"Noo!" Eliza exclaimed as Elle and Tess both smiled, listening intently as Eliza and Payton teased Remy.

"Yes," Payton said, nodding.

"How come I never heard about this?" Eliza asked.

"Because you never call your poor mother to see how she's doing," Remy said.

"In my defense, things have been a little hectic," Eliza said. "You forget what it's like to have three little kids—three little *boys* under the age of three!"

"I haven't forgotten," Remy said, "which is why I haven't called you. I never know if you're in the middle of something or if you have a little quiet time to yourself."

"Somehow," Payton said, "we've gotten off the subject . . . which was finding out how your weekend in Vermont with Dr. Sanders was . . . ?"

"It was nice," Remy said.

"Nice?!" Payton said in an exasperated voice.

"That's all we got, too," Sailor said, laughing. "Actually, we got *'fun.'*"

Elias peered through the screen. "Who wants cheese on their burger?"

They all raised their hands and he frowned, counting. "C'mon in here, cuz," Payton teased, "and tell us how the college boy is doing."

"I don't think so," Elias said, laughing. "There are way too many women in there!"

"Oh, c'mon," his older cousin pressed. "At least tell us what you're up to this summer."

Elias stepped into the kitchen, saw Logan—the only other male—on Eliza's lap, and smiled. "At least I'm not entirely alone!"

"So," Payton said, "other than growing six inches, what have you been up to?"

Elias shrugged. "Not much."

"He's been working on getting his pilot's license," Piper interjected.

"Well, that's something," Payton said. "How cool is that?"

"Pretty cool," he said, smiling.

"Are you working?"

"Just helping out at the sanctuary."

"Do you like it?"

"I do, but I don't know if it's what I want to do for the rest of my life."

"Shouldn't you have that all figured out by your senior year of college?" Payton teased.

"Probably," he said, grinning.

"By the way," Piper said, looking around the kitchen. "If anybody is still around tomorrow, we're going to be releasing a female loggerhead." She looked at Elias. "Did Dad say where?"

"Race Point."

Tess smiled. "Elliot would *love* to see that!"

"Okay, so nine cheeseburgers," Elias said, changing the subject. "I have to tell Dad."

Ten minutes later, they all gathered on the porch around the bountiful and festively decorated tables, and from the smallest to the tallest, held hands while David cleared his throat. "Dear Lord, we have so much to be thankful for this year. I do especially," he added softly, his voice filled with emotion. He felt Birdie squeeze his hand. "We are thankful to be together as a family, and for all these wonderful kids, especially our newest addition, Logan—look at that, I remembered his name—whose smiles and laughter and light fill our world with hope. We are thankful for the delicious food we're about to gobble"—he paused and listened to the kids giggle—"and we're thankful for this great nation. Please keep us safe and bless us with continued health and happiness. Ah-men."

"Amen!" they all chorused, clapping and cheering as the kids raced over to be first in line while the two dogs sniffed the table, wagging their tails hopefully—it was time for food!

An hour later, as the bright orange sun sank below the horizon and the yard slipped into shadow, Piper turned on the strings of glittering white Christmas lights she'd hung along the porch. "Oh, how pretty!" Birdie said, sitting down across from her sisters. Remy and Sailor both nodded in agreement and leaned back in their chairs. Just then, all the kids came running up the stairs onto the porch. "Aunt Piper, Aunt Piper," they called breathlessly. "Do you have any empty jars?"

"What in the world for?" she asked, looking at their flushed faces.

They pointed behind the house, and the sisters all turned and looked. The backyard was full of hundreds . . . if not thousands . . . of tiny yellow-green blinking lights.

"Fireflies!" five-year-old Maya explained matter-of-factly to Birdie. "We're gonna catch 'em."

"You're gonna *catch 'em?*" Birdie said, laughing.

Little Maya nodded.

"Yes, we're going to make lanterns," seven-year-old Elliot added.

"I think there might be some jars in the basement," Piper said. "Stay here and I'll go look." She disappeared into the house and came back a few minutes later with a dusty box of canning jars. The kids excitedly pulled open the top and reached in. "Be careful," Piper said. "They're glass."

They nodded as they gingerly lifted out the mason jars and fished around in the bottom of the box for lids and rings.

Elliot stood by waiting for the younger kids to get their jars and then knelt down to pick up the last one. He brushed off the dust and looked at the lid. "Hey, this one has a name on it," he said, cleaning off the top with his finger so he could read it. "Easton," he said, frowning. "Who's Easton?"

Piper looked at her sisters, and their eyes all glistened.

"Easton was our brother," Birdie said.

"You *had* a brother?"

She nodded, and the voices around them grew quiet.

"What happened to him?"

Birdie swallowed. "He died," she said.

"How old was he?"

"Seven . . . almost eight."

"Just like me."

She nodded.

Elliot traced the name on the lid. "How did he die?"

"In a drowning accident."

"How?"

"Well, we were walking on the beach one night, looking for stones, and he saw one that he really liked—a heart stone. Do you know what that is?"

Elliot nodded. "It's a stone that looks like a valentine."

Birdie nodded. "He saw a heart stone, but when

he reached for it, it tumbled away . . . and then he pulled his hand out of mine so he could find it . . . but when he wasn't paying attention, a big wave came in and crashed over him."

"That's awful," Elliot said, reaching out to touch her worn, freckled hand. His eyes were solemn and sad. "He shouldn't have let go of your hand."

Birdie squeezed his hand. "You're right . . . he shouldn't have."

"Here's a picture of Easton," Piper said, holding out the photo she'd found in the attic.

"Is that all of you?" Elliot asked in surprise, studying the picture.

Piper nodded.

"Wow—you were all so . . . young!"

"Thank you," Birdie said, laughing as Piper handed them each a framed copy of the old photo.

Remy looked at the picture and smiled wistfully. "Do you realize that Easton would've turned sixty this weekend?"

"That's right!" Sailor said. "I hadn't thought of that."

Birdie nodded, her eyes glistening.

"I did," Remy began, "and since we never got to celebrate Easton's birthday that year, I thought it would be nice to remember him by having his cake tonight . . . in honor of his sixtieth birthday."

Piper smiled. "Is that why there's black raspberry ice cream in the freezer?"

Remy nodded.

"I can't believe he would be sixty," Birdie murmured softly.

"What do you think he'd be like?" Remy mused.

"Oh, he'd be tall and handsome . . . probably an engineer—he was always so curious and smart."

"And full of life," Sailor added. "He'd be the life of the party if he was here."

Birdie nodded. "He would be. He would've made all of our lives . . . richer."

Just then, Maya trundled up the stairs, followed by her cousins. "Look at my lantern!" she said, holding out her mason jar. Piper turned off the Christmas lights and the lantern blinked and glowed, illuminating the innocent faces. "It's beautiful," Birdie said softly. "They're all beautiful," she murmured, as the years of guilt and sorrow slipped away.

❧ Chapter 63 ❧

It was still dark outside when Piper, Remy, Birdie, and David pulled into Sailor's yard. "I hope you made coffee," Piper said as she came into the kitchen.

"Of course," Sailor replied, pouring five steaming cups. "I also had a box of Munchkins delivered," she said, opening the box and pushing it across the island.

"I bet *you* did," Piper said, grinning as she took out a chocolate-glazed doughnut hole.

"How come the turtle has to be released so early?" Sailor asked.

"Because it's still the holiday weekend and we want her to be safely offshore before the boat traffic picks up."

Birdie looked around the neat cottage. "Where did Merry and Thatcher stay last night?"

"In a motel," Sailor said regretfully. "There isn't enough room for everyone here. That's the one downside of having such a small place."

"They could've stayed with us," David offered, sipping his coffee. "We have plenty of room."

"Or us . . . I mean, *me,*" Remy said, reaching into the box and taking a jelly-filled Munchkin, "if I didn't already have a house-full."

"Or *us,*" Piper added. "I didn't know they were staying in a motel."

"I didn't even know they were coming," Sailor said. "Otherwise, I would've made arrangements with one of you."

"I wish mine could've, too," Remy mused. "At least Sam and Tess were able to stay—Elliot and Maya are going to love this!"

"By the way," Piper said, taking a cinnamon Munchkin and popping it in her mouth. "We *really* have to make time to get through the attic.

It is *packed* and it won't be fair if something happens to all of us and Elias has to deal with it."

"We will," Birdie assured her. "In the fall, when it's cooler."

"Okay," Piper said, eyeing her skeptically. "I'm going to hold you to that."

Remy cradled her mug in her hands. "Is that where you found the old photo and the album Elias was showing everyone last night?" she asked.

Piper nodded. "I found some other things, too—letters Dad had written to Mom when he was in the navy . . . and the baseball cap Easton had on that night."

They were all quiet, remembering.

Finally, Sailor broke the silence. "Actually, that's why I wanted you to stop by this morning— I wanted to show you guys something." She smiled and motioned for them to follow her. She led the way down the short hall to her studio, turned on the light above her desk, and stepped back so they could see all the pictures.

"Oh my!" Birdie murmured while Remy just stood there, gazing in awe.

"What do *you* think?" Sailor asked softly, looking at David.

He blinked back tears and took a deep breath. "It's . . . stunning."

"It *is* stunning," Remy said softly.

Piper pointed to the newest addition Sailor had

hung in the empty spot when she'd gotten home the night before. "Here's where it all began," she said. "It wouldn't be complete without this one."

They all looked at the old black-and-white photo of the five laughing Quinn children with their arms around each other—a formidable crew!—and brushed back their tears.

⊰ Chapter 64 ⊱

"Elias, can you pick up the other side?" Nat called, motioning for his son to lift one end of the specially designed tank they'd used to transport the big loggerhead to and from the aquarium.

Sam and Piper trotted over to help, too, and as they lifted it out of the back of the truck and carried it down the ramp, Elliot ran over and put his hands under the tank to help bear the weight, too.

Nat nodded in Elliot's direction. "That's how you used to be," he said, smiling at Elias.

Elias grinned. "I still am."

The sun was just peeking up above the horizon when they set the tank down on the sand near the water's edge.

"Wow," Elliot exclaimed. "Look how big he is!"

"Actually," Elias said, *"he is a she."*

"It's a girl turtle?!"

"More like a lady turtle," Piper said.

"How do you know it's a lady?" Elliot asked.

"Her tail," Elias explained. "The male's tail is longer and thicker than the female's."

Elliot nodded.

"She's beautiful," Remy said, peering into the tank.

"She certainly is," Birdie agreed.

Piper pulled out her phone and scrolled through her pictures. "This is what she looked like when we rescued her." She tapped one of the photos showing the debris and lines tangled around her neck and flippers. She scrolled again. "And this was the buoy she was dragging."

"Oh my, that's awful," Remy said, shaking her head.

"It *is* awful," Piper said. "We are constantly rescuing turtles that have become tangled up in garbage. Last summer we rescued a little Kemp's ridley that was so wrapped up in fishing line, you couldn't even tell he was a turtle."

"I wish people would be more careful about leaving plastic bags and garbage around," David said.

"I'm going to pick up all the plastic bags I see," Elliot said, stroking the old turtle's scarred shell.

"Me too," Maya said, reaching for her mother's hand. Tess could tell she wanted to touch the turtle's shell, too, but just didn't have the courage.

"She won't hurt you, Maya," Elliot said.

Maya stepped forward and lightly traced her

finger over the scarred shell while David took the lens cap off his camera and took several pictures of Elliot and Maya with the old turtle.

Finally, Nat looked at Piper. "Shall we?" he asked.

"Don't you mean '*shell* we'?" Piper teased.

"Cute," Nat said as Elias rolled his eyes.

Piper laughed. "You know what? I think now is as good a time as any," she said, feeling her heart starting to pound, "and since I've just stumbled across *exactly* the right words to say, I'm going to say them."

Nat gave her a puzzled look and waited for her to continue, and Piper pressed her lips together. "I think, today . . . right now . . . while we're doing what we love . . . what we've loved doing all these years . . . with all the people we love most . . . is the perfect time to ask, especially since my sisters have always teased me when I've said I'm rescuing turtles with Nat." She took a deep breath, searched the slate-blue eyes she knew so well, and smiled. "Shell we, my love . . . shell we get married?"

Elias looked up in surprise and Nat shook his head in disbelief and laughed. "You're crazy, you know that?" he said, and then walked around the tank and lifted her off the ground. "We shell," he whispered, smiling.

"Well, that took a turtle's lifetime," Sailor said, laughing.

"Now that that's finally shettled," Elias said, grinning, "What about this poor turtle?"

"Oh yes! The turtle!" Nat said. He put Piper down and turned to help Elias lift the gate. The big loggerhead sea turtle, smelling the salty water and hearing the waves, made her way slowly toward the surf, and when she reached the water's edge and felt the wet sand under her belly, she paused and turned to look back at them with solemn eyes. Then, feeling the cold ocean water washing under her shell, she trudged resolutely into the surf until the tide washed over her and picked her up and carried her out to sea.

"What a beautiful grand old lady," Piper whispered, misty-eyed.

"She truly is," Sailor said, wiping a tear.

"Just like us," Remy added, smiling.

"*And* like us, she has learned," Birdie said, her eyes glistening, "that surrendering in order to be freed from what entangles us has a lovely, exquisite peace all its own."

Smiling and teary-eyed, they stood on the beach and watched the old sea turtle plunge through the waves.

"I can't believe you're finally getting married," Sailor said, kissing Piper's cheek. Just as she did, David called them and they turned, realized he was taking their picture, and pulled each other close, laughing and happy to be free.

With Heartfelt Thanks . . .

To Esi Sogah, my editor, and Deirdre Mullane, my agent, who are always ready with insightful suggestions and positive feedback; to everyone on the Kensington team who has worked to put together another wonderful book package; to my husband, Bruce, and our boys, Cole and Noah, whose love and support are beyond measure; and to my dear dad, who wasn't able to read *Firefly Summer*, but who was always interested in its progress. "How's it coming?" he'd ask. "It's coming," I'd reply. "You always say that." One week after I told him I'd finished, my beloved dad was in hospice care, and a week after that, he passed away, but his ready smile and unwavering faith will always inspire me, and for that I'm truly grateful.

Rhubarb Pie

Ingredients

4 cups fresh rhubarb, washed and cut into 1-inch pieces
1¼ cups sugar
2 tablespoons grated orange rind (zest)
¼ teaspoon (or less) salt
2½ tablespoons quick tapioca
2 tablespoons butter

Directions

Combine first five ingredients. Fold in rhubarb and mix well. Spoon into 9-inch prepared pie shell. Dot fruit with pieces of butter. Lay on lattice top—I cut the rolled-out dough into strips with a pizza cutter—and carefully weave the strips; fold under and make a decorative edge. With finger, lightly wipe a little milk onto the strips—will give it a shiny golden glaze.

Bake at 425 degrees F for 15 minutes, then at 400 degrees F for ½ hour, and check; cover the outer crust with a ring of foil if it's getting too brown, and continue baking for another 20–30 minutes. I also put a sheet of foil on the rack below to catch the overflow of juice.

Note: 1 cup sliced strawberries can also be folded in with the rhubarb.

Ingredients for Piecrust

2 cups all-purpose flour
1 teaspoon salt
¾ cup shortening (12 tablespoons)
5–6 tablespoons cold water

Directions

In medium-size bowl, combine flour and salt. With pastry blender, cut in shortening until mixture resembles coarse crumbs. Sprinkle with cold water, a couple tablespoons at a time. Continue blending with a fork until pastry starts to hold together. Shape pastry into two balls and roll out into circles on floured surface. Roll onto rolling pin and lay over 9-inch pie plate. Press down and shape to dish.

Rice Pudding

Ingredients

4 cups milk
Scant ½ cup regular long-grain white rice
¼ cup sugar
¼ teaspoon salt
2 eggs
1 teaspoon vanilla
½ cup raisins (optional)
Sprinkle of cinnamon

Directions

Heat milk, rice, sugar, and salt to boiling. Reduce heat to low; cover and simmer 45 minutes to an hour until rice is very tender, stirring occasionally.

In a small bowl, beat eggs lightly and stir in a small amount of hot rice mixture. Slowly pour egg mixture into rice mixture, stirring rapidly to prevent lumping. Cook, stirring constantly, until rice mixture is thickened, about 5 minutes. Do not boil, or mixture will curdle. Remove from heat and stir in vanilla. Add raisins, if you'd like, and transfer to bowl. Sprinkle with cinnamon. Cover and refrigerate or serve warm. Yum!

Discussion Questions

1. The author introduces readers to Birdie, Remy, Sailor, and Piper over the course of the first four chapters. How are the sisters different? What issues do they each seem to have?

2. As the story progresses, do you find yourself drawn to one sister over the others? Do you look forward to the next chapter focusing on this sister? Is there an attribute or concern you share with her that draws you to her?

3. Is there a sister you don't like? If so, why?

4. Each of the sisters has rescued or protected some kind of wildlife. Why do you think they're drawn to help wildlife in need?

5. Why do you think Piper never married Nat? Why doesn't Elias tell his friends they aren't married?

6. From what we know of Sailor's marriage, why do you think it failed? Do you think there's more depth to their problems than Frank's cheating?

7. Remy truly believes that she doesn't dwell on the life she and Jim would've shared if he had lived, yet she constantly thinks of him. Is she fooling herself? Why does she have a hard time letting go of her memories?

8. Birdie doesn't think she has a drinking problem. What events shake her world and her senses, and how does she change? What role does John Sanders play in her life?

9. The Quinn family has never talked about the tragedy of losing Easton. How, if at all, has each of them dealt with his loss? Has not facing his loss affected each of them in any way?

10. What events cause the sisters to finally face the past? What role do their children and grandchildren play? In what ways do the sisters change? How is the release of the sea turtle symbolic?

About the Author

Nan Rossiter was born in Mount Vernon, New York. She grew up in Pelham, New York, and in Barkhamsted, Connecticut. From a young age she loved to draw. After high school, she attended Rhode Island School of Design and graduated with a BFA in illustration.

After working in the freelance field and creating art for internationally recognized companies such as Viking, MasterCard, and UPS, Nan began writing and illustraing books for children. She is the author-illustrator of several children's books, including, most recently, *The Fo'c'sle: Henry Beston's Outermost House.*

Nan lives in rural Connectiuct with her husband and two handsome sons. When she's not working, she enjoys hiking with her family or reading a good book.

Visit her website at www.nanrossiter.com

Center Point Large Print
600 Brooks Road / PO Box 1
Thorndike, ME 04986-0001 USA

(207) 568-3717

US & Canada:
1 800 929-9108
www.centerpointlargeprint.com